THE CURIOSITIES OF PERCIVILLE HARPER

SIMON BATSMAN

CRANTHORPE
—MILLNER—
PUBLISHERS

For Niamh.

Remember that trip to Barcelona I promised you
for your birthday?

Well, anyway, I wrote you a book instead.

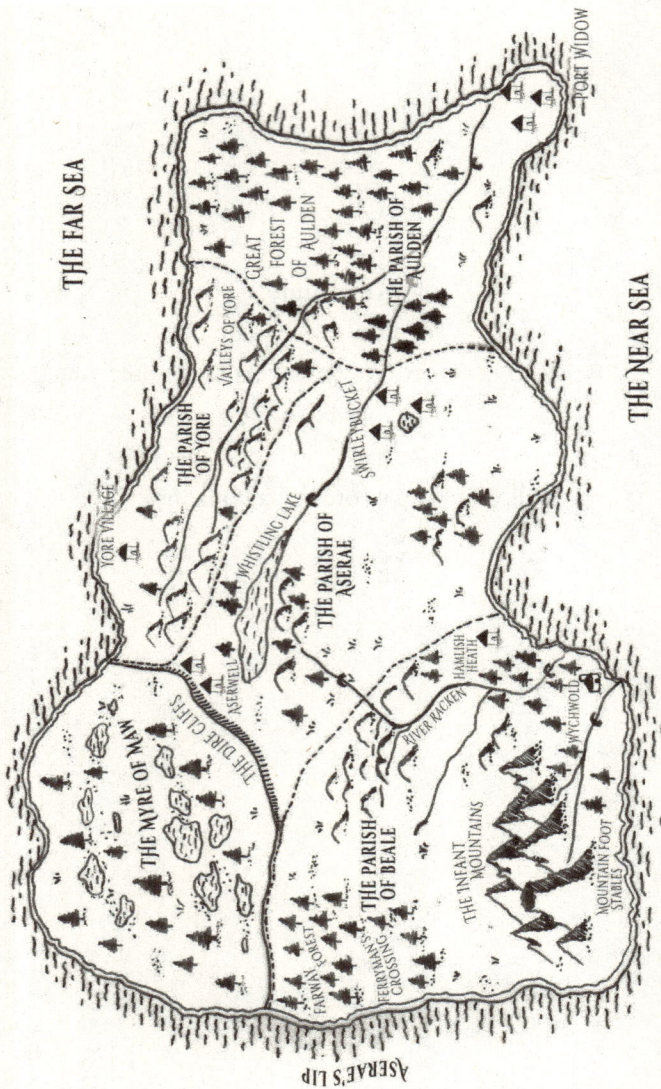

MARROW MYRE

THE FAR SEA

THE NEAR SEA

PORT WIDOW

GREAT FOREST OF AULDEN

THE PARISH OF AULDEN

VALLEYS OF YORE

THE PARISH OF YORE

SWIRLEY BUCKET

WHISTLING LAKE

YORE VILLAGE

THE PARISH OF ASERAE

ASERWELL

THE DIRE CLIFFS

HAMLISH HEATH

RIVER RACKEN

THE MYRE OF MAW

FARWA FOREST

FERRYMAN'S CROSSING

THE PARISH OF BEALE

WYCHWOLD

THE INFANT MOUNTAINS

MOUNTAIN FOOT STABLES

ASERAE'S LIP

THE ARVUM

THE FAR SEA

THE NEAR SEA

THE ULESTIC OCEAN

THE COLD SEA

THE ISLE OF RHIES

SATLISAI'MAE
(THE CARVED CITY)

SAVANNA

THE SAVANNION STRAIT

PORT WIDOW

MARROW MYRE

COLT

LYRIA

WILLOW'S BRUSH

ROSENSTED

MADDERMIRE

NAVINE

POLLEN

THE BLUE VALLEY OF EVENSONG

THE CUSP

PANAMAYA CITY

THE SLEEPING GIANT

SALAMANDER

BOUNDING CLIFFS

HORRI

THE PENTARI DESERT

DRAGONS

PENTARI CANAL

JACKDAW

PRECIPITOUS MOUNTAINS

SAVANNAH AND SCARP

THE SHATTERED LAND

THE ISLE OF FORTUNE

REVELIE

TWO SINNERS LAKE

SHALLOWDRAFT

THE ROCK OF CAEZNOR

THE HAUNT

BLAIR RIVER

PROSTRIDER WAY

THE STEPS

AUTUMN PENINSULA

LEAFALL

SPRATT'S ISLAND

HAVENSEND
(THE FREE CAPITAL)

LONGREACH

EAVE'S END

To most, it is impossible to picture absolute nothingness in the mind's eye. Not pure darkness, nor empty light, but actual, literal nothingness. And yet...

PROLOGUE

THE WOMAN AND THE CANDLESTICK

A voice of sorts, or perhaps rather a notion. Like a waning thought clinging to the underside of a single leaf being swept along in the wind.

Whatever it was, it said, "Imagine a light."

Then, of all things, a tall white candlestick appeared, as though it had always been there. It stood unassumingly, issuing a modest flicker of light, a hopeful beacon into that very nothingness.

"More," the thought said and, somehow, that lowly candlestick seemed to glow brighter, stretching out from its tender wick and spreading down its sides, to reveal an antique writing desk upon which it sat.

The flame bled into the pitch black surrounding it as if it were a stranger's hand, groping the stagnant air and reaching for something to touch.

Its light lapped about the deathly silence, soundlessly spilling over the top of the writing desk and swelling down its legs to illuminate a stone floor beneath. It clawed its way behind, up through the emptiness until it pooled into a

1

decaying cuckoo clock, seemingly suspended in the air. The wood of the clock, once beautifully carved, was warped and rotten. Its hands, bent and twisted from a timeless neglect.

The light cast shadows across its broken façade as it climbed down the chain of a rust-mottled pendulum.

Then, across the floor, it festered between the cavities of the stones, eroding away the darkness where it settled in front of the writing desk.

Here, the last thing one might have expected, had they the misfortune of being present, was a young woman. She lay on her side, knees tucked up to her torso, cheek resting dreamlessly on her pale hands. The veritable sleeping position, in the most unlikely of places.

The woman, pretty in the face with a river of mousy brown hair flowing midway down her back, was clad in a simple white gown held tight by a tattered rope belt around her slender waist, and on her feet, she wore plain sandals that were fastened up to her ankles. She had long ears that were softly pointed at the tips, and her skin shimmered slightly as if she were cast of bronze.

The voice, or thought, spoke again. "Wake now."

The first chime was deafening as it pierced the silence, the second clashed dissonantly. As the pendulum swung arrhythmically, the twisted hands spun furiously over the clock's disfigured face.

From within the clock came a loud knocking as if somebody were trapped inside and wanted to break free. It knocked again, this time harder, competing with the ringing of the torturous chimes. Moments later, a miniature door sprung open, though not a cuckoo emerged. Instead, a model of a figure in a black robe, its hood obscuring its face but for a gruesome smile and snarling eyes.

Each time the figure shot out of the door, it dangled freely at the end of its cord like a broken limb. In and out, it sprung to the cacophony of chimes whose tempo was desperately chasing its volume. Louder and louder it chimed, enough to make one's ears bleed.

Louder and louder into that small but enormous nothingness.

Louder and louder until, in a fraction of a moment, the chimes stopped, the hands ceased, the figure disappeared, and the young woman's eyes shot open.

Nothingness and silence.

CHAPTER 1

WYCHWOLD

It was often remarked that the people of Marrow Myre were a strange and ancient race. That their blood was the most closely related to that of people from an age long past and, to most, long forgotten. A time of chaos and confusion, of greed and war, but a time also of great art, music, science and romance. Long before the world became too marred, too complicated, and people yearned for a simpler way of life.

Though if one were to broach the subject to a Myrish local, they would most likely regale a more traditional narrative of mighty gods, weaving together their unintelligible charms in order to create the most perfect and peaceful land in all of the Arvum.

Then, perhaps, one might ask, "But what about the rest of the Arvum? Why not make the whole world perfect and peaceful?" and most likely they'd be presented with a dismissive shrug, a coy smile, and another pint of Swirleybucket ale plonked on the table in front of them.

The Myrish were a kind and hospitable people, devoted to their land and forever opening their doors. They gladly welcomed travellers of all kinds, elves and such, from across the continent to visit this large but humble island, to sample the local ales, the cheeses made from the thick milk of the Beale goat, and smoked salmon from the shimmering waters of the Whistling Lake.

Perhaps the Myrish people were too devoted to this land, one might suggest, for though they may have frequently crossed the parish boundaries or ventured into the Infant Mountains, it was most unusual that they should ever cross the sea into the wider world. Not for a long time had the inhabitants of Marrow Myre left this remarkable, though sometimes lonely, island.

Remarkable and sometimes lonely was a fitting description for Fjona Sarsen. She lay dreamlessly on a cotton mattress, wrapped up tightly in a goose feather duvet with one pale arm hanging over the edge of the bed, her knuckles nearly brushing against the floorboards. Her face was hidden beneath a veil of deep brown hair, though it almost appeared maroon under the soft rays of sunlight that crept between the gaps of the window shutters. Her hair was cut short, only as far as her shoulders, and was lusciously thick and curly, somehow the gold standard of a tidy mess.

Although old enough to live alone, Fjona occupied the loft of her parent's house. Their home was a roundhouse with a near-conic thatched roof, except for where the straw had been parted to accommodate the timber loft. It was situated on the top of a hillock in the shade of a mighty oak tree, itself a city of wallowbird nests.

Already the wallowbirds, a native species to Marrow Myre,

were whistling harmonically to signal morning. Their call had begun as a subtle tweet here, a trill or two over. Then, as more and more of these illustrious purple and green birds picked up the call, their song became more uniform. Every day, they would synchronise a different tune and, every day, wallowbirds across the island would raise the sleepy Myrish people from their beds.

Mostly, except for Fjona who required a firm knock at the door from her mother, Dharla. In a whirlwind of velvety chestnut hair, Dharla welcomed herself into Fjona's room, carrying a long evergreen dress over one arm. She herself was wearing a handsomely fitted blue dress with a swirling pattern of red vines interweaving upwards from hem to collar, and upon her head she wore a cream-coloured sunhat with an overly wide brim.

Had it not been for a slight stoop, Dharla would have needed to duck beneath the roof truss as she strode across the floor with the grace of a deer.

"Morning greets you," she said sweetly, as she draped the dress over the back of a chair before walking past the bed to open the window shutters. A warm light spilled into the bedroom, reflecting off dust motes that floated in the air. Then, with a slight edge to her voice, she added, "I was embarrassed by the same old tattered rags that you normally wear so I fished this out of the wardrobe for you." Dharla proceeded to swat a net of cobwebs away from the beams with her hat. "Your father is already outside helping the villagers set up for breakfast. He's still very grateful for you herding all the goats back in last night." She continued as if they were having a conversation.

"Mind you, it was your fault that they escaped in the first place." She furrowed her thick brow and retreated to the door. "Come now," she said decisively as she left the room and made her way downstairs, welcomingly replaced by the fragrance of freshly baked bread.

Fjona, like many young adults, had the exceptional ability to both be listening and not listening at the same time. She rubbed away the sleep from her eyes and kicked off the duvet before stretching her entire body out on the bed like a spider anticipating a hug. Groggily, she slid off the mattress and stood embracing the crisp breeze, now circumventing the room from the wide-open window. She found herself staring forlornly at a wallowbird, which was treading carefully along a narrow branch of the oak tree and whistling along to the morning's melody as if it hadn't a single care in the world. Moments later, another wallowbird landed beside it in a plume of colourful feathers. They started to sing together until flapping their wings and disappearing somewhere over the village.

Fjona released a long, heavy sigh then, coming around to the idea of being awake, looked disdainfully at the hideous green dress. Hideous, at least in Fjona's eyes, for she had never held a particular affinity for garments that were designed to be free of crinkles and free of dirt. At least the evergreen matched her eyes, she reasoned.

Reluctantly she put it on. Even if she'd had a mirror in her bedroom, she would not have bothered to check herself before making her way downstairs. Not that she would have needed to. Fjona was just one of those people who could wake up looking herself; even if that did mean unbrushed hair, bags beneath her eyes, and a smudge of dirt across her cheek.

As she spiralled down the staircase, Fjona could hear her mother opening drawers and banging cupboards, the murmuring of water boiling on the kitchen stove, and the sizzling of eggs in a pan as Dharla frantically prepared platters of food and hot drinks. Enough to feed a village. After all, breakfast was regarded as a very important meal across Marrow Myre. It wasn't just about fuelling the body before a day of tilling the fields, tending to livestock or constructing new barns. It was about community. A social gathering that took place each and every morning, no matter the weather. In the villages and towns that made up the island, the Myrish people would be sure to don a nice frock or coat and catch up with their neighbours over a vast spread of fruits, cheeses, breads, cured fish and cold meats. Then at the end of the meal, they would tidy everything away, change into clothing more suitable for their work, and start their day with a fresh bout of energy that often follows a good conversation.

"Morning greets you, Mother," Fjona said as she stepped down into the wide-open hub of the roundhouse.

Still feeling groggy, she almost had to squint as the sunshine poured in through large oval windows, casting a crisp, golden hue over the furnishings.

Blinking her eyes into focus, Fjona felt Dharla thrust a platter of food into her arms and plant a soft, loving kiss on her cheek.

"You look beautiful, my *derine*. Now please take these fruits down to your father. I will be with you all in a few moments," Dharla told her daughter, swiftly returning to the kitchen area.

Fjona sucked in the sweet smell of cinnamon that hung beneath the rafters, then proceeded for the door, though not without pinching a square of white cheese from the table.

Outside, she was welcomed by a bustle of neighbours from the village, the hubbub of chatter, clattering of crockery. She breathed a heavy sigh, preparing herself for the monotony of yet another day in pleasant little Wychwold.

Fjona found herself leaning on a fence, looking down the scarp to the village green where several long tables were being laid with cutlery and plates. Beside it, on the opposite side of a fishpond, were Carlé Doe, the village bard, and her grandfather Meris, who had played his pan flute at breakfast for nearly a century.

Fjona could hear the same jolly performance that they seemed to play every morning. Along with a flock of wallowbirds, who had subsequently picked up this tune, were several children from the village who were kicking up their heels and spinning around animatedly to the music. They knew this one well. The music started to increase in tempo, gently at first though it very quickly picked up the pace. The children were swirling around, clapping their hands in chaotic fashion. They received a few disgruntled looks from the adults of the group, though most were grinning with anticipation and many were clapping their hands in time with the music too.

Just as it was getting faster, it was getting louder. Both Carlé and Meris had a relaxed but definite look of concentration, furrowed brows and straight face. Faster and faster. Louder and louder in a swelling crescendo, and then, perfectly on cue, the music peaked. It stopped on a single powerful but short note, at which point the children all collapsed onto the grass, giggling and throwing themselves around, while the adults applauded with a smattering of laughter.

Fjona was distracted by the scuffling of little shoes on gravel and turned to see a small boy, well dressed in a smart coat but dappled with dirt.

"Why didn't you want to join in, Peter?" Fjona asked, gesturing to the children by the green with a nod of the head.

Peter climbed up on the fence and scoffed. "I'm much too old for silly games!"

It was enough to make Fjona smile from ear to ear. "You sound exactly like your brother."

Peter returned her a contemplative look.

"Which brother?" he asked curiously.

"Why Todie, of course," she replied, to which Peter just rolled his eyes and theatrically buried his head in his hands. "Where is Todie, anyway?"

"He's with my dad and Rodmear," Peter replied glumly, "and my grandma." His face turned as sour as an underripe blackberry.

"And you didn't want to join him?"

Peter just shook his head, then wiped his runny nose on the back of his sleeve.

"Hey!" Fjona encouraged, her eyes wide with excitement, "How about a race down the hill?"

Suddenly Peter was attentive. He looked up, a beaming smile across his sullied face.

"First one to the bottom gets the biggest fig," Fjona added, tipping the fruit platter towards him, in the middle of which was a succulent purple fig the size of Peter's fist.

Fjona had barely finished speaking before, in a scuffle of dirt and gravel, Peter raced off along the path that gently curved down the edge of the hillock.

With Peter helping himself to a head start, Fjona had little choice but to clamber over the fence and take a shortcut down the steep scarp. Clutching the fruit platter closely to her chest, she skidded down the dewy grass and weaved between the bare rock, all the while keeping her balance. At the bottom of the first slope, she hopped over a fence into the Wiskins' vegetable patch, carefully planting her feet between the rows of parsnips. On the far side, she came back onto the path just as Peter was running past. He shot Fjona a bemused look, nearly tripping up on the cobbles as he did, but determinedly continued along to the next slope.

Fjona didn't waste a second. She crossed the path, hopped another fence and carefully descended the second slope. As she climbed down through a blanket of wildflowers, butterflies and bees flurried about her but Fjona remained unperturbed. The bottom was in sight and she could see Peter only just now coming back around the bend. When she glanced up briefly, several villagers were looking at her disapprovingly, owl-like heads crooked to one side, arms crossed.

Then, as her feet landed on level ground, Fjona had too much momentum to stop. She leaped over yet another fence, this time passing through Iser's stables, and plummeted her face into a big, broad shoulder.

Dazed and with a ringing in her ears, she could hear Peter calling, "You cheated, you cheated," and another voice saying,

"Fjona? What in the Arvum are you doing?"

When she peeled back away from the shoulder, Fjona looked up to see a kind face smiling back at her, his wispy auburn hair waving in the breeze like tall autumnal grass in a meadow.

"Todie! Fjona cheated!" Peter complained, his face bright red with fury.

Todie looked first at Peter, then to Fjona with an enquiring expression. "Is my brother speaking truthfully?"

"Hey, I never said you had to stick to the path," Fjona teased, "but you're right, I shouldn't have taken the shortcut." She plucked the fat fig from the top of the platter and dropped it into Peter's cupped hands.

Todie ruffled his brother's floppy hair, and without so much as a thank you the young boy raced off towards the village green with his prized possession.

"You know you needn't keep entertaining him like that," Todie said as he removed a stray leaf from Fjona's scraggly hair.

"He's having a hard time," she replied.

"I know."

"It seems to help him."

"I know," Todie repeated with a sigh.

"How are you?"

"A little nervous, but otherwise not too bad."

"Did you speak to Lasmee?"

Todie forced a smile. "I did, but she was never much of a listener *before*."

Together they headed through a thicket of twisting pine trees whose boughs shivered in the breeze and followed a brook that led down to the village green.

Once there, Todie said, "Find us a good seat. Need to check if my mother could use a hand." He wandered off towards a two-tiered roundhouse opposite the pond, where his mother stood unsteadily carrying a towering tray of bowls.

Meanwhile Fjona headed over to her father, Ascerat, who was busy polishing cutlery at one of the tables. He was bent forward, thick-rimmed spectacles perched precariously at the end of his long, pointed nose as if they may tumble off onto the table at any moment.

In spite of the sunshine, he was wrapped up in a winter coat, so thick that even the moderate wind couldn't ruffle it.

"Morning greets you, Papa," Fjona said cheerfully, to which there was no reply but for a quiet muttering.

As Fjona put down the fruit platter, she noticed Ascerat's veinous hands trembling as he attempted to polish a sharp knife, and she grabbed him by the wrist to prevent him from accidentally severing himself.

"Papa!" Fjona exclaimed, startling her father. The knife clattered to the table; a loud ringing echoed from the rim of a plate. Not that anybody else could have heard it over the music and their own conversations.

Ascerat turned to Fjona. In the morning sunlight, and just for a moment, his eyes appeared almost yellow as he pushed his spectacles up to the bridge of his nose.

"Sorry, my dear, I was utterly lost in my thoughts. A silly old fool, I am!" he said. "Not that I can even remember what it was I daydreaming about," he added, frowning deeply with his gums pursed together like a doll. "Anyhow, what was it you were saying?"

Any concern Fjona had harboured in that moment for her father was immediately extinguished when he smiled fondly.

"I just came over to say morning greets you," Fjona repeated.

"Ahh, morning greets you too, my *derine*." He kissed his daughter on the cheek.

It was only once Ascerat's cold lips met her skin that Fjona realised how hot her skin had become from running down the scarp.

"May I assist you at all, Papa?" Fjona asked feigning politeness while she surreptitiously pilfered a plump red grape from a nearby bowl.

"I do believe we are quite ready," Ascerat replied as a crowd of rosy-cheeked villagers flocked towards the table.

With them they carried plates and platters, stacked high with freshly prepared food. To an onlooker who hadn't seen such an event, they would likely have perceived the procession of food-bearers as manic and disorganised. How a rubble of people, seeming to be constantly getting in one another's way, could possibly lay a table in such a manner was near impossible. Yet, like a murmuration of starlings, the well-rehearsed choreography of plate-laying was successful and, minutes later, the table was set.

"Please..." Ascerat gestured to Fjona to take a seat next to him, as he struggled to pull his own chair out from beneath the table. Receiving a curious look from Fjona he added, "Leg must have got caught in a tuft." Then he plonked himself down.

Fjona just shrugged, then waved Todie over to join her.

By now, Carlé and Meris had put their instruments away and the whole village was seated. There was much excited chatter as the Myrish people of Wychwold tucked into a breakfast banquet. Cold ham dripping in a thick lather of golden honey, smoked salmon on a bed of bright lettuce leaves and covered with a zealous sprinkling of dill, and rich cheeses in all tangs and tastes. There were bowls brimming with ripe, juicy plums, and hazelnuts collected by the children from the nearby woods, which had been toasted and seasoned with salt and sweet peppercorns. Pots of tea and strong coffee were spread evenly across the table, though not for Mrs Wiskins who, at nearly ninety years old, was partial to a half pint of stout with her breakfast.

As the meal wore on, Fjona contentedly slathered butter over a thick slice of crusty bread while engaged in a heated debate with Todie about the best way to spear a fish.

"Miss Sarsen, how wrong you are! The best way to spear a salmon is to wade out into the river as far as you can, let the waters roll in quietly around you, take a deep breath, and..." he paused "... there!" Todie stabbed his knife into a tantalising piece of salmon. "Speared! That's how you—"

Before he could finish his sentence, Fjona had slipped her own knife horizontally through the thick slice of salmon and whisked it towards her own plate.

"Lose a perfectly good bit of fish," she concluded casually, and stuffed the whole piece into her mouth.

Todie considered her in equal part admiration and disgust. "Well played, Miss Sarsen. Next time we go up to the Racken, we'll use your technique," he conceded.

Fjona smiled a great, *salmony* smile, prompting Todie to pretend to faint. That made them both fall apart with laughter.

Although their table manners were clearly lacking, everybody was too wrapped up in their own meals and conversations to notice.

All in all, it was a very pleasant morning in Wychwold. Very pleasant indeed. Though perhaps not for Dharla Sarsen, for had someone taken the time to look away from their bountiful plates of food or paused for a breath from their intimate conversation, they may have looked up to see her staring intensely at her husband, a deeply troubled and pained look of consternation frozen across her sullen, ashen face.

CHAPTER 2

THE SAGE

Perciville Harper found himself pondering that same conundrum that most men find themselves asking at least once in their lives: "What in a thousand moons was her name? Nephalise? Tenia? Llaminya?"

Now that he came to think of it, 'what in a thousand moons' might not even have been a real expression, and she may not even have been a *she* after all. That did happen from time to time, depending on what mood he was in and, when it came to the even folk and twelve doubles of Myrish whiskey, to be frank, Perciville found it hard to tell. What didn't help the matter was that in the wider world, Myrish whiskey, while readily mocked, was as cheap as air. Earthy brown sewage water was one of the nicer descriptions he'd come across, and that was by a Grugan who drank liquefied horse liver. Though, to give the Myrish distilleries some credit, their whiskey did taste fractionally nicer once he'd downed the first three or so, and it was one of the few drinks that seemed to be available wherever he went.

Perciville had hoped that his drinking habit would

naturally improve over time but now it had got to the point where if he could wake up and his crotch was still dry, he would consider that a victory. As far as he knew, there was no such enchantment for extracting a urine stain from a pair of trousers. It was simply chuck them and be done with it, or grin and bear it and hope that nobody notices.

His head thronged like an endlessly vibrating bell and he felt so dehydrated that even had he been able to bathe his tongue in icy water, it still couldn't have stopped it from feeling like sandpaper. It was also far too soon in the morning to be awake – the early hours when the moon was still in the sky as the sun was just peeking over the horizon.

Perciville rubbed his bleary, crystal eyes in the hope that he could squeeze away his headache and decided just to brave it and get out of bed. He rolled over to one side and... fell out of a tree.

"Ahh cockles," he cried as he tumbled down through the branches and landed twenty feet below on a bush of gorse. "Urgh," he moaned, spitting brambles out of his mouth and pushing himself up with his staff. At least he still had that, he considered.

The staff was nearly two metres tall, about the same height as Perciville, and was made of a rich, dark oak. Its long, narrow shaft had more than a couple of knots and whorls, and its head peeled out into four wooden hooks that bent up into the rough shape of a teardrop. A fifth arm erupted from the neck of the staff and spiralled partially around the head like the bottom coil of a spring.

A sage's staff bore unfathomable power. It could conjure

18

and heal, hurt and reveal. It could shift mountains and islands, even toy with the very fabric that bound the world and, in this particular circumstance, it could aid a severely hungover man to just about stand up on his own feet.

Perciville removed his long, dark purple robe and sullied white shirt beneath. He cast them to one side, kicked off his boots and discarded his trousers.

Shakily, and with enough caution to suppress his need to throw up, he raised the staff just above his head. He felt his pulse race from his heart to his arms, through to the tips of his fingers and into the wood of the staff. Then above his head, in a flash of green light he created a small, personal raincloud as easily as though he were pouring a glass of water. Next, Perciville thrust the staff into the ground and, just like that, it started to rain around him.

Perciville relished in the cool water. He felt it swell into his thick, dark hair and trickle down his pale, skinny body. It cascaded onto his shoulders and pooled in the gaps between his toes. He turned his head up to it and drank in as much as he could until his water to alcohol ratio began to feel more tolerable.

After a few minutes, Perciville was much more refreshed. He thrust the staff into the ground again and the rain ceased. Then, he whipped his tangle of earthy brown hair about like a dog, closed his eyes, felt the pulsing through his body, and leaned the staff in one direction. This time a strong cool breeze embraced him and swirled about his frame. Leaves and dirt billowed in the air about him, along with a spray of rainwater as it blew away from his body like a breaking wave.

When Perciville felt sufficiently dried, he tapped the staff on the ground again and the wind stopped as abruptly as it had begun.

"Ahh, much better," he said to himself, taking a satisfactory breath, though his tongue still felt scratchy.

Now the ground in this wooded area was swamped in a pool of muddy water, and sticks and leaves had been blown all about the place. At least Perciville felt better as he put his clothes back on.

Somewhat revived, he took stock of his surroundings.

"Okay. Woodland..." He glanced around contemplatively. "Guess I'm not in Sallisai'Mae anymore. Shame, it was nice there." He crouched and placed a hand on a dry patch of grass. "Ground, a little warmer here too?" It was both a question and a statement. "Blimey, I'm not even in Bouanda anymore!" He chuckled to himself. "How did I manage that?"

Scrunching his eyes up and probing his temples with two fingers, Perciville attempted to recall the events of the previous night.

"I was on a terrace looking out at the Far Sea. There was a—" He paused, desperately trying to retrieve something from the chasms of his memory. "—somebody with me. We were drinking, talking. Laughing, perhaps, and she – they – invited me back to their home?"

The cogs of his brain were spinning now, but to no avail.

"Doubtful."

He began pacing up and down between the trees, kicking specks of moss aside and tapping his staff frustratedly on his head as if it might knock the pieces back together.

"So what then? I wandered off by myself and got on a boat to—"

He was snapped out of his stupor by a flock of wallowbirds racing overhead. Even this early in the morning, they were beginning to sing.

"Oh, sages no," Ferciville murmured, the realisation beginning to dawn on him. "Not here... anywhere but this place! The whole of the Arvum yet I find myself beneath the dog's tail, on the dullest island of them all." He took a resigned breath of contempt. "I need a drink."

Having spent the previous evening in the elven city of Sallisai'Mae, Perciville Harper may almost have been forgiven for his abject disappointment in finding himself in Marrow Myre the following morning. Sallisai'Mae, or the *Carved City*, was built into the marble cliff face on the shores of Bouanda, an island to the north of the Arvum. Each building and column, staircase and balcony was built with a breath-taking intricacy that resonated with unrivalled beauty. Images of the city were burned into Perciville's memory. He could practically hear the waterfalls that cascaded over the cliffs and plunged into sapphire pools. Could almost taste the salty air as he'd crossed the elegant, arced bridges that spread over the pools like the wings of a dragon. In his mind's eye, he could picture the marble city shining like exquisite pearls in the day and reflecting the moon at night.

Not that Marrow Myre didn't possess a charm of its own, but very few places in the Arvum could compare with the Carved City. Consequently, Perciville kicked his heels and trudged through the forest. Dawn was only just beginning to break and, although the moon was full and almost as bright as if it were the sun, the light amongst the trees was dampened by a purple hue. The ground was pocked by patches of pink moss and strange bulbous grasses. Perciville fervently chose his way between the trees, no discernible pathway in sight. The trees rustled glumly and the wallowbird song had been replaced by the intermittent cawing of a raven.

"To think that no more than a few hours ago, I was feasting on oysters and wine on an elven veranda," Perciville muttered. "Probably," he added as an afterthought, his recollection of the day before still very much in stanzas. He sighed deeply through his crooked nose.

Then his heart lurched. Footsteps. A lot of them. Tapping around him like rats inside a wall.

"Who goes there?" he asked, desperately trying to sound more confident than he was.

He focused his mind and clutched tightly to his staff. It began to glow at the top like a torch.

The scurrying of feet was encircling him and he could almost make out the sounds of muttering and chatter, but, as he arced the staff around him, all he could see were trees, grass, and the occasional toadstool that he was certain would be poisonous.

Perciville tried to ignore the sounds and convince himself that it was just the trees, rustling and clattering in the wind. A perfectly plausible explanation but for the lack of a breeze.

The footsteps continued and they seemed to be getting nearer.

He knew what he had to do. He wasn't proud of it but he

was a sage and with that comes a particular palette of skills and a certain responsibility to do the right thing.

He clutched his staff even tighter, felt the weight of it in his hand. He took a long, deep breath and nurtured the energy pouring from his heart to his hand, and into the polished wood. Electricity pulsed through his very being, the signature of spirit and power.

Then, with great ferocity, Perciville ran. He wasn't a coward by any means, but he was lost, still suffering from the effects of the night before, and had decided which of his fight or flight instincts he would listen to.

He darted between the trees like a gazelle, ducking under branches and leaping over logs. His staff was still lit up like a beacon and he used it to guide his way through the suffocating forest.

As fortune would have it, the trees soon parted and Perciville fell out onto the banks of an open bog. It gurgled with a thick, peaty hunger. It was then that a snippet of the night before returned to him and he realised where exactly he was.

"The Myre of Maw. I had a friend here once," he said to nobody. On the off chance that his friend may have been present and listening, Perciville called out, "Bosmar? Bosmar Fodd? Are you out there?"

Silence, of course, followed. That and the cawing of the raven.

"No, I didn't think as much," he said, surprised by how lonely he suddenly felt.

The footsteps at least had faded away and Perciville took some comfort in the fact that he now had a vague idea of where he was.

The Myre of Maw was a forested bogland in the north-western corner of Marrow Myre. It was an unsettling place and somewhere that the Myrish people avoided. It was of course a buffet for speculation and rumours such as children straying too close to the forest boundary and never being seen again, or swamp monsters living in the depths of the viscous marshes and preying on unfortunate visitors who had taken a wrong turning or two.

With that in the forefront of his mind, Perciville kept a sizeable distance from the nearest bog and clung closely to a line of trees around the outside.

"I swear if I ever get out of here, I will never drink Myrish whiskey again."

He waved the staff gently in front of him, illuminating the areas where the moon just couldn't appear to reach. His heart leaped up into his throat when, at one point, it lit up two bright white eyes at head level next to a tree.

Perciville froze as a chorus of cacking ensued and two dozen more pairs of eyes appeared. Large bat-like creatures, their bodies as big as a sack of potatoes, swooped out towards Perciville and up into the air, voicing their dissatisfaction at having been disturbed with a shrill, echoing cry. His robe billowed under the gusts generated by their enormous, fleshy wings; each one easily the length of one of Perciville's arms.

It took him the best part of a minute to regain enough composure to start moving again. Deeper into a thicket of tall trees he went, only the glow of his staff to guide him. He was very much in the heart of the forest now and the space between the trunks was narrowing. Just as the air seemed to be depleting and the darkness enshrouding, Perciville felt a morsel of promise. Round ears straining, he listened to the faint sound of singing that had sorely disheartened him not so long ago.

"Oh you wonderful, brilliant wallowbirds!" he said now, completely changing his tune, not unlike a wallowbird, in fact.

He held his staff directly in front of him, closed his eyes and focused his ears. Perciville channelled his energy, and gently tilted the staff in each direction until he was able to pick out the faint, but definite, call of the birds. Deep in concentration, he felt a tap on his shoulder.

"Not right now please, I'm trying to—" He cut himself off, eyes snapping open. He swung around on the spot only to be presented with .. nothing at all. "I hate this place."

But just as his emotional leaves were settling and his heart rate dropping, something or someone said, most clearly and definitely, "Run!"

Perciville did not need to be told twice. This time in the vague direction of the wallowbirds, he slipped between the trees and under low-hanging branches. Over exposed roots, kicking mushrooms aside and clutching his staff as firmly as he could. He really wasn't a coward, Perciville Harper, but the Myre of Maw had a strange energy about it. A choking, deafening atmosphere. It would take someone with no sense of fear at all to be able to cope with the suffocating fog of the forest.

Then, finally, hope was on the horizon. The forest fizzled out to a smattering of trees here and there, and the moonlight could wash over the landscape in full spirit.

Perciville inhaled deeply, relieved to be able to breathe again, his heart pounding against his ribs, but there was little worse than succumbing to premature celebration.

As his eyes adjusted to the natural light, he followed the sound of the wallowbirds. They were a short way in front of him, fluttering around the top of a great mossy cliff.

Perciville stared up at the cliffs with disdain. "You have got to be kidding me... what is this ghastly place?"

Nonetheless, he was a sage and a relatively good one at that. He had a sizeable repertoire of enchantments, though even his abilities were only scratching the surface.

He looked up at the cliffs, about twenty times the height of the forest, leaned his staff against the stone and trained his energy. It demanded a vast amount of strength and Perciville, still tired and hungover, was exhausted. On a good day, perhaps, he may have conjured something a bit more impressive, but today was evidently not a good one.

Instead, a rickety ladder started to form from the ground up, materialising in a wave of silvery green light. Up it went above Perciville's head but stopped only at the tenth rung, a long way short of the clifftop.

"Great," Perciville said, the bare cliff all but laughing at him. "Well, better than nothing I suppose."

The sage focused his energy again and a ruby light enveloped his staff. He released his grasp on the smooth wood and the staff swooped behind his back, hovering in the air as if his spine had a gravitational pull on it. As Perciville moved, the staff followed him, always an inch or two behind his body.

He placed his hands a few rungs up and stepped onto

the lowest. As he climbed to the next level, the lowest rung disappeared and was replaced by a new one above him. It wasn't the most dignified approach but Perciville would be damned if he didn't get results. Despite his shortcomings, the ladder seemed to hold its own, and even the heavier gusts nearer the top of the cliff proved inadequate to make it sway.

Conscious not to look down, Perciville trained his eyes above and before too long the end was in sight. Up here, the distant wallowbirds were a little less distant, the stale air far less stale. His mop of hair flopped about in a stiff breeze, and his staff bobbed up and down behind his back as he gracefully hopped off his enchanted ladder and planted his feet onto solid ground.

Perciville looked back to where he had come from and sighed with relief.

The top of the cliff was starkly different to the bottom. The landscape had opened up and Perciville could see for miles in all directions. The air felt fuller up here and there was a particular blend of peacefulness that accompanied the chirping of crickets in the tall grass and the fidgeting of tree branches in the wind.

After dematerialising the final top ten rungs of the ladder with his staff, Perciville moved away from the clifftop and over to an earth track nearby where a horse and cart were pootling along. The cart was stacked with sacks and barrels, and a young woman was navigating from the reins. She was a modest height and broad in a muscular way, most likely from the laborious job of loading and unloading her cart. Her face was rounded with plump, rosy cheeks and she had an expansive nose that resembled that of a pig's. Her blonde-brown hair was tied into a tight braid through which her scalp could be seen, and around her forehead she wore a red-and-white bandana.

"Morning greets you," she said, a warmth to her voice and a kindness in her eyes. Then, with a giggle, she added, "Or perhaps rather the night greets you." She continued to chortle as if she'd said something genuinely amusing.

"Umm. Sure, okay," Perciville replied, taken aback.

The horse whinnied, perturbed by the stranger. He was a tall hazelnut stallion with a long, dark mane that swayed either side of his thick neck.

"Don't mind ol' Molligue here," the peculiar woman said once she'd regained her composure. "He just don't like me stopping when we're in an 'urry!"

Perciville forced a smile.

"Anyway, you be lost my *derin?*" she asked, looking Perciville up and down.

For a heartbeat he was tempted to say 'no' and relieve himself of this intolerable woman, but good sense intervened and he realised how much he could do with a ride.

"As it happens, I am not quite where I'm supposed to be," he said, unnecessarily cryptically. "Where are you headed?"

"Why Molligue and I are making haste to the fine town of Port Widow!" the unbearable woman said as if she were auditioning for a play. "Delivering these barrels from Aserwell for the Lullatide Festival, and I need to be back in Hamlish Heath in time for breakfast. Lullatide's not for me, really – not that I've the coin to spend there." She wiped her nose on the back of her sleeve. "Still, p'raps it's your scene?"

A festival? That caught Perciville's attention as he weighed up the options. Keep wandering until he ended up somewhere more palatable? Or join this overly enthusiastic woman on a tedious journey to a town he'd only heard about from drunkards of little taste and thieves of little moral? Mind you, ports meant people and people meant taverns.

He sighed deeply in his mind so as not to offend his new travelling companion.

"Port Widow it is!" he said, a little too passionately to sound sincere.

"Terrific!" the woman replied. "There's room enough in the back for a skinny man as yourself. Should be able to squeeze in between the barrels."

Perciville looked at the cart in dismay. There wasn't a whole lot of space but it beat slogging his way across the island and finding himself in the company of somebody even more annoying.

"Thanks," he said quietly and hopped aboard.

The woman kicked Molligue and the cart started rolling along the trackway. Port Widow wasn't where Perciville had expected to end the day, but at least it was somewhere he could get a proper drink.

Just as he was about to close his eyes for a moment's kip, the silence was yet again broken.

"I'm Rosalyna Foster, by the way. Pleasure to meet your acquaintance."

Her upwards inflection at the end invited Perciville to introduce himself.

"That's nice," he said instead, and dozed off.

CHAPTER 3

THE SULTAN OF PANAMAYA CITY

The forum swarmed with all manner of folk from across the Arvum. There were half-giants from the Blue Valleys of Elkensen, island elves from the glistening Sallisai'Mae and spring elves from the town of Rosensted. There were even tipids, a diminutive race, who had ventured south from their village of Nouwa not so far away.

Although Panamaya City was located on an isolated mountain rock in the heat of the Pentari Desert, it was a hive for travellers and merchants, and more or less the centre of the world. The passage through to the city could be treacherous but the rewards for crossing the hazy sands would nearly always outweigh the risks. Every day, caravans of traders would cross the desert like ants to a picnic. Carts from all over the continent would be overflowing with wares in hope of exchanging them for something more valuable to return home with. Silk from Bouanda, minerals from the Blue Valleys, or exquisite foods from Havensend would be amongst the goods bought and sold, leaving many a merchant laden with a pocketful of *summits*.

This great dance of negotiation and trade took place in the Lower Gate where the majority of the population lived in square, flat-roofed sandstone houses, all squashed together in the fear that any open space might be perceived as wasteful. It was a jungle of buildings and narrow streets, rooftop cactus gardens and trickling gullies. It was a bit like a mathematical equation; at first glance it appeared a chaotic mess, but if the right people looked closely enough, somehow, it all just seemed to make sense.

The Upper Gate was a very different place. The spring that provided the only source of water to the city was located here in the courtyard of the Sultan's palace: a beautifully ornate, cool blue stucco building surrounded by four columns, each capped by a solid gold-winged statue. On the roof of the palace was a gold dome, cast so finely that the sun could shine through it into the great hall beneath, and from the outside it could be seen glistening across the desert.

Sultan Ayermune Dahller Sé had ruled over Panamaya City for nearly six decades and was highly revered by his people. He was like a respectable teacher; if you kept in his good books then he would openly value you and be willing to share his knowledge. However, if you were to find yourself in the Sultan's bad books then disciplinary action may result in the loss of a finger, if you were lucky.

Ayermune was a summer elf, a native of Panamaya City. He had rich, dark skin and a pebble-shaped nose, and had a plaited black beard that was as long as his wiry neck. Being of such wealth, the Sultan wore the finest garments made by the Arvum's most expert tailors. His long cyan robe was bejewelled with rare stones from across the continent. It had a gold leaf collar and cuffs, and was emblazoned with a silver giant wielding a hammer, the symbol of Panamaya. Upon his head he wore a tall silken hat that matched his robe in both colour and adornments.

The Sultan was pacing, agitated, in his audience chamber, accompanied only by his steward Oolia Khamun, an unusually short summer elf, with long, pointed ears, and a shock of white hair that was tied up neatly into buns. She wore a simple, though pretty, tunic and a shell necklace around her slender neck.

Oolia was fervently trying to console the Sultan. "Perhaps they don't mean anything at all," she suggested levelly. "What makes you so sure that these aren't just dreams?"

Oolia regretted making such a remark the moment the Sultan's fiery eyes turned on her. She could feel them burning through her skin and her face reddened.

"Just dreams?" he said, his voice bubbling with anger. "These are not *just dreams*. Peasants fantasising about becoming a Sultan are *just dreams*. A whore believing her last affair was love, is *just a dream*. What plagues my mind, night after night, is not merely the imaginings of a child!" He was shouting now. Words so short and sharp they could draw blood. Saliva frothed at the corners of his mouth as if he were a rabid dog. "I understand dreams, and these are something wildly different, so do not dare to patronise me."

Anyone else would surely have been whimpering under the wrath of Ayermune Dahller Sé, but not Oolia. She had served as the Sultan's steward for a third of his tenure and had suffered many of his tantrums during that time. This was one of his calmer performances.

She had found that the trick to dealing with the Sultan's bad mood was to do nothing at all. Submission could lead to a loss of respect and banishment from the Upper Gate, as was the case with Oolia's predecessor. Retaliation, however, could result in missing limbs or worse, as was the case with Oolia's predecessor's predecessor. Until Oolia's appointment, the role of Steward to the Sultan was reputably short-lived with career prospects that could only be considered as bleak.

Pacifying the Sultan was all about finding that sweet spot between cowardice and bravado, and Oolia had learned it to a fine point. She pulled out a velvet chair from beneath the long table, gracefully took a seat, lifted her chin up, and waited in silence with a stern expression.

Ayermune gritted his teeth. His eyelids twitched as if there were something more than just his amber eyes beneath them. He raised a hairy fist and prepared to slam it on the table but, just as his hand was about to make contact with the recently varnished wood, he stopped himself.

A long breath squeezed through his pursed lips and the Sultan looked down ashamedly at his steward – his anger dissipated.

"I'm sorry, Oolia, I did not intend to lose my temper." He walked over to a large, arched window through which he could see the forum and the thousands of people penned in, trying to make their ways in the world. "I fear that this enchanting city of mine could find itself in peril and I simply do not have the solution." The Sultan remained at the window for a while, quietly brooding in the still, hot air.

Oolia stood and took a place next him. "If I might offer you counsel, my Sultan, perhaps there is somebody in the city who can help you? A Proprietor of Intellect, most likely. I would gladly visit the Archivus for you to find out." Her tone was soft but assertive.

For a moment, Oolia thought her suggestion had appeased the Sultan. His thin lips parted as if he were about to reply and his eyes twisted up in contemplation. But before his utterance of appreciation, he merely shook his head, his beard swinging from side to side like a pendulum.

"They would only think me crazy," was all the Sultan said, before the main doors to the audience chamber flung open and two soldiers appeared.

They were wearing long, open white coats bearing the Panamayan Giant on the left side of the chest, the insignia for the Noble Guard of the Sultan. Beneath the coat shone a polished breastplate that clung tightly on to their muscular frames. They each wore a tall crimson helmet which partially covered their faces, and carried a silver cutlass on their belts.

The soldiers marched in purposefully, removed their helmets and knelt before the Sultan, their heads bowed and their right, gauntleted arms held in a fist over their chests.

One soldier lifted her head. A summer elf with clipped garnet hair that was held in place by a simple cotton bandana. Her face was severe and firm, and she appeared broad beneath her coat and armour.

"Your Divine Excellency, please forgive our intrusion," she started.

"Yes, yes, you may cease your tedious formalities," the Sultan said, waving his hand dismissively. "Since you've the urgency to disturb me without so much as a knock, I suggest you get on with it."

The soldier didn't hesitate. "There has been an attack on the workers at the Pentari Canal. Two of them have been killed and another three, wounded. The assailants got away before the Guard could get to them. It seems they had planned the attack while we were out on an expedition to a nearby outpost. We have no idea who they are or where they came from but before they left, one of them allegedly said" – the soldier took a moment to retrieve the words that were stored somewhere in her memory – "*Sil'yhab forlein.*"

Silence hung in the air like a bad smell, the soldier hoping for the Sultan to react and the Sultan hoping for the soldier to embellish.

"Please," he said, in a tone that invited the soldier to give her name.

"Lais Stone, Corporal of the Fourth West Division, my Sultan."

"Thank you, Stone, and what exactly is *Sil'yhab forlein*?"

More silence. The tension was so palpable that even a knife would have struggled to cut through it.

"I'm sorry, your Excellency, we have no idea. We left the rest of our division at the construction and came here as soon as we could. I had first intended to report to Captain Lahsilli but he is on an excursion with the Fifth West, and nobody seemed to know where General Kheller is. Since you are the next in the chain of command, I—"

"Yes, yes, okay. You did all you could, Lahsilli and Kheller are preoccupied." Another wave of the hands. "Tell the workers to pick up their pace. The sooner the canal is finished, the sooner we can alleviate this threat of bandits. In the meantime, return to your post with the division and keep close guard of the construction. They are under your watch. I will arrange council with the general to get his view on the matter, and you are not to leave your position until the works are complete. If there's any more trouble, then I want to hear about it before it has even happened, do I make myself clear?"

"It is done, my Sultan," the corporal replied.

Ayermune clapped his hands. "Then be gone." A shadow of venom laced his voice.

With that, the two soldiers bowed, turned and vacated the room. A sour quietness filled the void.

Oolia broke it first. "Is that the kind of peril you were worried about?"

The Sultan was contemplative. He shook his head solemnly. "No. Far worse. Oolia, I'd like to take up your offer from before. There must be someone in this city who can help me."

CHAPTER 4

THE INFANT MOUNTAINS

No sooner had breakfast started than it was all over and the villagers of Wychwold, bellies nourished to a near-comfortable level, were awaiting the morning sermon from the new town cleric which would conclude the meal.

Fjona looked at Todie who was facing down and looking at his knees, trembling. He was fumbling with an amulet of black metal and running his fingers over its engravings. Fjona leaned over to get a closer look. The amulet was in the shape of a rose, no bigger than the palm of Todie's hand, and the petals were decorated with intricate etchings of mountains, valleys, forests and lakes: the sanctuaries of the Four Good Gods. At the core of the rose was a square of crystal glass that shimmered with a silvery hue whenever it caught the sun.

"It's beautiful," Fjona whispered in Todie's ear.

"It belonged to my grandmother," he replied without looking up from his fingers.

Fjona gave him a moderately gentle nudge in his side. "You'll be great!" she said, urging him to stand. "Just try not to swear."

Todie returned her smile, pocketed the amulet, and mouthed the words 'thank you' as he stood up before his eager congregation. Fjona could practically hear his heart pounding through his chest and his nerves were only exacerbated when the chatter faded and a silence consumed the tables.

The quiet seemed to last for minutes though in truth it was probably no more than a few seconds, occasionally interrupted by the bleating of a nearby goat.

Fjona nudged Todie again and he immediately seized his confidence and began to speak.

"I wanted to take a moment there to reflect on the recent passing of our former cleric, and my beloved grandmother, Lasmee," he said confidently, completely winging it. "I know how much she would have loved to have been here today. Not for giving a few peaceful words, nor for enjoying your delicious food" – so far so good – "but for taking great pleasure in watching Mrs Wiskins getting pissed."

Silence again.

"Oh my," Fjona muttered under her breath, looking away as if to deny her friendship with Todie.

Had there been crickets out in the neighbouring fields they would surely have been heard chirping but the only sound was Meris, who was in a fit of coughing having swallowed his tea down the wrong pipe. Even Todie's mother, Angine, avoided making eye contact with her son.

That being said, Todie wasn't wrong. Mrs Wiskins was too busy nursing another half pint of stout; she hadn't even heard her name being mentioned.

Credit to Todie, whose face had turned a little red in

places, he persevered. "It is by breaking bread together as a community that we can truly appreciate all that the Four Good Gods of Marrow Myre have provided us. We must of course thank Aserae, the eldest sister, without whom there would be no world in which we could live. We thank you, Aserae, for creating the lands and oceans, mountains and rivers, and everything in between."

The rest of the villagers had now settled after Todie's introduction and responded in unison, "To Aserae, we thank."

Todie too was beginning to settle into his role and continued. "We must thank Yore, the master of the elements that bind this world, for he designed fire and wind, fed power to the waters and forged the climates within which we live. For that, we thank you, Yore."

The villagers responded again, "To Yore, we thank."

"To Aulden we must thank for she created life and without her we simply would not be. We thank you, Aulden, for the birds and bees, flowers and trees, and all the inhabitants with whom we share this world. It was, after all, in the soils that Aserae laid, Aulden who breathed life so that we can live off the fruits and harvests of Aserae's creation."

"To Aulden, we thank," the villagers replied.

"And to Beale we must thank you for bestowing upon us the power of emotion, without which we and all the beings of this world would lack the ability to feel. Without emotions, we as a village could not come together for breakfast and care for one another as we all do." Todie, now brimming with confidence, looked around the tables of strange and wonderful people. "And most importantly," he added, "we would not have the capacity to forgive, say, a young cleric who perhaps got off on the wrong foot!"

Redeemed, now all of the villagers were smiling and many went so far as to chuckle a little which, though perhaps forced, was at least audible.

"So we thank you, Beale, who resides in the mountains of this very parish for giving us the power to emote."

"To Beale, we thank."

"It is with Kalzeth, the deceitful sibling, who tarnished the work of Aserae, Yore, Aulden and Beale that we remember the pains of this world, and we must use this knowledge as motivation to bring good to us all. So please be mindful of others, kind and respectful as the Four Good Gods themselves wished, and do all have a blessed day here in Wychwold," Todie surmised.

Fjona could practically feel an air of relief washing over Todie as he quietly seated himself back down.

There was a mumbling of thanks to the young cleric and words of agreement to his final message as the villagers excused themselves from the table and proceeded with clearing up.

The same efficiency with which the table had been laid was applied to cleaning and, soon enough, a conveyor of helpful hands was collecting in the empty dishes and bowls, cups and saucers, and feeding what little food scraps remained to the goats.

Fjona abstained from being helpful and stayed seated for a moment with Todie.

"Just so we're on the same page," he eventually said, breaking the silence, "in my first ever morning testament as cleric to the village, the role I have aspired to since I was a young child, and spent many long years of devoting myself to learning the doctrine of Myrish religion, beneath the watch of my late grandmother and everybody I have ever known... I said the word *pissed*. That is what happened, right?"

"Amongst other things, yes. Though it could have been at lot worse..." Fjona mused before giving a wide grin. "You could have told Mrs Wiskins to f—"

"Fjona!"

The two friends looked behind them to see a palomino horse with a long, flowing mane trotting towards them. Riding the horse was a *helven* woman: part Myrish and part elf. She had an endearing, plump face with dark eyes, round ears and long, silver hair. Her skin glowed with a golden hue and her body was tall and spindly like a birch tree.

"Aserae, save me," Todie said to himself as Fjona leaped from the table and raced towards the visitor.

"Hey, Evelyn, what brings you to Wychwold?" Fjona asked with a broad smile. She petted the horse and ran her fingers through its hair.

"It would appear the fates have presented me – nay – *us* an opportunity. A neighbour of the village received some Common money for a menial errand. She had no use for it herself, so proffered it to me," Evelyn said as she shimmied off the horse and dug her hands into the pockets of her suede riding jacket. She opened her palm to reveal two dozen polished round coins.

"Wow!" Fjona exclaimed, cradling the bronze and silver coins as if they were newborn chicks. "How did your neighbour even come across these?"

"I'm none too sure, truth be with you. Rosalyna has a tendency to speak a lot without really saying anything. Something about a traveller who'd washed up here from the mainland and she giving him a ride to Port Widow," Evelyn explained, "but it should bother us, not! For once, we have a little money to spend at Port Widow ourselves. I have heard the spring elves are in town for Lullatide, bringing with them sweet music and sweeter concoctions. Fare wishes and farewell Myrish privy water; you and I may taste the real thing."

"Come on!" Todie scoffed having wandered over. "Surely you have better things to do than go to Port Widow just to get—"

"Pissed?" Fjona teased as Todie blushed yet again.

Evelyn looked at Fjona, perplexed.

"I'll fill you in later," Fjona replied with a grin, "and to answer your question, Todie, no, Evelyn and I do not have better things to do than to get drunk in Port Widow. Besides, when else might we get a chance to join in with the festivities?"

"Twas the rocks, indeed, the bow concedes,
a sleeping captain, lost at sea.
'Til Myrish fishmen, strong of head,
did save the elves of Rosensted," recited Evelyn. "Or so does say the poem."

"Well if that doesn't persuade you... " said Fjona after a brief pause.

Todie pondered it for a moment.

"Okay fine. Please let me come along too."

Several of the villagers were looking over at the three youths disapprovingly for not helping clear away after breakfast, though none of them were willing to say anything.

"Forgive me, my sweet Todie, but why the abrupt change of heart? Have you got little better to do with your time?" Evelyn said with only a hint of derision. "Or perhaps you dare not trust two helpless young ladies alone, but for each other, in a tavern crowded with unsavoury gentlemen?"

This only encouraged Fjona. "Yes, oh please do protect us," she said, in a mocking tone. "Why whatever would we do without a big strong man to keep watch over us?"

Now Evelyn and Fjona were in hysterics at the expense of Todie whose face, somehow, reddened further.

"Relax, my sweet Todie, you may have the pleasure of our company," Evelyn assured him as she climbed back onto her horse.

"Well I will gladly join you both," said Todie, "but in the meantime, I should best lend a hand to the other villagers before they complain to my mother. I can also speak to Iser about borrowing a couple of horses for this evening."

"Your astute attention to planning makes you ever more interesting," Evelyn said, though the heavy sarcasm was not missed by Fjona.

Todie merely rolled his eyes as he walked away.

"You ought to be nicer to him, Evelyn. You know how much he and his family have been through lately," Fjona said but the helven was too preoccupied with petting her horse to listen.

"We shall gather in Hamlish Heath this late-afternoon and together ride to Port Widow for moonrise," Evelyn said as she pulled the horse around, "and be sure sweet Todie doesn't remain, for we may need a recipient for our japes when we're inebriated!"

Fjona smiled. "Todie will be there, don't you worry. We shall see you later, Evelyn."

With that, Evelyn and the horse clattered off away from the village.

Fjona, feeling a nervous excitement for the evening to come, headed back up the hillock to her house to offer some assistance to her parents and get out of that horrible dress.

She had hardly taken a step through the door before her mother, Dharla, was on to her. "Fjona, your father and I need to speak with you," she started, but Fjona was already striding away towards her bedroom.

"Of course, I shan't be a moment. I am just going to get changed out of my *beautiful* frock," Fjona replied with practiced sincerity.

She was up the ladder and into the loft before she could hear Dharla's response.

As soon as Fjona was in her room she pulled the green dress over her head, only to reveal that she had been fully clothed beneath it all morning. She was now just wearing a grubby, cream sleeveless shirt that was fastened by wooden buttons of which at least a couple were missing. The shirt was tucked into a pair of narrow, black trousers that stopped midway down her calves and were tightened by a brown leather belt.

Fjona threw the dress ungraciously over the back of the chair and returned to her mother downstairs.

Dharla didn't comment on Fjona's appearance. "Your

father and I have decided to go away for a while."

This piqued Fjona's interest. "You're going away? Not once have you stepped outside of Wychwold in all the time I have been alive. Where do you intend to go?"

Ascerat could be heard fumbling around in the master bedroom downstairs, presumably already packing bags for the suddenly announced trip.

Dharla invited Fjona to take a seat at the table and proceeded to pour them each a cup of freshly brewed tea.

"Todie's..." Dharla hesitated for a moment while she gathered her thoughts. "*colourful* testament this morning reminded us just how disconnected your father and I feel we have become from our spirituality. We intend to make a pilgrimage to Beale Cahn, the stone circle in the Infant Mountains where Beale's spirit resides. I realise this is very abrupt but we plan on leaving today. We expect to be home within a couple of weeks."

Fjona pondered this. "Just so that I am hearing this correctly, Todie's sermon this morning has inspired you and Papa to drop all that you are doing here in Wychwold to travel countless leagues into dangerous terrain, all in search of a stone circle so that you can find yourselves?"

Dharla looked away, perhaps afraid that her daughter might feel abandoned. They each took a slow sip of tea.

"I think that's fantastic!" Fjona eventually said, having concluded that an excuse would no longer be necessary to visit Evelyn later that day.

Dharla's face lit up and she placed a soft hand over Fjona's. "Are you sure? I know how sudden this decision has been made but we didn't want a moment's delay. Besides we both know that you can handle everything here and I suspect that you may enjoy a little time to yourself."

"Mother, this really is wonderful. I think a spiritual journey will do you and Papa a world of good and you can certainly trust me with the house. I ask only that you travel safely."

"Of course, my *derine*, you need not worry about us," Dharla replied, although Fjona sensed a faint breath of uncertainty in her mother's voice.

It was then that Ascerat entered the living room, feebly dragging a bulging canvas bag. He was muttering quietly to himself, completely oblivious to the presence of both Dharla and Fjona.

"Let me help you with that," Dharla said, springing to her feet and striding over to her husband.

"Yes, yes very good, tip top," he mumbled as he turned to find Fjona sitting at the table. "My *derine*!" he said, surprised, before quickly settling into conversation. "Has your mother shared our wonderful news?"

Fjona stood and embraced Ascerat firmly in her strong arms. "Yes, she told me everything. You have both worked so hard around here and I agree that you deserve a chance to rediscover your spirituality. Please do keep safe, though. As you know, I have never been to the Infant Mountains myself but I can only imagine how treacherous it can be out there."

"You have nothing to fear, my *derine*, your mother is a fierce woman," he replied with his trademark smile before they were interrupted by a knock at the door.

Fjona turned to see a young stable boy, covered from head

to toe in a thin coat of manure and straw. He had light hair and a face as freckly as a currant bun.

"Welcome, Tomis," Dharla said, the bag strapped comfortably over her back.

"My father has prepared the two horses for you, Mrs Sarsen," Tomis informed her.

"Thank you, my *aerin*. Ascerat and I will be over shortly," Dharla replied as Tomis raced off back towards the stables, kicking up dirt in his wake.

Despite looking forward to having some time to herself, Fjona felt an unexpected pang of sadness at the departure of her parents.

"We shall be absolutely fine," Ascerat said, as if sensing Fjona's apprehension.

"I know," Fjona replied although she couldn't quite shake off her doubts.

They went outside and Dharla began filling the saddlebags of two stocky horses with food, waterskins and cooking utensils. Iser, the stable keeper, was checking over the horses and chatting amiably. Fjona could only be impressed by how quickly her mother had prepared for the journey.

She glanced over to see Todie strolling towards her, auburn hair flopping freely in the wind.

"What's going on?" he asked Fjona as he watched Dharla adjusting the saddle of her horse.

"It seems your morning testament was more successful than you first gave credit," Fjona replied.

"What do you mean?" Todie asked, puzzled.

"My parents were inspired to rekindle their spirituality," she said simply. When Fjona realised that Todie was only becoming more confused, she added, "They're going on a pilgrimage to the Infant Mountains for a couple of weeks. Something about connecting with the spirit of Beale."

Todie was dumbfounded. "I cannot believe that my words have had such a profound impact on your parents!"

Brimming with joy, the young cleric bounded over to Dharla. "I understand my sermon this morning has encouraged you to explore your own spirituality," he said. "I cannot tell you how flattered I am that you have been so touched by what I had to say."

Dharla regarded Todie, though her thoughts were elsewhere.

He continued nonetheless. "I would like to wish you the safest of journeys and pray that you will find in yourself what you are searching for."

Dharla finally acknowledged Todie. "Yes, thank you, cleric," she said brusquely, and rushed back into the house murmuring, "blankets" to herself.

Todie was standing resolute and blushing again when Fjona placed a gentle hand on his shoulder. "Yes, thank you, cleric," she mocked.

Todie had clearly taken just about as many jibes as he could for one day. "I wonder exactly what your parents plan on doing many leagues away that they felt they couldn't do in their own bedchamber," he said and made off towards his own house, smirking from ear to ear.

Fjona's stomach lurched.

CHAPTER 5

THE SLEEPING GIANT

Down in the Lower Gate, Kaikura Kendi was attempting to make her way through the throng of tradespeople and travellers. She was a summer elf with dark skin and velvety black hair tied up in a casual ponytail. Tall by most standards, though a little short for an elf, and scrawny around the bones. Her eyes were dark, and her pointed ears were slightly folded at the tips and decorated with simple copper earrings.

"Excuse me, forgive me, thank you," she said, brushing past a Grugan who was a very long way from home.

The Grugan, tall and broad with waxy orange skin and sharp teeth, snorted back at Kaikura in a seemingly rude way, though being well studied in most Arvish languages, Kaikura knew the sound to express an apology. He turned back to a stall where a second Grugan was chopping up a slab of strange purple meat with a large cleaver. The two Grugans grunted and snarled at each other in an apparently informal way as if they were discussing the weather or which desert outposts they had visited on their journey down to Panamaya City. A short while later, the unusual meat was chopped, coins exchanged and the Grugans parted ways.

Kaikura had spent the best part of the morning teaching at an alleyway school, a short way beyond the forum. There, nearby children could freely attend to learn about the Arvum from a small band of volunteers who dedicated whatever free time that could to bettering the lives of the youngest generation. For the children, Kaikura was a perfect role model. A former pupil of an alleyway school herself, she was now a scholar at the Archivus: the oldest university and library in the Arvum, which just happened to be in the Upper Gate of Panamaya City.

From Kaikura's perspective, she relished the opportunity to share with the children what she had learned from her mentor, Proprietor of Intellect Sialah Bouwer. Under Proprietor Bouwer's wing, Kaikura had studied everything from mathematics, modern and ancient languages, and life sciences, to historical events, geology and politics. With a wealth of knowledge that could have afforded her a palace of her own, could it have been converted into money, the impoverished children of the Lower Gate were beyond fortunate to have someone of Kaikura's esteem to guide them.

Yet, somehow, elven politics and Arvish geography did little to titillate their fleeting enthusiasms. As such, Kaikura now found herself juggling a stack of books from the Archivus that leaned towards mythical monsters and curious stories of the past in the hopes that she could steal her pupils' attention for even just a morning.

As Kaikura slipped between two traders, her green tunic flapping behind her, an island elf inadvertently elbowed her in the ribs, causing her to spin on her heels just to keep her balance.

Unlike the Grugan, the island elf was less polite. "Oh do mind yourself," he said without so much as a cursory glance to check that Kaikura was okay.

She cursed as she watched the tall, golden-skinned elf disappear into the crowd. Somehow, she had managed to hold on to everything she was carrying, including her purse that was slung over one shoulder – though it contained only a handful of *bassals* and *clines*.

It was the middle of the day by now and the forum was sweating under the searing heat of the sun.

After bumping into backs and shoulders, tripping over feet and animals, Kaikura finally crossed the gallery that surrounded the market and into the labyrinthine, cobbled avenues of houses that sprawled across the Lower Gate.

She took a relieved breath. "All things considered, I believe that went rather well. Would you perhaps agree, Bobassa?" she said, as her pet sandkat slinked out from the shadows of a narrow alleyway, barely discernible between two hovels.

Sandkats were feline by all accounts but differed from their domestic cousins by their colourful coat of incredibly fine and deceptively soft scales. Their ears were large and rotational, and they were known to have anywhere between one and four long tails with a brush-like tip. Bobassa had two tails and wore a copper and coal coloured coat. He'd been a devoted companion to Kaikura since she rescued him from poachers nearly four summers ago. Since then, he had rarely left her side and, although he was reluctant to go into the forum himself, would keep a watchful eye on her from the surrounding rooftops.

Bobassa gallantly strolled over to Kaikura and affectionately brushed up against her leg, letting out a warm purr.

"I would be most obliged if you could lead the way home," Kaikura said, gesturing to the sandkat.

In a flash of shimmering scales, Bobassa leaped ahead of Kaikura and set off down the steep, bumpy road between the houses. The streets were relatively quiet but for a few passers-by, mostly summer elves heading up to the forum and the occasional beggar waiting at alley junctions in the hope they could get a coin or two from the passing traffic.

They followed a gully trickling with water that became increasingly murky the further down the mountain they descended, then cut across a flimsy, wooden bridge that led over a quiet street below.

Eventually they stopped at a row of indistinguishable buildings, all with simple wooden doors and small windows behind closed shutters. Carefully balancing the books between one arm and her chest, Kaikura climbed a ladder that was precariously attached to the façade of the houses and made her way onto the roof where Bobassa was waiting obediently. Together they headed to a red-brown wooden hatch, midway across the rooftops. It was covered in a dusting of fresh sand and had a wrought iron handle on the nearest edge. Around the hatch were four barred shutters that allowed at least some natural light into the confined room beneath.

Kaikura opened the hatch door and clambered down a rickety wood and rope ladder into her cosy little home. It wasn't much by anyone's standard but it was Kaikura's space and that was all that mattered to her.

The hovel comprised of just one room but with a separate wooden terrace on the far side that could be accessed by its own ladder. The terrace was big enough only for a small bed and side table and was bordered by a low wooden banister to prevent Kaikura from rolling off it in her sleep. Bobassa slept in a small crate at the foot of the bed. It had been layered up with sand and pearl-swan feathers that Kaikura had purchased from an island elf in the forum.

The main floor was roughly divided into basic amenities. One corner housed a small clay oven and simple stove, behind which were shelves stacked with jars and ceramic crockery. A couple of small pans hung from hooks on the wall alongside some tea leaves and drying herbs. Adjacent to the kitchenette was a privy chamber that Kaikura had segregated with some red and purple sheets attached to a wooden post. Inside it contained just a chamber pot and small wash basin, neither of which were particularly fun to carry up the ladder to dispose of outside.

In the centre of the room was a large, round wooden table that was well loved and well used. It was stacked high with piles of books, scrolls and old maps, and a metal lantern dangled on a long piece of rope that was attached to the ceiling above so that Kaikura could still be absorbed in her reading material after dark.

"Finally some respite, Bobassa," she said and took the bread over to a store cupboard in the kitchen.

With a couple of flint flakes, Kaikura lit the wood-burning

stove in spite of the heat pouring into the home through the open shutters. She proceeded to make herself a cup of tea, grinding up the leaves with a pestle and mortar, and boiling spring water that she had collected the day before. Bobassa, meanwhile, was satisfied with a dish of cool water and a fat, juicy rat that he'd killed in the streets outside.

"Well then, Bobassa, I am burdened with the search of discovering material more befitting the mind of a child," Kaikura said, sifting through her newest books on the table.

She pushed aside a dense tome about anthropology and replaced it with one of her new books. It had the title *The Myths of Music by Edwar Polst* inscribed on the front in swirling gold calligraphy.

Kaikura flicked through the first few pages, her brow furrowed with concentration. "I wonder if perhaps this may stimulate their young minds," she said to Bobassa, who was now tearing through the tough flesh of the rat with his long, sharp teeth. *"It was said that during the eleventh Dynasty of the Sagedom, the tipids of Nouwa sang songs of worship to honour the Sagen Master, Thannilius the Thirsty. Although, in most cultures, the worship song as a whole bears no evidence to success in respect of reward, the tipids were in fact blessed by Thannilius. It is alleged that the Sagen Master bestowed upon the tipids an enchanted brass flute that, when played, could rejuvenate wilting plants and put giants into slumber. Giants likely referred to anyone from outside the village who were natively bigger than the tipids. No such flute has ever been discovered; however, even until as late as the sixteenth Dynasty of the Sagedom, the tipids continued to worship this long since deceased sage who had vowed to protect them."*

Kaikura gently folded the book over her hand, a habit that helped her process what she had read.

"Whatever do you think, Bobassa? An enchanted flute with the capacity to coerce a giant into slumber..."

A disinterested Bobassa was more preoccupied ripping apart the rat's tiny head than listening to tales of a magical instrument.

"Hmm, I think perhaps you may be right. I fear it may be a little too dense for the children and it's somewhat abstract. I must find something with a broader educational scope..."

Kaikura closed the book and pushed it to the side, then pulled another towards her. *The Intriguing Peoples of Marrow Myre,* this one read on the cover.

Again, she flicked through the pages reading aloud phrases such as, *"five gods and only four parishes"* and *"mysterious disappearances in the Myre of Maw."*

Then, as before, she closed the book over her hand.

"An interesting locale, it must be said. Folklore and religion, strange inhabitants and unusual traditions" – she paused – "but Marrow Myre is much too far away. How could I expect the children to relate to something like this?"

She was beginning to lose hope. Although Kaikura wasn't due to teach in the alleyway school for another couple of weeks, she was afraid that she might not ever find a subject that would keep the children engaged.

Then her eyes settled on the spine of a red-covered book buried in her new stack. As if time were seeping away, she quickly retrieved it and plonked it on the table in front of her. In big, garish letters it read *The Sleeping Giant and Other Pentari Tales* with a faded drawing of the mountain below.

"Well this is rather fortuitous," Kaikura said, beaming from ear to ear. Sweeping a stray strand of hair away from her eyes, she delved into the book's crisp pages, reading aloud, "*Legends tell of a man of such stature that he could amble from Eave's End of Longreach, to the northmost coast of Bouanda in merely an afternoon. With the entire Arvum to play, he would rip trees out from their roots to eat as if he were plucking carrots out of the earth, and bathe in lakes with his feet resting on one bank and his head on another.*

The giant was an inquisitive being who loved exploring the Arvum, stepping up mountains and splashing in the ponds like a child might splash in a puddle. He was docile and kind, and took pleasure in visiting the tiny villages where the small people lived.

However, although the giant had never shown any signs of harming the villagers, they were afraid of him. The moment they could hear his pounding footsteps echoing from the surrounding hills or forests, the villagers would flee into their homes, bar their doors, and hide under their tables. All except for one young man who took pity on the giant.

The young man was an outcast himself and harboured great sympathy. One day, while the giant was sitting over a cliff above the Near Sea and skimming boulders across the waters as if they were small stones, the young man came to his side.

'Thou shalt know, this that plagues thy mind, plagues my very being. We might both be cured were those villagers to accept us,' the young man said, startling the giant who, before now, had never been engaged in conversation.

56

'Who are you?' he asked the man in a warm, booming voice.

'I am but a lonely soul, as I know you are too,' the young man replied, 'and I wish to befriend thou, for we might both be accepted.'

'Why don't they accept you already?' the giant asked. 'I thought all the small people accepted one another.'

The young man was contemplative for a moment as if weighing up the possible answers.

'The villagers accept only those who are exactly alike,' the young man said. 'They distrust me for I am special.' With that, the man gently waved his hand over a wilting wildflower amongst the grasses next to him. A moment later, its stem started to stiffen and the flower's head folded backwards and sat firmly upright. Blue petals burst outward in a sprinkling of silver dust that shone in the sunlight.

The giant gawped at the flower.

'What is your plan? How can we make the villagers accept us?' he asked the young man, seemingly convinced.

The young man smiled; a flash of deceit passed through his eyes."

By now, Bobassa had completely devoured the rat and was licking his fat lips satisfactorily. He had climbed up onto Kaikura's lap and was purring sweetly, a look of expectancy on his face which roughly translated as 'let's go out hunting', but that Kaikura read as 'please proceed with your story'.

"The young man had persuaded the giant to take him to the Bounding Cliffs of the East which formed a great ridge between the Near Sea and the Pentari Sea. Surrounding the Pentari Sea were hundreds of villages, the people of whom depended on all that this vast expanse of freshwater provided.

'Thou has doubtlessly heard the villagers' complaints. How fish of the Pentari Sea are scarce, how many fear of starvation,' the young man said.

The giant uncertainly agreed. 'I am sure I have heard such whispers.'

'Well I've a plan to welcome fresh fish in bountiful proportions to fill the stomachs of the villagers. We need only to collapse the Bounding Cliffs, thus allowing the waters of the Near Sea and the Pentari to coalesce,' said the young man. 'How grateful the villagers shall be. Little choice should remain but to accept us as their own. Perhaps even as more than their own,' he considered, 'like gods!'

The giant pondered this for a moment. 'I yearn not to be a god, but merely to be accepted. Though already I can hear their cries of gratefulness as we provide them with such fruits from the sea.'

It wasn't cries of gratefulness that the giant would come to hear but cries of devastation and doom. For the young man took a regular sized hammer and cast a spell upon it that enlarged it into one that would befit the giant, and with it the giant tore down the Bounding Cliffs of the East. With each mighty swing, great chunks of the ridge were flung faraway into the ocean, tidal splashes erupting on the horizon.

After the cliffs were no more than flakes of rock and dust, the giant waited in eager anticipation for the Near Sea to feed into the Pentari, but it never did. Instead, the water drained out of the Pentari Sea until there was nothing left but a vast blanket of sand.

'I don't understand,' the giant said, with his enormous head buried in his enormous hands. 'I thought the seas were supposed to meet?'

The young man chuckled cruelly. 'Worry not, my dear friend,' he said, 'for it is with fear that we can govern the villagers.'

It was then that the hard truth dawned on the simple kind giant. 'There never was a shortage of fish in the Pentari, was there? You tricked me so that you could become powerful and control your people!' His eyes flared with rage.

'Never were they my people!' replied the young man, his disdain frothing at his lips.

The giant barely heard the young man for he was already racing towards the villages to beg for their forgiveness and offer his help. The villagers of course did not take kindly to his appearance.

It is said that the small people could be heard crying in pain from ten leagues away and when the giant turned up at their gates, they accused him of draining the sea and blamed him for the anguish they now suffered. They threw rocks at him and frightened him with torches burning with angry fires.

The giant, scared and ashamed, raced away from the villages to a quiet spot in the now Pentari Desert.

Then, while the giant was sulking alone on the open sands, the manipulative young man appeared again before him.

'Cry not, my friend, those villagers were cruel to thee. Their suffering is deserved,' he said.

'I did not want to bring them harm. This is all your fault,' said the giant.

'My fault?' the young man asked, innocently. 'Was it not

thou whose hand held the hammer, and was it not thou who vanquished the cliffs, and was it not thou who released the Pentari Sea into the great oceans. I was but merely a spiritual advisor. I held no such hand in its destruction.'

The giant thought about it for a while. Perhaps it was true, although the man had provided the hammer, it was in fact he who had wielded it.

'You're right!' he said. 'This is all my fault! How can I live in the knowledge that I have caused such harm?'

The young man feigned to consider this for a moment, though of course he was conspiratorial by nature and knew exactly what he intended. For the time being he no longer needed the giant.

'Here,' the young man beckoned, 'take a seat upon the sands. From here, thou can repay thy debts to the villages and keep guard of the desert. Should any ill befall, thou may rise from the dusts and defend them.'

Distracted by the depths of his shame, the giant was oblivious to any ulterior motives of the young man and agreed. He sat down on the burning sand, tucked his knees up to his head and rested his hands upon his legs.

The young man clapped his hands together firmly, and dust and sand swirled around the giant and tucked him in like he was being tucked into bed.

'Thank you, my friend, for all that thou have done for me.' The young man cast a spell over the giant that put him into a deep, undisturbed slumber. 'If ever I am in of need your help again, return I shall to wake thou from thy sleep, but until then...'

Over generations and generations, the giant's body was battered by sandstorms and became buried in a dense rocky mountain. Then generations more passed and settlers discovered this lowly outcrop in the middle of the desert. They climbed to its peak and established, at first, a village which over time grew into the city known today as Panamaya.

As for the young man, we know not what happened to him, but it is said that should he ever return he will awaken the sleeping giant and mark the beginning of the end."

There was a stillness in the air by the time Kaikura had finished reading the tale. Bobassa was now curled up on her lap, most likely dreaming of hunting vermin in the streets outside.

"That is how the mountain got its name *The Sleeping Giant*," Kaikura concluded and shook Bobassa off her lap.

He screeched at her at the shock of being disturbed, but quickly softened when he realised he was safely at home.

"The children will certainly enjoy this tale," she added. "After all, it tells the story of where they all live."

Later, at the base of Panamaya City, Corporal Lais Stone and her five rangers of the Fourth West Division pulled up alongside the trench where the workers were constructing the canal. The trench was as about as deep as the Sultan's palace was tall, and at least twice as wide. Inside there were around two hundred men whose sun-kissed skin was matted with sand and sweat from a day of working.

Lais leaped from her tall red stallion and marched purposefully towards the labourers, expecting to find them waiting around with shovel and mattock, eagerly anticipating the go-ahead to continue working, but she was mistaken.

As she approached the trench, she could hear two of the labourers talking agitatedly in Kelnish, the tribal language of the Kelner elves who lived in satellite settlements across the Pentari Desert – often the first to take up cheap work when they could find it. She climbed down a series of rope ladders, then headed towards the crowd of workers.

"What's going on?" Lais demanded.

The two labourers continued arguing in front of a rabble of other workers who were muttering quietly to themselves. There was a lot of gesticulation and pointing of long fingers, often in the direction of two white palls, beneath which Lais could only presume were the bodies of the men who had been killed during the attack.

"I said, what is going on?" she called again with a force that echoed down the trench. This time she did get the attention of the two men.

The first, a broader elf with paling skin and a black cloth shirt that symbolled superior status, spoke up. "My men, refuse work," he said simply in the common tongue.

The second, in a dusty white cloth shirt, interrupted in Kelnish but the superior cut him off. He looked scared.

"The Sultan says you are to pick up the pace and get the job done," Lais said matter-of-factly.

The labourers looked around at each other, many with a look of horror. Their grasp on Arvish may have been limited but they certainly knew phrases like *pick up the pace and get the job done*.

The superior attempted to placate them but to no avail. They continued to talk amongst themselves, their voices raising as more and more of them spoke up with something important to say.

"What is the issue?" Lais asked impatiently.

"They afraid. They refuse work," he replied.

Lais looked around at the bedraggled group of labourers. "Tell them they no longer need to fear the bandits. My name is Lais Stone. I am the corporal of the Fourth West Division for the Noble Guard of the Sultan," she replied patriotically. "My rangers and I are here to protect you. We will keep away any trouble so that you can get the job done safely."

The superior shook his head in dismay.

"No, no, my Guard. My workers fear not bandits," he said.

"Then what is the problem?"

"*Sil'yhab forlein*. It is Kelnish for *the worst is yet to come*. My Guard, they are afraid of waking the sleeping giant."

CHAPTER 6

BEHIND THE DOOR

Mattis was very brave for his age. His reputation in the alleyway school had earned him the nickname of *the scorpion* having developed quite the affinity for the blood red, venomous arachnids. While the other children would scream at the intrusion of the strange, little creatures with their blackened pincers and beady eyes, young Mattis would lay face down on the floor and wait for them to scuttle nearer to him. With soft words, he would chat boyishly with the scorpions until they appeared to relax, then carefully collect them in his open hands and sit for a while to show the other children that they need not be afraid.

He was never a coward when it came to pinching food off the stalls in the forum or running between the houses in the dead of night, and what was so scary anyway about waking a giant that had been asleep for thousands of years?

Although Mattis only just needed two hands to count his age, he had found himself enrolled with the Noble Guard of the Sultan, in a sense. Twice a day, between school lessons and food acquisition, he would sweep the floors in the barracks for the grand total of one *bassal* at the end of the month. Sweeping may result in a smog of dust settling on his head of thick black hair but he had a pocket in his rag clothes that was heavy with coins, and that really wasn't bad for a homeless Panamayan orphan.

However, like most things, Mattis' reputation for immense courage took a dramatic beating when he reported to his classmates that there was a monster living in the barracks. He and his broom were busying away in the dank, gloomy cellars which served as a storeroom for old equipment. Around him were stacks of old robes, cracked shields and broken cutlasses, old riding boots, rotting saddles and rusting horseshoes dumped in the low-ceilinged cavern deep in the belly of the Noble Guard's domain. Although it was essentially a graveyard of military apparel, often the relics of deceased soldiers, Mattis generally enjoyed visiting the cellar in hopes that he may find a friendly rat or spindly spider hidden away in a secluded corner with whom he could play.

However, on the day that his bravery was severely questioned, the cellar felt colder and quieter than ever before.

At the far end of the dark basement was a red door that was always locked; Mattis had tried it before. Curiosity had lured him in but never had he found a way to see to the other side.

He was minding his own business, wafting the dust under a dilapidated crate when a sudden and loud bang caught his attention. Heart pounding in his small, pointed ears, Mattis stared, frozen in horror. Months of tending to the barracks and not once had he ever heard so much as a squeak from behind the red door. When his blood began to settle again, he harnessed whatever confidence he had and crept in the direction of the loud bang, careful to not make a sound of his own that might draw attention to himself.

Nearly within touching distance of the door, Mattis could hear a quiet moaning from beyond. It sounded like a distressed animal and reminded him of the butcher at the forum who would slaughter sheep right there in front of the throng of potential customers. The moans seemed to be intensifying, a monster hungry and raring to kill its prey. Mattis was preparing himself to tear the door down and rescue whoever was inside from the clutches of the fiendish beast. He could picture it clearly: taut face, huge frothing fangs that drooled with blood, and great claws that could rip apart a small building, and yet Mattis was still brave enough to confront this beast and save its victim from the brink of death, whoever that victim may have been.

Then he found out. Just as his steady hand reached out for a tarnished brass doorknob, Mattis heard the most piercing of screams from the other side. The monster had made its move, shredded through flesh and bone, and was drinking the blood of a pallid, wilting corpse. It was all too vivid in his young, imaginative mind.

Legs shaking, he ran as fast as he could towards the stairs and never looked back. From that moment onwards, Mattis vowed to never again pay a visit to the monster that lurked beneath the barracks.

On the other side of the door, Sigmund Kheller, General to the Noble Guard of the Sultan retreated from beneath the dress of Lady Lucinda Denvillier. She cried out again in an expulsion of energy, a tingling sensation prickling her body as she lay back on a conveniently placed hay bale in immense satisfaction.

Her breaths were sharp and heavy, and her slender, olive-skinned body felt cold beneath a film of passionate sweat.

General Kheller's dense black beard was glistening in the candlelight and he wiped it with the back of his strong, bare arm.

Lucinda looked up and saw that the general was as stiff as a tall glass of Myrish whiskey.

"Your turn," she said, and shakily got onto her knees as she peeled her dress off over her head.

Afterwards, they lay naked together on the hay, panting like two excited dogs.

"Remind me how long you are in the city?" General Kheller asked between deep, heaving breaths.

Lady Lucinda rolled over and stared at him with enticing, deep blue eyes. "My dear Sigmund, I regret to inform you that I will be departing for Rosensted in the morning. I have a meeting to attend in the Upper Gate but then I must be on my way."

The tense, muscular frame of the general seemed to deflate a little. With a long, pointed finger, Lady Lucinda traced an ancient scar from Kheller's abdomen up to his shoulder before laying a gentle kiss on his thick neck. He made a satisfied sound not unlike that of a cat purring.

"When will you be back?"

"I cannot say exactly but you will be the first to know when I am," Lady Lucinda replied with a whimsical look in her eyes.

This seemed enough to satisfy the general who rolled back over on top of her.

"Now, now," she said quickly, patting the eager soldier on his chest, "were I to stay any longer I would miss my appointment and would have no reason to return to Panamaya."

For a moment, Kheller hung over her, his dark tangled hair brushing Lucinda's forehead, a hungry expression on his stern angular face. With anyone else, Kheller may not have shown so much restraint, but there was something powerful about Lady Lucinda that discouraged him from pursuing his urges. He submitted and rolled back over into a slight dip in the hay that roughly outlined his broad frame.

Lady Lucinda swiftly stood, her modest breasts swaying as she reached for her honey-coloured linen dress that had been discarded on the dusty stone floor beside her. Surrounding the dress was a silk chemise and a pair of delicate leather sandals. Her clothes were mixed in a bundle along with the general's ruby and gold coat, breeches, helmet, and one black leather boot, the other of which had been thrown against the door in a hasty attempt to undress.

She proceeded to pull on her undergarment, comfortably aware of the general's black eyes fixed upon her.

"Must you go?" he eventually said when he snapped out of his lascivious gaze.

Lady Lucinda turned back to the general while tidying her wavy, pine-green hair with her fingers. "Perhaps, Sigmund, I shall be able to return," she said conspiratorially. "My appointment shan't be long but I must be punctual to join my caravan back to Rosensted. If you can promise not to leave that bed before I get back, then I may just have time to pay you a visit before I head off."

The general's mouth opened into a lustful grin. "I can be patient," he said. "The Guard can manage without me for a while. Who exactly are you meeting?"

Lucinda shot him a sharp look, but quickly softened her expression and smiled sweetly. "You need not be troubled by my affairs."

The general opened his mouth as if to question her further, but no words came to his mind. Instead, and despite his instructions, Kheller made to get off the hay bale bed, but was quickly interrupted.

"No, no. You must not leave that bed, General. You know the rules."

"I just thought that if I stayed in this room—" he began, but Lucinda cut him off.

"Do not get off that bed," she said sternly, though only fractionally raising her voice.

Her words cut through the general and he retreated back to his former position, naked and unashamedly vulnerable.

"Very good," Lucinda said in a much softer tone. "I will be back before you know it."

Without so much as a kiss on the forehead, she scampered towards the door and left Sigmund Kheller alone in the dim candlelight.

Lady Lucinda hastily made her way through the basement, shivering in the cold gloom, and up the stairs that led into a quiet corner of the barracks. On light feet, she cautiously navigated the winding corridors so as not to bump into anyone, although she knew that most of the divisions would be out on patrol at this hour of the day. Before long, she stepped out into the glaring Pentari sun and had to squint as it reflected from the pale buildings of the Upper Gate.

Her eyes caught a hooded figure, surreptitiously hovering by an alleyway on the opposite side of the spring. They appeared to notice Lucinda before fading into the dark space between the two buildings. Lucinda dusted off her dress and hurriedly made for the shady character.

The azure water of the spring glowed beneath her as she crossed over a stone bridge that forded it. There were a few people about, mostly garbed in elitist attire and lackadaisically strolling about the spring without a care in the world, too busy to notice anyone up to no good.

At first, Lucinda couldn't see anybody when she stepped into the alleyway, but then she noticed the hooded figure emerge from the shadows.

"Feldin, be snappy, we don't have a whole lot of time. I need to return the original to the general before he notices," she said as she revealed a small package from a discreet pocket of her dress.

"Of course, my Lady. I shan't be long," Feldin replied in a croaky voice.

Without a moment's hesitation, Lucinda handed over the parcel.

"What are you going to do in my absence?" Feldin asked, placing the parcel inside his cloak.

Lucinda smiled with her eyes. "I'm going to see whether I can coax my way into the palace," she replied, spinning on her heel.

She headed back out into the Upper Gate, the Sultan's palace looming over her like a great monster, while the shady Feldin slipped away into the dark of the alleyway.

CHAPTER 7

HAMLISH HEATH

Word of Dharla and Ascerat's spontaneous journey to the Infant Mountains had spread around the village like a flu and many well-wishers had congregated about the roundhouse, armed with cakes and biscuits, to see them off. The Sarsens were showered with trinkets meant for good fortune and all manner of items to aid them on their quest, though most of the gifts were left in the house for lack of room in their packs.

Angine Farren gave Dharla a long, loving hug. "Travel well and may the Four Good Gods be forever with you." She brushed both of Dharla's cheeks with the backs of two fingers, a gesture of good faith among the Myrish people.

"Thank you, Angine. I will tell you all about it when we get home. Please watch over Fjona," she said in a hushed voice that only Angine could hear.

Angine smiled in a way that said 'of course'. "And you" – Angine moved over to Ascerat and wrapped her arms around his big coat – "look after your wife."

Ascerat looked blankly at Angine for a moment and then smiled warmly as he embraced her. "You have my word," he said.

"You've a fine pair of horses here, Mrs Sarsen. You can trust them to get you safely to the mountains," said Iser whose long face closely resembled the animals in his keep.

Dharla replied with a simple, "Thank you."

"I trust you know where you are headed," Iser continued, to which Dharla nodded.

"We should arrive at the base by moonrise, though it is the passage through the mountains where" – Dharla paused for a heartbeat – "where our spiritual recuperation will really begin."

After a series of hugs and kisses, Dharla and Ascerat were ready to head off.

Fjona was the last to say goodbye and wish them well.

"Ride safely, Mother. I hope you find what you are looking for," Fjona said, resting her head on Dharla's shoulder.

They remained that way for a while until Dharla replied, "We shall see you when we return, my *derine*." Then, as any mother would be sure to say in such a circumstance, "Please look after the house and don't forget to feed the goats. Oh and remember not to let the hearth burn overnight or forget to wash any blankets and give yourself a chill, and don't—"

"Mother!" Fjona interrupted. "I'm going to be absolutely fine! I know how to look after myself, and I have Todie to help me out should I need him. Don't spend your break from home worrying about me. You'll end up wasting this incredible experience by concerning yourself over whether or not I've eaten my vegetables."

Dharla beamed at her daughter and released her from her tight embrace. She cupped Fjona's face in two hands and kissed her fondly on the forehead. "May the Four Good Gods watch over you," she said and made for her horse.

Ascerat then wrapped his arms around Fjona. "Stay safe, my dear."

"You too, Papa," Fjona replied as a single tear rolled down her cheek, for reasons she couldn't quite put her finger on.

With that, the villagers waved off Dharla and Ascerat, and watched the two horses trot off in the direction of the mountains.

Todie stood beside Fjona as a figure of support. "Incredible, isn't it?" he said.

"What is?" Fjona asked, wiping away the tear.

"Your parents are so disappointed in you gallivanting off to Port Widow that they packed their bags, left town and disowned you."

Fjona slapped him across his chest. "I didn't tell them, you toad." It was an insult he used to suffer daily at the schoolhouse when they were young. Fjona smiled. "Come on then, Todie, we had best be on our way to Hamlish Heath or else we won't make it to Port Widow at all!"

Todie shrugged. "Very well," he said, and the two of them strolled over to the stables where the horse Todie had saddled earlier was munching on a thinning bale of hay.

Fjona looked at the dishevelled animal. "This is it? I thought we were taking a horse each, not squeezing onto a big sheep," she said, desperately hoping that Todie was playing an excessive, though not unlikely, prank.

"I'm afraid your parents took the two I'd set aside for us," Todie admitted, though he didn't seem too bothered by their last resort. "Iser tells me that Shagwell here is a finer beast than he appears."

As if on cue, Shagwell passed wind, belched and urinated all in one beautiful symphony of ablutions. Fjona looked sternly at Todie, arms folded across her chest as if to say: 'we're talking about the same horse, right?'.

"He's still finer than he appears," Todie professed, and proceeded to pet the goofy animal.

Shagwell released a wheezy bray, coughed, then resumed eating the hay.

"Look, Iser assured me that Shagwell is strong enough to carry us both as far as the east coast and he's a damn sight better than walking," Todie assured her.

Fjona watched the horse keenly for a second before conceding. "Fine, we'll take this helpless thing but you're responsible for him if he buckles and dies," she said flippantly.

"Phew!" Todie replied, "because I've promised Iser a bottle of elven liqueur as a thanks for letting us take Shagwell and he'd be very upset if I failed to deliver."

Fjona rolled her eyes and went over to stroke the horse's coarse mane. "Please don't collapse under me, Shagwell," she whispered in the horse's ear as she climbed onto his back.

Todie led them out of the stables and along a dirt path that took them to the edge of the village.

Most of the village folk were tending to their gardens and animals, or in the houses preparing yet more cups of tea and cakes. Only Mrs Wiskins, half asleep in a rocking chair outside her hut, was aware of them leaving the village, though she was in no coherent state to say anything.

At the entrance to Wychwold, Todie hopped on behind Fjona who shuffled forwards a fraction to make room. Shagwell wobbled for a moment but somehow found enough strength to carry the two of them without toppling under the weight.

They talked amiably as they followed the path through the treeline that bordered the village and up to the River Racken, which they could then follow upstream to Hamlish Heath.

"What did *your* mother say when you told her that you're travelling to Port Widow?" Fjona asked, ducking under a few low branches along the riverbank.

"I didn't exactly tell her," Todie replied.

Fjona's eyes widened. "A man of the cloth, the cleric for the village, deceiving his own mother?"

"Please don't. I feel bad enough about it as it is."

"I'm just surprised, that's all. I thought Beale, or one of those Gods at least, frowned upon lying."

"I didn't lie," he said. "I just didn't tell her precisely where I'm taking you."

"Where you're what?"

Todie was hesitant for a moment as the path before them twisted up a steep bank. At the top, he eventually said, "Well see, I told my mother that I would be taking you to the Parish of Aulden so that you could explore your own spirituality. I said that, with your parents going away for a while, I felt you could benefit from visiting the Great Forest where Aulden's spirit resides and connect with your inner self." Again, he paused as if his thoughts were flickering away like sparks from a flame. "Perhaps we could swing by there on our way home."

"To settle your conscience?"

"That too, but really it is an extraordinary place. My grandmother took me to see the Great Forest when I was little, and it was the first time I realised that there is more in life than all we see around us. That was when I knew I was to become a cleric. I guess I'd like to share that experience with you."

They trotted on in silence as Fjona debated whether or not it would be fair to tease Todie when he was so vulnerable. She chose not to.

"Would seem a shame to travel all the way to the Parish of Aulden and not visit the Great Forest," Fjona said, "but keep your expectations low. I don't imagine I'll be fully subscribing to your religion on the back of one woodland."

Todie smiled. "Of course, consider my expectations at rock bottom."

Shagwell took them across a narrow bridge that forded the Racken. The water swelled around pointed rocks that reached out of the river like miniature mountains.

"Did your siblings say anything about our expedition?" Fjona asked, making conversation as the horse slumped off the bridge on the far side. She felt more than a little uncomfortable atop Shagwell with Todie pressed up tightly behind her.

"Peter is too young to suspect anything. I think he was excited to be the man of the house for an evening, although there's only so many responsibilities one can have at the age of seven," he replied.

Fjona chuckled.

"And nothing gets past Flo. You know that as well as I do. I can pay for her silence with a bottle of crystal gin."

"How many alcohol debts have you collected for this?"

Fjona asked, rolling her eyes.

Todie laughed. "Just Iser and Flo," he said as they came through a canopy of vines that led into the village of Hamlish Heath.

It wasn't unlike Wychwold albeit with several fewer houses, mostly rectangular and made of stone with wooden or thatched roofs. There were a couple of more traditional roundhouses around the outskirts of the village, a number of which had loft compartments similar to Fjona's house. Whereas the residents of Wychwold farmed mainly wheat, corn and fowl, the people of Hamlish Heath were more preoccupied with long stretches of vineyards and orchards. A sweet fragrance of fruit hung over the village like a floral mist, to which Todie and Fjona found themselves being drawn to.

They followed a stone track leading up to a long, two-storeyed house, fronted by a big timber porch. There were several elegantly carved wooden sculptures and shrubberies shaped to perfection. It was the sort of building affordable only to those who had made their wealth on the mainland.

Todie and Fjona had hardly made it to the door before it swung open and Evelyn charged out to greet them, dolled up in a stunning silver-blue dress that came down only as far as her knees and fitted trimly to her slight frame. Her made-up face was flawlessly balanced and she wore fine jewellery of necklaces and bangles that only emphasised her innate beauty. Her exquisite face sunk into a look of horror as she was greeted by Fjona in a filthy top and trousers, twigs in her straggly hair, and specks of mud on her pale face. Todie had at least thrown on a clean jerkin and breeches.

Evelyn didn't hesitate for a moment.

"Inside, now," she said firmly, gesturing for Fjona to enter the house.

Fjona and Todie exchanged a quizzical look before following Evelyn into the enormous building.

They stepped into a grand lobby where a candle chandelier suspended from timber beams over an ornately decorated rug that covered much of the open floor. A wooden staircase tapered up to a mezzanine floor that formed a ring around the entranceway and allowed light in through a tall glass window at the top of the stairs. Every visible piece of wooden furniture and fitting had been polished to a glossy sheen, and various statues and artefacts had been placed around the room as if it were a museum.

Although Todie and Fjona had known Evelyn for many years, this was the very first time either of them had been invited into her house. They couldn't help but gawp at the vast interior as they treaded carefully over the rug for fear of smearing mud over the embroidery.

"Come on!" Evelyn beckoned from the top of the stairs and stormed off through an open door.

Fjona started towards the stairs.

"I should probably wait down here " Todie said shyly.

"Afraid of seeing a woman dressed down?" Fjona teased, though she continued up the stairs regardless.

Todie just shrugged and explored the museum pieces. He was drawn to one in particular. A figurine, no bigger than the palm of his hand and carved delicately into hard stone. It appeared to be a caricature of sorts, depicting a person with an unusually large rectangular head and stick-like body. He couldn't resist picking it up and admiring its surprising weight in his hands.

"I should hope, child, you might exercise caution, for I've a particular fondness for this piece."

Todie was startled and fumbled with the statuette. He carefully put it back down on its velvet pedestal before it could come to any harm. He turned to see an elven man who looked only a few years older than himself but spoke with the resonance of age and wisdom. Todie, who was tall himself, only came up to the elf's narrow shoulders from where an elegant green robe hung loosely around his slender frame. His skin radiated a soft golden glow and his eyes were closer together than most with pupils the colour of the night's sky. His face, though, had a hint of pallor as if the elf were dehydrated or feeling a little under the weather.

"I'm sorry, truly. I just wanted to—"

"I should encourage you to not fret, child," the elven man said. "It is a rare privilege to be able to touch history itself, though we should be mindful to hold it with gloves of respect." The elf stood by Todie and picked up the artefact himself. "Your heart sings of your friendship with Evelyn," he said, with a look that was both kind and stern. "By the name of Malwei Tussel, I am Evelyn's father."

"Todie Farren," Todie replied offering a hand, though Malwei seemed to not notice the gesture and instead politely dipped his head.

"Through virtue of chance, may it be that we should meet," Malwei said; then his expression softened and Todie could see a dampness in the island elf's eyes. "My soul aggrieved in hearing of you father and brother. A terrible tragedy no offer of condolence may heal, but for you fare strength and fare wishes."

Todie suddenly went very solemn and, when he didn't reply, Malwei offered a sympathetic smile then abruptly changed the subject.

"I gather my daughter and you who stands before me had something of an intimate, though perhaps short-lived, relationship?"

The tips of Todie's ears flushed pink. "Yes, sir. I don't know how much Evelyn has told you but I really do apologise for any—"

Malwei cut him off again. "It is not the place of a father to judge all those whom Evelyn has been acquainted but to protect her from those who may wish her harm. I trust that is not you, else you would not be here." He looked down at Todie.

"Of course, Mr Tussel, I could never harm her. I guess I was just unable to be as present for her as she needed."

Malwei was quiet for a moment before letting out a contented sigh and placed the figurine carefully back down. "An artefact of the fifth dynasty, several millennia past. This statuette came from Havensend, today the Free Capital of The Arvum though, at the time, only but a large town. Meticulously carved by the hands of an autumn elf; cherished as a totem of faith. Such discovery has been few, so fortunate I was to acquire this from an old merchant in the desert."

Todie stayed motionless for a while, transfixed by the

diminutive artwork until he was called back to his senses.

"Elves of old and man anew, my pleasures sing to present: Miss Fjona Sarsen," Evelyn announced from the top of the stairs.

Todie swivelled around on the balls of his feet, quietly alarmed to find that Malwei had disappeared and he couldn't help but wonder just how long he'd been staring at the statuette.

Fjona hopped down the steps, two at a time.

"Admittedly the transformation is but subtle," Evelyn said, following closely behind, "but the eyes of an outsider may perceive you to have made an effort."

Fjona had simply thrown a pine-coloured linen shirt over her top and buttoned it up to her breasts. She wore a matching neckerchief and a burgundy cap; perhaps an unusual ensemble but somehow it seemed to work. Crucially, Fjona's face had been washed and delicately made up by the hands of Evelyn, and her hair had been stripped clean of straw and leaves, and tied up into a neat bundle.

Todie gawped at her, jaw down to his knees as she marched past him saying, "Off we go then."

Outside, Evelyn ushered them around her pristine palomino horse and swung gracefully onto its back. It was here that she acknowledged Shagwell for the first time.

"Blessed Bouanda, what is that?" she asked, a cocktail of judgement and intrigue.

"Shagwell here is a finer horse than he appears," Fjona replied with a glancing look at Todie, "though I think I'll hop on with you, Evelyn, if that's okay?"

Evelyn gestured invitationally at the space before her and Fjona willingly climbed up onto an exceptionally comfortable saddle.

"Don't listen to them, Shagwell," Todie whispered as he carefully climbed into his own saddle, and they headed off for the east coast.

Shagwell let out a relieved wheezy breath.

CHAPTER 8

THE WOMAN AND THE BELL

She had been asleep for a very long time, though exactly how long she could not tell. The young woman picked herself up from the cold floor and took stock of her surroundings. It was a small box of a room, about the size of a typical bedroom albeit without a bed. It was akin to a log cabin with red-brown timber walls and ceiling, and a grey flagstone floor lain out in an irregular pattern.

She felt strange – a clear head, undazed and fully cognitive but with no sense of identity, least of all her name.

The woman gasped as she knocked something behind her and spun around to find an old writing desk. Upon the desk was the only source of light in the room: a candlestick of which the wax curiously showed no signs of burning in spite of the yellow flame that was sufficient enough to illuminate the entire room. She tentatively reached a hand out to the ember, as if to test whether she had all her sensations, and was relieved to feel the gentle heat radiating from its soft glow.

Beyond the flickering flame, her eyes were drawn to the silhouette of an object hanging from the wall behind the table.

The woman stepped away from the candle to stop her eyes from burning and walked over to the object, now coming into focus. It was an old, derelict cuckoo clock that seemed to bear some familiarity. The wood was warped and decaying, and its pendulum suspended forlornly into the stiff and stale air as if it hadn't swung for a very long time. The clock took the form of a tall house with a collapsing gable roof, and intricately carved leaves and vines descended either side from the roof to a narrow platform, upon which perched a little wooden bird. The bird's head was turned up towards a small hatch near the top of the façade as if waiting for its friend to appear. What digits remained on the dilapidated clockface were of an ancient language and the two hands, both pointing to midday, were as thin as sewing needles and made of tempered bronze.

This was the kind of fastidiously made furniture that was near-irresistible to touch, in spite of its rotten appearance, and the young woman found her hand reaching, as if not by choice, towards the small model bird, when she was distracted by the loud creaking of a door behind her.

She turned, startled by intrigue rather than fear, surprised in herself that she had failed to see the door there in the first place. The young woman removed the candle from the table and made purposefully for the door.

"Hello?" she called into the silence, more out of wanting to hear her own voice than in the expectation that there may be someone close by.

There was no response.

It was a simple battened and ledged door made in a dark, worn wood and hinged to the frame by two narrow, iron braces. There was no handle or knob on the inside, though, being ajar, the young woman was able to pull it open at the edge.

Still clutching the candle, she stepped through into a moody corridor walled by dull grey bricks with speckles of moss and mildew. The strong scent of dampness hung in the humid air as if fusty water was leeching through the cracks in the mortar.

The door slammed shut behind her, despite the absence of a draught, and the young woman felt her heart lunge. She pushed against it with her free hand but found that the door was securely in place and would not budge.

"What is this place?" she thought as she turned back to face the corridor and continued along it.

She stopped after several paces when she noticed that the walls were adorned by four picture frames on either side. They were most unusual, not least for the fact that they had been carved in a most ostentatious and meticulous design of swirls and knots, but because the empty frames were obscured by iron bars like that of a cell. The sight alone sent a shudder through the woman, though for what precise reason she could not tell.

The young woman found herself being drawn to one of the frames, a frightful intrigue luring her in. She stared at the blank canvas between the bars.

"That can't be..."

The canvas appeared to ripple with movement like that of a bug beneath a sheet. Or bugs, rather, as the canvas was undulating in multiple places and though it was discomforting for the young woman, it was equally and dangerously mesmerising. She found herself being pulled into the dancing waves and ripples as if she were analysing the most spectacular of paintings until, suddenly, a face appeared through the frame, distorted horribly by the canvas itself. A great white toothless mouth screamed and two scaly hands squeezed on the bars from the inside, the arms disappearing into the frame.

The young woman leaped backwards, echoing the scream of the atrocity. She fell back against the wall behind her, panting like a dog, wailing like a banshee. Her heart pounded against her chest.

"Who *are* you?" she cried at the screaming monster.

The only reply was a long, harrowing laugh.

"Where am I?" she yelled back, but this just encouraged it to laugh louder and harsher.

Its eyes were two vacuous pits that grew wider and more terrifying as the discordant screeching amplified to a near-deafening pitch.

Then it just stopped. No more screaming, no more laughter. Instead, it twisted its disfigured head, grimaced cruelly and slinked back into the canvas from whence it came. An unsettling silence ensued.

Adrenalin rushed through the young woman with a warming buzz as she sat, huddled against the bricks, trying to catch her breath and completely unaware of a long, spindly finger stretching out of the frame behind her and groping the flat air around her shoulder. It had barely touched her before she shot to her feet and flew down the corridor to the backdrop of cackling. Until now she had managed to hold on to the candle, but here she released it as all of her strength was poured into her legs to carry her along.

"Please," she whispered as she approached another door and was desperately relieved to discover that, not only did this door have a knob, but that it was unlocked and she was able to escape through it.

On the other side, she slammed it shut and leaned against it, keeping the demon at bay. After regaining some sense of composure, she reluctantly turned to inspect the new room.

It was starkly different from where she had just been and the young woman felt greatly at ease as a warm sunlight streamed through the stained-glass windows of a grand, circular chapel. Iridescent greens and blues, bright oranges and soft purples from the windows, reflected over the aisles of pews leaving a comforting haze of light which filled the room. There was still a quietness in here but it was a kind and peaceful quietness that instilled a sense of tranquillity in the woman.

The woman walked carefully along the aisle, gazing across to the windows and admiring the beautiful colourful images they portrayed. She silently speculated over the narrative being told from frame to frame; the first of tiny yellow stars glistening in a mulberry sky; the second of a warm green hill scape before a glistening azure ocean. Then an image of a woman and a man, each with cocoa skin, wearing simple, sparse clothing and standing tall before a great olive tree. The next depicted an impressive ship with crisp white sails, battling with waves over an icy sea. A fleet of smaller vessels could be seen on the horizon and a bright yellow sun hung low in an empty sky.

The young woman marvelled at each window as she

treaded slowly along the nave towards the lectern. One image seemed to illustrate a conflict with soldiers and men baring bright torches, another showed a palatial building engulfed in an immense orange flame. The following showed a barren landscape, proceeded by several windows that appeared to show people travelling across different terrains: snow-capped mountains, lavish green valleys, and a hazy sandy desert. The next few showed people with pointed ears, engaged in various activities such as fishing and tending to farmsteads, weaving cloth and erecting houses.

The penultimate window showed simply a tree with a young child apparently tugging at a single branch not far up from the bottom. The tree had a twisting trunk and a thicket of ruby and jade-coloured leaves which cast a warm shadow over the child, depicted wearing a blue cloak and red scarf.

The final window, above the door through which she had entered, was much larger than all the rest and showed a woman with dazzling, golden hair holding a silver staff above her head. Rays of sunshine radiated off her and upon her face she wore a stern and powerful expression. In the sky above the golden-haired woman were two glistening meteors; one, a cold sapphire blue; the other, a burning blood red. They seemed to be suspended in the air as if the woman in the grand window were tracing them through the sky with her staff.

The window itself was so enormous that the young woman found herself reversing up the aisle on her toes in an attempt to view the whole image.

"I know this place... but why?" she wondered, still walking backwards, admiring the stained glass until her rear bumped into the lectern behind her.

She turned hurriedly and noticed a single sheath of parchment on top containing a scrawled message, decorated by splotches of purple ink as if written in a hurry. It seemed to be addressed to her.

Marseiha,

Should slumber ever release you from its strangle and your eyes ever settle upon these words, so it will be that time is seeping away. You know already what must be done; find the door beyond the altar.

"Marseiha," she mouthed, a flake of recollection drifting through her mind.

The note was for her memory as an egg was for baking: not nearly enough to make a cake but one could at least cook up an omelette. She was a long way from understanding where she was, and who, for that matter, though some voice deep inside filled her, Marseiha, with a sense of purpose.

Without a moment's hesitation, she left the lectern and made for the altar. It was little more than a tall sheet of blue marble, absent of carvings and decoration, yet as captivating as if it were the most exquisite of paintings. It was several times the height of Marseiha and many times as wide, polished and smooth on the faces but jagged along the narrow edges. It glowed as if all the windows were pointed at it, though only a couple were. Most strikingly, to the uninitiated the marble seemed to be completely unfunctional as an altar owing to the severe lack of any table upon which to make a sacrifice. For that very reason, Marseiha was sceptical as to whether this strange monument was indeed the altar mentioned in the letter yet, somewhere inside her, she knew that it was.

"Find the door beyond the altar," Marseiha repeated as she stepped around it to inspect the wall behind. She chuckled gently as she looked up at an impressive curtain that concealed the wall. It was a rich green velvet, the colour of pine needles. "A cunning disguise," she said as her hand gripped the fabric and pulled the curtain to one side.

Marseiha was quickly disappointed as she revealed only a white stone wall, glaring ashamedly back at her as if she had just stripped it nude. She cursed quietly under her breath.

She glanced about her in a swift arc to make certain that she hadn't missed anything before turning back to the empty wall. Nothing stood out as being beyond the ordinary. No grooves or blemishes in the stonework to suggest a hidden lever, no stone appearing out of place. It was just a wall.

Marseiha muttered those same words to herself again, "The door beyond the altar..." but could make no more sense of them. This was the altar, of that there was no doubt.

Delicately feeling the stone wall with her fingertips, she hoped to discern some clue as to the whereabout of this elusive door. She ran them cautiously along the grain of the stones, feeling the cool smoothness beneath her fingers. Some repressed instinct reassured Marseiha that she was in the right place though even that soon started to wane.

Just as she was starting to lose faith in herself, Marseiha felt one stone budge very slightly. The stone was level with her chest, about four times the size of her hand and, though it was near-perfectly square, it blended in with its peers.

Marseiha applied a little more pressure and felt the stone push back into a cavity in the wall. It went in about a hand's length until it dropped down, revealing a small chamber, far too small for anybody to climb through. Marseiha reached in, expecting to find a handle or lever with which to open a hidden door somewhere in the wall and was relieved when her fingers wrapped around a wooden object.

She pulled it towards her and, to her dismay, discovered a simple hand mirror.

She sighed, fondling the strange object. "What am I to do with this?" Frustrated now, Marseiha stared at her reflection in the small glass panel and yelled, "Who are you? What is this ridiculous place? Why am I being held prisoner here?"

She raised her arm with the intention of flinging the mirror on the floor but found some restraint just as she was about to release it. A thought sprung into her head.

Marseiha held the mirror up before her face, looked solemnly at her sallow reflection. "Show me the way."

She paused with bated breath; a sense of optimism engulfed her as she felt a power emanating through the handle of the mirror.

Nothing happened. The optimism faded and Marseiha was once again subjected to an intense disappointment.

"Open the door," she tried, still looking into the mirror. "Reveal to me the way."

But it was all in vain. She was close, something told her that, but still missing the point.

Then, just as she was about to succumb to her frustration

again and project the mirror in the direction of the wall, something in its quiet reflection caught her eye. Marseiha adjusted the mirror so that she could see the reverse side of the marble altar directly behind her; except that instead of a sheen face of blue marble, a staircase appeared to be spiralling upwards, inside the altar itself and continuing beyond the top of the monolith.

She spun on her heels and, to her surprise, found that the staircase had vanished and the blue marble returned. Marseiha reached out to touch it and felt only the cold stone of the altar. She removed her hand and looked back at the reflection in the mirror. Sure enough, the staircase was visible behind her but, when Marseiha turned to look, all she could see was the marble altar.

An idea came to her. She maintained an eye on the staircase via the mirror and reached out behind her with her other hand. She felt nothing, only the empty space inside the altar. This time, when Marseiha turned to face the marble, the staircase was fully in sight, as clear as day, and her hand was deep inside the hidden vessel.

She tucked the hand mirror into her rope belt, in the event that she may require its services again, and stepped fully into the altar. It took her into a tight and gloomy stairwell, wide enough only to inhabit the staircase that spiralled upwards beyond Marseiha's vision. Her feet cautiously made contact with the first step as if she were expecting it to collapse beneath her weight, though she was quickly reassured otherwise and began the ascension up into the unknown.

"You know already what must be done," Marseiha said,

reminding herself of the letter as she climbed the staircase. She ran the words through her mind several times over in an attempt to decipher them. "How could I possibly know what to do when I don't even know where I am?"

She was desperate to find some sense of resolution in this nonsensical place. Her memory was as fragmented as the mosaic panels of the stained-glass windows and Marseiha found her thoughts drifting to the golden-haired woman and the powerfully iridescent meteors. So bright, in fact, that they still burned in Marseiha's retinas.

She paused to peer down through the eye of the stairs and felt a wave of fear when she discovered that the entrance was now out of sight and she glanced up to see the staircase twisting into darkness. Onwards, she climbed, her thoughts now turning to the recovery of her identity.

"I would not have invited myself into such a wicked place," Marseiha pondered, "so someone else must have brought me here. Imprisoned, more likely, with nothing but a note baring little in instruction." Her feet continued to tap, step by step. "Why?" she yelled, enveloped by her own voice as it echoed around the brick-built tower, reverberating down the smooth wooden banister.

Marseiha persevered despite the encroaching feeling of despair, her head mostly drooping down towards her feet. Up she went until, a long while later, a shimmering speck of golden light could be seen peering back down at her from above. In spite of her aching calves, she pushed herself on further, propelled by the comforting knowledge that the end was in sight.

Then, like a bird breaching a canopy of clouds, Marseiha stepped into a bright, domed chamber. There were no windows and the remarkable light appeared to be coming from an enormous gold bell which hung motionless in the centre of the room. It was so dazzling to look at that Marseiha had to shield her eyes with the back of her hand to keep from being totally blinded.

On the far side of the chamber, furthest from the top of the stairs, Marseiha could just discern the bell rope and felt a rush of knowing through her body as if she had been aware of her purpose here all along. She immediately made for it, ducking under the bell's wooden frame. With both hands, she gripped tightly to the rope and thrust down with all the strength she had, though to little effect. Not only was the bell exceedingly heavy but its mechanism was stiff and tired from an ageless abandonment.

The wheel that supported the bell began to gently roll and the bell itself swayed lethargically, though without music. Marseiha persisted, now feeling the momentum of the contraption and the clapper brushed softly against the lip of the bell, issuing an ambient ring not unlike the sound produced by the running of a finger around the rim of a wine glass.

Her muscles tightened and the wheel turned more animatedly. Finally, the clapper made full contact with the bell and a powerfully vibrating ringing exploded from within, strong enough for Marseiha to feel inside her chest.

It felt as if the bell rope was pulling Marseiha and soon the chamber was drowning in a volcanic ringing. The tone itself was rich and bold, really quite beautiful and, though the immense volume hurt Marseiha's ears, she felt compelled to continue pulling on the rope.

The bell rang several more times, each chime as impressive as the one before until, after about eight or so, Marseiha felt that it was time to stop. She held firmly on to the rope and eased the bell down until it hovered softly in its frame. The air around Marseiha seemed shaken and there was a palpable uneasiness in the chamber as if the dust had been unfairly awakened.

"Well I suppose that's it then," she said and started back to the top of the staircase, anxious for the long descent to the bottom, but she was stopped in her tracks.

Without anyone pulling the rope, the bell struck again. This time, however, the rich and beautiful tone was no more and a sheer, discordant clang screamed out of the golden bell. The floorboards seemed to be vibrating under the weight of the ringing and the dazzling light that had filled Marseiha with hope was beginning to fade.

The bell struck again and a shadowy plume of darkness began to encircle it, enshrouding the frame in a black cloud. Marseiha's face turned the colour of snow; her heart thundered against her rib cage.

"Oh no!" was all she could mutter before a ravenous fracture split across the now tarnished bell like a family of lightning forks.

It suddenly felt very cold and lonely at the top of the bell tower but Marseiha had no time to process what she had done before the step beneath her gave way and she found herself tumbling down the stairwell. She bounced from step to step, down the spiralling staircase, her arms outstretched in a futile attempt to hold on to something, but all she could do was scream and hope that she'd make it to the bottom in one piece.

Echoing down from the top of the staircase, Marseiha could have sworn that she could hear a cruel, hungry laughter.

Finally, her slender frame plummeted against the stone floor at the foot of the tower and Marseiha rolled out of the altar through a gap between the broken steps that were piling up at the bottom.

She could hear the staircase crumbling behind her until she was fully away from the marble monument and the door had resealed. After that, it was as if it were nothing more than a large stone and no knowledge of what lay within it could be heard.

Marseiha remained on the floor for a moment as she regathered her strength before eventually pushing herself up on her forearms. She dazedly stood on her wobbly legs and patted down her simple dress as if, by sweeping away the dust, she may also sweep away the horrors of where she had just been. She was pleasantly surprised that she had come to little harm and, though she ached in one or two places, she had suffered no bruises or broken bones.

Having regained herself, Marseiha looked up at the chapel around her and yet another flourish of fear shot through her.

The radiant sun that had previously encapsulated the room had seemingly clouded over and now a dim haze resided. The walls were no longer clear and white, but a dull grey, pocked with mildew and cobwebs. An unsettling chill flowed through the cavernous space. Row upon row of pews were in disrepair, the wood warped, stained and rotten.

A sickening feeling took hold of Marseiha as she stared in dread at the windows. They no longer depicted beautiful images of opulence and triumph, but instead conveyed scenes of suffering, disease and death. The jewel-like colours from before had been replaced by black and blood red, and the themes of genesis, diaspora and resurrection had all been lost to reckoning and destruction.

The portrayal of the woman and man now showed two muscular, horned beasts with long, pointed ears and sinister, possessed eyes. The palatial building was now a whole city being ravaged by flames, and instead of tending to farms, the village people were preparing graves and digging trenches.

Most heartbreakingly, the transcendent tree displayed in the penultimate window was now wilting, bare of leaves and colour, and a hooded figure in the grand window above the door stood over a pile of bones, wielding a black staff.

The only thing that remained seemingly unsullied were the two dazzling meteors that, if anything, appeared to be bursting with more radiance. A radiance that seemed to escape the mere confines of the window.

As Marseiha stared on, the glass surrounding both of the sapphire and blood meteors began to ripple as if it were melting back into sand. Then, in the breath of a moment, the two meteors shattered out of the window with so much force that Marseiha was thrown with her back crashing against the lectern. From her dazed position, she could barely look up at the dazzling, burning bodies of light that hovered in the stagnant air of the chapel. They had an energy about them like a wolf restraining itself before the pounce.

Finally, with seemingly no rhyme or reason, the two meteors shot upwards, soaring towards the high ceiling of the chapel, penetrating the roof with ease and disappearing beyond.

With the immense light of the meteors now faded, a cold gloom washed into the chapel.

Marseiha's heart fought so hard against her chest that she was afraid it might burst through in the same way the meteors had the chapel.

"What of Hell have I unleashed?"

CHAPTER 9

PORT WIDOW

The coastal town of Port Widow was named so nearly three centuries ago when young, hopeful sailors left their wives behind in search of riches across the Far Sea, only to succumb to the hands of crafty pirates or monsters, and never to return again. Or so the story goes.

Before then it had been a lucrative trading town, attracting merchants of all flavours from across the Arvum, particularly spring elves from its sister town of Rosensted off the east coast of the mainland. Through several dynasties, Port Widow served as a sanctuary for the elite, providing lavish hospitality, artisanal food and only the classiest of after-hour companionship. Most patrons were oblivious to the extortionate prices for even the least opulent of cuisines available to them, and those who weren't oblivious simply didn't care. The town was a living organism – a cultural soup, alive through the wealth of those visiting Marrow Myre.

However, its reputation dwindled along with the missing sailors, and merchants became reluctant to the pay the town a visit, instead making their fortunes in the likes of Panamaya

City, Havensend or the Blue Valley. Since its golden age, Port Widow had plummeted into decline and become infamous for hosting a sour class of frivolity. Now the streets stank of piss, the piss stank of ale, and the ale stank and tasted like piss.

To some of the local Myrish population, Port Widow was an exciting affair with the opportunity to sample exotic produce from across the Arvum, but to outsiders it was only worth the trouble if one's ship happened to be passing by.

That's not to say that the whole town was awash with toxicity. If there was one establishment that had maintained some semblance of decorum, and really there was only the one, it was The Tipsy Mercer, a tavern that sat atop the chalk cliffs overhanging the Near Sea.

Within its stone walls was a symphony of chatter, the swishing of fresh pints, and the ringing of tankards as inebriated customers jostled between one another and the low-hanging eaves.

One such customer, a corpulent island elf with frosty eyes and a thick yellow beard, slumped down on a stool across the bar. His belly creeped out of the bottom of a rust-coloured doublet of which the buttons could scarcely fasten together, and his thinning hair was matted from grime and dirt.

The elf had a nose like a hard-boiled egg and his skin, which would have once radiated with a golden sheen, was as dull and tarnished as an old, neglected kettle.

His big head flopped on to the bar with an audible thump and through foaming lips he slurred to the barman, "One ale, if you could please..." before trailing off into a low frequency murmuring.

The barman, an uncharacteristically tall and slim Myrish local with a thick head of blonde, curly hair replied in a soft, patient tone, "Have you the coin t'pay, Gruno?"

With big sausages for fingers, Gruno fumbled with the thread of a small black purse. Determined, he attempted to prise the opening apart, though it was obvious from the outside that the purse contained very little, if indeed anything at all.

"Two of whatever he's drinking," a voice said from the adjacent stool, the occupant pushing several *bassals* across the bar.

The barman looked over at Gruno, who appeared to have completely passed out, then shrugged and said resignedly, "Your money," as he swept up the loose coins.

A short while later, the barman placed two glasses of rich, velvety mead in front of the two weary customers.

"Thanks, sir," the stranger said as he raised his glass to the barman.

"Please, call me Jat," the barman replied.

"Perciville," he said, and toasted again before taking a long swig of the sickly-sweet beverage.

Gruno snorted in his stupor, a long vine of drool reaching over the sleeve of his doublet.

"Here for Lullatide, are you, my friend?" Jat asked as he poured himself a tumbler of Myrish whiskey.

"Not really," Perciville replied. "Thought I'd have a look since I'm here but it didn't interest me much."

Jat nodded politely. "So what did bring you to Port Widow? You don't seem to be a local." He gestured to Perciville's unusual robe with his eyes.

Perciville took another sip of mead as he considered his response. "I'm not entirely sure."

"Ahh, try'na find your purpose in life? Been there before," Jat replied as he poured the whole measure of whiskey into his mouth. He smiled warmly as the burning liquid cascaded through his body.

Jat's response seemed to resonate with Perciville. "Soul-searching, I guess. Though quite what I hope to find here remains to be discovered."

"Where are you from? I've seen all manner of folk in 'ere over the years but never one in a robe like yours. Can I ask, what does that symbol mean?" Jat asked in the nosy way that barmen often do. He was referring to a small emblem stitched on the chest to the left side of Perciville's robe. It depicted a tree with an unusually slender trunk that, at least to the knowledge of a sage, resembled a staff.

"I am a man of learning," Perciville began. "It would be remiss of me to deprive you of asking questions."

He said no more though and a silence fell between the two of them until Jat got the hint and proceeded to reorganise the tumblers on a shelf beneath the bar.

Gruno snored himself awake and sucked the drool back into his throat which made him cough and splutter ferociously. Once he'd cleared his lungs, he took a swift draught of his mead before his head collapsed back onto the bar.

Perciville and Jat exchanged a jovial look.

"What's his story?" Perciville asked, gesturing to the simple oaf beside him.

"Gruno? Truth be told, I ain't too sure. Been washed up in Port Widow for fifteen years, mostly drifting from tavern to tavern. Some rumour he was once a wealthy merchant in Sallisai'Mae, others say a *mercen'ry* and a fraudster. Even heard *consort to the sov'rin* though that seems a stretch," Jat replied as he wiped the bubbling drool from Gruno's fat lip with a dirty old rag. "Whatever the case, he turned up 'ere with a crate full'a coin which he squandered on drink and women. Obviously dried up now. I give him the occasional pint on the house but I've a business to help run and, besides, it does him no good to keep him *permantly* on the sauce." Jat gave another shrug.

Perciville took a cursory glance around at the heaving establishment, quietly pondering how much truth there was in what Jat was saying. After all, the business seemed to be going well, though perhaps it told a different story for the rest of the year

A rotund barmaid whose belly protruded further than her generous bosom squeezed theatrically behind Jat. Her hair was short, bright red and curly like the tail of a pig, ironically since her face bore the same resemblance.

"Stop natterin' to the customers, Jat, there's a queue needing drinks," she crowed with more than a hint of aggression.

Jat rolled his eyes, catching a grin from Perciville as he glanced over to the couple of patrons waiting patiently at the bar.

Jat bit his tongue and replied, "Course, Derethy," as he proceeded to take orders and prepare drinks for the customers. "My sister and co-owner of the Mercer," he stated to Perciville as he exchanged the freshly poured drinks for a couple of *bassals.* "She's a particular way of runring things round 'ere, namely not *intracting* with customers but fer quenching their thirsts and takin' their coin." He expelled a heavy sigh. "So really, where are you from, my friend? Rosensted like the rest of 'em or somewhere a little more exotic?"

It was ultimately a very basic, unloaded question but it somehow got Perciville thinking. "If I'm honest I'm not sure I'm from anywhere," he replied, and in that regard, he was being truthful.

"Say no more! I can tell when a merchant on business is wise to keep his *animnity*," Jat said, waving his hands dismissively.

"No, truly. It's nothing like that," Perciville protested. "My origins go back a long way and I'm not even sure of them myself. The last few" – he hesitated as his mind raced to offer the simplest of explanations – "years, I suppose, I've been between places."

This answer evidently didn't quite satisfy Jat's curiosity but the barman was polite enough to not push it further. "Here, have a Myrish whiskey. On the house."

Perciville's stomach recoiled just at the thought of more whiskey.

The three companions had been travelling for several hours and Fjona was greatly relieved when their horses finally trotted over the threshold into Port Widow. A bright moon lit up a hazy purple sky and a stark chill rattled through the empty streets, save for a few early leavers who were stumbling across the cobbles and ricocheting off the stone houses.

It was a sizeable town, lit up by hundreds of street lanterns which, to Fjona's eyes, looked like giant, motionless fireflies. Dozens of rectangular buildings rose up gently on one side to the top of a cliff in the near distance and dropped steeply downwards on the other to the port itself.

"This is it?" Fjona teased as the palomino inched further into town. "I was expecting rivers of honey, gold-skinned elves and manors made of marble."

Evelyn slapped her playfully on the arm. "A river of honey may sound delightful upon your ears but would surely be infested with wasps and flies. Port Widow may compare little to Sallisai'Mae, or so my father tells me, but where else in Marrow Myre might we reside without being judged by our neighbours?"

Shagwell let out a wheezy cough as his stumpy legs folded beneath him and Todie toppled off his back. He half managed to twist his body in a way that could make the fall appear graceful until his hand slipped on a wet cobblestone and he landed face down next to a steaming pile of manure.

"Well that was a close encounter," he said, unusually calmly considering just how close his nose was from the faeces.

The other two were crying with laughter as Fjona hopped from her horse to assist Todie back on to his feet.

"Come on, Todie, I'll walk the rest of the way with you and Shagwell," she said, wrapping a gentle arm around his shoulders.

Evelyn clapped her hands impatiently. "Might we best get a move on else the hour of the climbing sun will arrive and we should be returning home."

They made their way between a row of houses just as the clouds gave way and an icy rain began to fall. Todie complained that all of the taverns appeared to have closed down, rendering the whole journey a waste of time. He wasn't wrong, though. They walked past half a dozen public houses right on the street front or hidden in discreet nooks and crannies, all of which seemed to have been run down into dereliction.

Evelyn was vocalising her dismay at suggesting this adventure in the first place when they heard a gentle humming somewhere in the distance.

"Listen," she said in a hushed tone, and her two companions trained their ears into the silence. "Music, atop the cliffs."

They persevered onwards, the faint melodies becoming more distinct: the obvious pulse of a small drum; the rapid waves of a fiddle; the smooth wooden timbre of a pan flute.

Suddenly Port Widow seemed alive as the young travellers reached the top of the cliff to find a smattering of taverns built around a busy stone courtyard with hundreds of folk singing and dancing merrily in spite of the rain. It was lit up with a combination of warm candlelight and strategically placed mirrors that reflected the moon around the whole plaza. The music was coming from a trio of minstrels who were playing on a wooden step outside one venue with a sign saying *Rump and Roody's.*

To one side of the courtyard stood a scaled reconstruction of a ship, angled with its bow tipped towards a pile of rocks. A straw effigy dressed in a sailor's outfit dangled over the edge, rocking back and forth in the wind. A sleeping captain, lost at sea.

The word LULLATIDE was engraved into the ship and illuminated, somehow, as if the letters were on fire. Beneath it read: 42 YEARS' GRATITUDE TO THE MYRISH SAVIOURS. Fjona was entranced. She had never seen such a crowd of strange and wonderful beings. She watched as, every so often, a spring elf would stand before the ship, respectfully dip their head and place a hand on the hull. Following this, they would head around to the effigy and thrust the dregs of their drinks, gradually dowsing it in alcohol.

Beside her, she heard Evelyn say, "For the captain's recklessness, many a sailor's life was stolen. Succumbed to the drink, they say of him, and so the elves offer peace to the fallen and grief to the shamed captain."

Before long, Fjona's attention turned elsewhere and it took a sharp elbow in the ribs from Todie for her to stop staring at a couple of spring elves who were garbed in long, flowing green dresses and swirling around like petals in an updraft. They had alluring olive skin and big bright eyes that sparkled in the moonlight. Their ears were pointed and as slender as their bodies, and soft brown hair flowed delicately onto their sharp shoulders.

"Now this my heart had longed for," Evelyn said, hopping from the palomino and leading them through the crowd. She was nearly shaking with excitement. The energy emanating from the revellers was infectious. "Take this," she instructed Todie as she handed him the reins to her horse and grabbed Fjona's wrist.

Together, they went bundling into the dancing frenzy and

were soon spinning and moving to the addictive, beckoning music.

It was a different style to anything they had heard before in their own villages. The rhythms were more syncopated and sporadic, and the melodies leaped around in big intervals unlike the more conventional scalic motions they were used to. It mattered not to Fjona and Evelyn who were entirely enveloped by it and having far too much fun to quibble.

The two spring elves were quick to invite themselves over and soon the four of them were holding hands and spinning around in an elegant circle. Without even saying a word, the elves, who were more familiar with the choreography, took it upon themselves to teach Fjona and Evelyn a few moves. With outstretched arms, they kicked back their left legs and spiralled downwards on their right like a whirlpool. Their beautiful, luscious hair swayed about like a ceremonial flag as the two elves rose upwards, while still spinning, and returned to their starting positions.

Other folk had joined in now as Fjona and Evelyn attempted the routine. They started well enough: arms in the right position, posture straight and stable; however, both lacked the finesse for the next stanza. Evelyn, who was a little more elegant, was able to complete a full spin before falling over, but Fjona, who lacked all the necessary grace, tripped up immediately.

This only added to their enjoyment and the spring elves were kind enough to help them back onto their feet to continue dancing.

After a while, Fjona and Evelyn were beginning to feel

fatigued and decided that a drink was necessary to revitalise themselves.

"We are most gracious for you sharing a dance with us," Evelyn said to the two elves with a respectful curtsey.

"The pleasure was most certainly ours," the first replied with the silkiest of voices.

"*Mesier florya lo'mas, sen carier la'mas*" added the other before translating. "Dance is to the spirit as breath is for the lungs."

Fjona and Evelyn stepped away from the growing crowd and made for the centre of the plaza, both looking around, concerned, for Todie.

"Wherever has that useless boy disappeared to?" Evelyn asked, scanning her surroundings.

"That *useless boy* has been tending to your *enormous steed* while the two of you were busy ditching me to party with complete strangers," Todie replied, coming up behind them.

Evelyn sighed. "Forgive me, Todie, for we are just far too interesting to be content merely watching the fun."

"Leave him be, Evelyn, let's go get a drink," said Fjona, sensing a little tension. "Where do you reckon?"

"*Rump and Roody's* has a lively atmosphere," Evelyn suggested.

Todie waved his hands. "No, no, while you two were busy cavorting with exotic drunks, I was off tying up the horses in the only available stable I could find. The owner said we could leave them there in good faith so long as we provide them our custom."

He pointed over to a humble, little tavern at the furthest

point of the cliff, just beyond the main courtyard.

"The Tipsy Mercer?" Fjona said, reading the wooden sign above the door.

"It's nice in there, I promise!" Todie added fervently. "And far less rundown than the rest, I assure you."

He had a point. Despite the energy, the music, and the enticing blend of candle and moonlight, the taverns surrounding the plaza did show signs of disrepair and more than a couple had boarded up windows. The Tipsy Mercer, meanwhile, seemed much better preserved with a new slate roof and freshly painted façade.

Although aware they were leaving the party, Fjona admitted that The Tipsy Mercer did have some appeal, and the fact that their horses were happily sheltered and muzzle-deep in a bucket of hay was enough to persuade her.

"Looks good to me," she said, feeling a trickle of rain down the back of her neck, and she eagerly led the way.

Perciville was a very well-travelled sage and had had the opportunity to visit much of the Arvum and the eclectic occupants of each great city and town. He had broken bread with Grugan chieftains, drunk sweet wine with autumn elves in Havensend, and spent more than his fair share of nights with the golden-skinned island elves of Sallisai'Mae. However, until that murky, drizzling evening in Port Widow, not for many years had he laid his lonely eyes upon a helven.

As he watched, the door to The Tipsy Mercer seemed to

fly open on its hinges, and a palpable silence filled the tavern as every head turned in expectation to look at the band of strangers who stepped inside: first the slender, pale young woman with a nest of curly hair, followed closely by a big, broad man with an auburn mop. Then, finally, time seemed to pause as a beautiful woman, tall and slim, hair like a silver river, entered, enveloped by a radiant glow of moonlight.

In reality no-one but Perciville had paid the sodden and windswept newcomers any attention, and if anything, the volume only increased as conversation fought over the intrusion of the gusts from outside.

"Who is she?" Perciville asked aloud, though more to himself than his new acquaintances.

Gruno turned his fat head to the door and mumbled something completely unintelligible.

"No idea, not seen 'em out this way before," Jat replied, looking up from a bottle of wine he was pouring for an aged spring elf. "Do you recognise them, Derethy?"

Derethy turned from cleaning the floor behind him and her usual frown that made her head look like a turnip curled up into a great smile. "Oh yes, yes," she muttered excitedly, adjusting the apron around her wide hips, and shimmying her breasts about as if she were plumping up a cushion.

She bounded towards the entrance, her enormous rear wobbling like a bowlful of chicken stock.

"Come now, my *derin*! Let me show you to a table," Derethy

said, her sweaty palm gripping firmly onto Todie's hand.

She tugged him through the bustling crowd to a quiet table at the rear of the tavern, closely followed by Evelyn and Fjona who each carried a quizzical expression.

Derethy pulled out a chair for Todie and invited him to sit.

"Umm, thank you," Todie said, hovering beside the chair for a moment too long before awkwardly taking a seat.

The other two pulled out their own chairs and sat themselves down, invisible as ghosts.

"Now if you need anything at all, I'll be just over there," Derethy said, addressing the table but looking only at Todie. "And that's my brother, Jat, there by the way, not my husband or anything." She added this so quickly that the words practically melded together. "But if you come to me, I may be able to sort a little discount or something..." She trailed off before snorting like a piglet.

There was a long silence. Todie was unsure how to reply and looked to his companions for help. They were far too bemused to comment and did little more than stare uncomfortably in his direction.

"Thank you, madam," he eventually said.

"Name's Derethy, please," she replied, attempting to smile endearingly but instead just twisting her face into an ugly, toothless squint.

Evelyn had evidently had enough and said decisively, though not without etiquette, "Why our hearts serve a deep gratitude, Derethy, for your exquisite hospitality, and we most certainly look forward to sampling much of your menu."

Derethy shot her a scornful look. "Glad to hear," she said

with a double helping of sarcasm before turning back to Todie and saying, "See you up there."

She giggled like a strangled pheasant and waddled off back in the direction of the bar, to the backdrop of Evelyn and Fjona bursting with laughter.

"So who are they, then?" Jat asked as Derethy returned to cleaning the floor.

"If I'd to guess I'd say some kind of Arvum angel," she replied with a shiver of excitement and biting her lip.

"And the girls?" Jat insisted.

"I don't know, ask 'em yourself," she barked back.

Jat rolled his eyes. "Sorry Perciville, you're on your own."

By now the attractive young newcomers had indeed drawn some unwanted attention and were getting glances from less savoury-looking characters crammed into the tavern, Perciville included.

Derethy picked up a pail of filthy water and made for a back door. As if on cue, the Arvum angel took the opportunity to sweep up to the bar, apparently eager to get a round of drinks before his new admirer returned.

"What can I get you, my friend?" Jat offered before the angel had even got to the bar.

"I'm not too sure, to be honest. Just three drinks that I couldn't get anywhere else in Marrow Myre."

Jat barely hesitated. "How about a Rosensted Root Beer, a crystal gin from Bouanda, and an Elkensen Ale?"

"Perfect," the angel replied, drawing a purse from his jerkin pocket. "How much will that cost?"

Jat seemed to consider it for a moment. "Well ordinarily that would be eleven *bassals* but since the ordeal with my *intolable* sister. let's call it nine."

The angel fumbled through the coins, closely examining them to pick out the right amount while Jat proceeded to make the drinks.

"Here, allow me to help," Perciville offered, to which he received a sceptical glance. "Don't worry, I've no need of your money," Perciville added. "I won't pinch any."

There must have been something convincing in the way he spoke as it appeared sufficient enough to reassure the man.

"Thank you," he said and emptied a number of coins onto the counter in front of them.

"Not seen this kind of money before, then?" asked Perciville.

"Never. We don't have currency in my village, rather just communal spirit. Everyone chipping in to help out."

Perciville rolled the copper coins around his fingers. "Here, this is a *cline*, you don't need that. Or this one, put these back in your purse." He pushed them about, counting as he went. "There you go, nine *bassals*."

The spare coinage went back into the velvet pouch.

"Thank you for helping me, sir."

"Please, call me Perciville."

"Todie."

They exchanged a smile and a cursory nod.

"So tell me, Todie, what brings you to the back end of the

world?" Perciville asked.

"My two friends over there, Fjona and Evelyn." Todie gestured to his table where the two women were engaged in a heated discussion, unperturbed by the audience watching them. "Evelyn was given a handful of coins from a neighbour. We don't often get Common money out here so we decided to come down for the festival and spend it in the one place we can."

"And where did the neighbour come across Common money?" Perciville asked, although he sensed he already knew the answer.

"She helped a traveller get across the island on her wagon, apparently."

Perciville smiled knowingly. "And your helven friend, is she Evelyn? Very unusual bloodline, you know. What's her story?" He tried to keep the tone of his voice on the safe side of curiosity.

"Her father was a wealthy merchant, I believe. Came from Sallisai'Mae many years ago and—"

"Here you go, my friend. Nine *bassals*, if you will," Jat interrupted, pushing Todie's drinks across the bar and scooping up the coins.

Todie said his thanks to them both for their assistance and returned to his table.

Perciville, meanwhile, quietly considered what Todie had said. A helven woman living right here on Marrow Myre. Perhaps waking up here wasn't as bad as he'd first thought.

"What took you so long?" Fjona asked as Todie presented the table with the three drinks.

"I was accosted by some strange robed guy at the bar. Asked what we are doing here. Seemed perfectly harmless to me, just feeding his curiosity. Wanted to know how a helven came to be in Port Widow, that sort of thing."

He was oblivious to the concerned look that Evelyn and Fjona exchanged as he carefully placed the glasses on the table.

"Anyway, I've got ale from somewhere on the mainland, a Rosensted Root Beer and gin from Bouanda. Take your pick."

Fjona proceeded to take a sip of each drink before welcoming Evelyn to do the same. She settled on the ale, Evelyn on the gin.

"The finale of three, it would appear you are left with the root beer, my sweet Todie," said Evelyn.

Todie took a contented sip of the cool, citrusy tonic and smiled heartily. It was light and fizzy with a bitterness that faded into a sweet aftertaste, like nothing he had every drunk before.

"Not bad," he muttered.

Wiping foam from the top of her lip with a sleeve, Fjona asked, "What makes you say that robed man is perfectly harmless?"

Todie considered it for a moment with another swig of beer. "I don't know. He seemed genuine. Spoke out of fascination, not out of desire. Besides, I'm a cleric. I am learned in understanding people at their roots."

"Or seeing only the best of them," Evelyn suggested.

The three of them were quiet and contemplative, gently

sipping their exotic drinks.

"Look, we can just keep clear of him, okay? We stick together," said Todie.

This satisfied the others and, before long, they were back to excited chatter and wholehearted laughter. The purse of Common money was becoming increasingly lighter as Todie and Fjona relieved Evelyn from any awkwardness with the stranger and took it upon themselves to fetch drinks from the bar: a dangerous mix of wines, beers and spirits from all across the Arvum.

Derethy, who had taken an obvious and unrequited shining to Todie, came over on a couple of occasions to give him an ale on the house. It led to an uncomfortable silence as she hovered around the table like a bad smell until either Fjona or Evelyn plucked up the courage to ask her to leave.

The night continued in a spiralling descent from sobriety to inebriation and they were all soon feeling the hazy cloud of incoherence seeping into their minds.

Todie was lying back dazedly in his seat with Evelyn's head gently resting on his shoulder like a sleepy kitten.

It was now that Fjona broached another question that had been playing on her mind. "What happened to you two? How come you went back to being friends?"

Todie's cheeks reddened slightly, though that may have been a flush from the last glass of thick red wine he had been drinking. Evelyn's body, however, noticeably stiffened a little. She half opened her mouth as if to explain, but no words came out.

"Wow, touchy subject. You don't have to explain if you

don't want to," Fjona said, turning away her gaze slightly.

"Wisest is to speak up, sweet Todie," Evelyn slurred. "She will find out eventually. She always does."

Now Todie was definitely turning red, whether through embarrassment or shame. He was quietly praying that Derethy could interrupt them again, just to take the heat off. Then, when he realised he was praying in vain, he cursed to himself in repentance.

Perhaps his prayer was answered as they were indeed interrupted, though not by Derethy.

"*Toby*, my *derine!*" Perciville exclaimed as he stumbled over to the table, leaning heavily on his staff for support.

"It's *Todie*," Todie replied, fervently.

Evelyn giggled and said, "He swore you a girl! *Derine!*"

Fjona corrected the intruder. "*Derin* is for the men and boys," she said, only encouraging Evelyn to howl with laughter.

Perciville, evidently unperturbed by his faux pas, continued. "Evelyn, I gather?" He was swaying on his staff now, barely able to hold himself up. "How does such a beautiful helven end up in such a place as Marrow Myre?"

"What's wrong with Marrow Myre?" Evelyn asked.

"Lay off her," Todie added.

Fjona didn't say anything, standing up between the stranger and her friends.

Evidently flustered, Perciville quickly backed away. "Forgive my intrigue, please. I did not intend to cause offence. It has been a very long time since last I stood in the presence of a helven and I was taken by surprise to meet one here. Look, let me provide you with something more to drink as a means of apology."

With that, Fjona expected the stranger to return to the bar but, instead, he pointed his staff towards the table and went solemnly quiet. He was clearly very unstable on his feet and desperately trying to focus. Then, moments later, a subtle green glow emanated from the end of his staff and a sparkling light appeared in the centre of the table. It whirled around conically, forming a round bottle with a narrow spout. Inside it contained a blood red liquid.

Todie and Evelyn were suffering too much from the effects of the night and seemed completely unaware of what they were witnessing, but Fjona's head was clearer. Evidently she had a higher tolerance for alcohol than her friends. She stared dumbfounded at the materialising object.

"Autumn Elf Old Port," Perciville said, his voice sticky with drunkenness, "from Havensend. Can't get that anywhere outside the citadel. Very valuable."

He nodded in affirmation, then tumbled back towards his seat at the bar.

Fjona slumped back into her chair and popped loose the cork from the top of the bottle, releasing a sweet, inviting fragrance from the deep liquid within. She sloshed the bottle around and saw how the contents flowed viscously, nearly sticking to the curved edge of the glass.

Before she knew it, she was taking a sip straight from the spout and could feel the warm port trickling down her throat and tucking into her stomach like it was climbing into bed. It was truly delicious, easily the most palatable drink she had sampled during the evening, and she had sampled a lot.

When eventually she looked up, Todie and Evelyn were fast asleep.

Fjona kicked them under the table. "Wake up, you two!"

It had no effect on Todie who only snored, but Evelyn came to.

"What happened?" she asked, peering out through bleary bloodshot eyes.

"You fell asleep!" Fjona replied. "The night is still so young! Don't leave me now."

"Forgive me, dear Fjona, but my soul weeps for slumber. A room upstairs I shall pay for with remaining coins."

Evelyn slid off her chair and slinked uneasily over to Derethy at the bar. She stumbled well clear of the robed stranger as she drew the attention of the repugnant barmaid.

Back at the table Evelyn added, "You may wish to rest your own soul, Fjona."

"I'm not ready yet but thank you. I shall follow you up later."

Evelyn was practically already sleeping as she replied, "Very well but be safe alone. Room four, upstairs."

She brushed Fjona's cheek with her fingers before helping Todie onto his feet and together they made their way over to a staircase in the far corner of the tavern.

It was the early hours of the morning and, by now, most of the patrons had disappeared. Locals to Port Widow had returned to their houses and those passing by had either crashed in a room upstairs or were sleeping in their boats down at the dock.

For Fjona, however, the night really was young. She found herself staring over at the enigmatic stranger who had crafted a bottle of port only with his mind and a big stick.

She grabbed the bottle and joined him at the bar.

"My name is Fjona," she said. "Fjona Sarsen."

The robed man glanced over at her and straightened his back. He had been snoozing for the past few minutes, evidently just long enough to feel a little refreshed.

"Perciville," he replied, offering his hand and a big, welcoming smile.

CHAPTER 10

TO UNEXPECTED COMPANY

Fjona slammed the bottle of port on the bar in front of them; the liquid leaped up the glass on the inside under the force. "What is the meaning of this?"

A look of shock turned Perciville's face ghostly pale. "Hide that thing away, now! Don't you know what Jat could do to us he if saw that we had *conjured goods* on the premises! Or Derethy, for that matter."

He shuddered, swept the bottle off the bar and tucked it underneath his robe.

"Then explain it to me! Who are you and how did you make that bottle appear out of thin air?"

Perciville was defiant. He remained unmoved, analysing Fjona through squinted eyes.

"I swear, Perciville, tell me who you are or I will show that bottle to the owner," Fjona said, glancing over to Jat who was busy mopping the floor around the tables.

Perciville shared her gaze, then turned back to Fjona. "Very well," he said, splaying his hands in defeat and taking a long, controlled inhalation. "My name is Perciville Harper and I am a sage. I deal in *the art of manipulation*. I can cast spells from my mind, body and soul, and channel them through this staff, here." He showed her the dark, oaken staff that had been leaning against the bar next to him, somehow unnoticeably. "My tale is long and filled with many a twist and turn, but in years gone by I have found myself wandering the Arvum alone, residing in the great cities and towns that define it and cavorting with the folk who inhabit it."

Fjona was dumbfounded. She had never heard of a sage before, let alone met one. She found herself staring at him as if he were an illusion she was trying to comprehend.

"And that's why you came to Marrow Myre? Another destination on your itinerary?"

Perciville's pale lips twisted into a great smile, his straight, white teeth sparkling in the gloomy candlelight.

"Not quite," he began. "I didn't exactly plan on stopping by here. Another lengthy tale involving oysters and wine in Sallisai'Mae, culminating with me waking up in the Myre of Maw and falling out of a tree with a devastating hangover."

The story sounded completely implausible to Fjona, yet there was something in his telling that reassured her it was the truth.

She returned his smile. "Okay, I won't mention the port to Jat."

Perciville didn't reply but nodded softly to show his appreciation.

Moments later, they were interrupted by Derethy. "Closing time, off you go," she said succinctly and with a sharp huff.

It was said in such a tone that Fjona wouldn't have been

surprised if Derethy had proceeded to sweep them out with a broom.

Fjona and Perciville stood and made for the door.

"I better head upstairs and find my room," Fjona told Perciville, "but it was nice to meet you."

She really meant it too. Perhaps it was just tiredness, alcohol or both but she was beginning to feel that she had been too quick to judge this man and felt a wave of disappointment wash over her from not being able to get to know him more.

"You can finish your drinks outside, if you like. Just put the latch on when you come back in," said Jat as he beckoned them towards the entrance.

"Thank you, although I'll probably just go and find somewhere to sleep," Perciville replied matter-of-factly as if sleeping outside was a common occurrence for him.

Fjona pondered Jat's invitation and said, "Actually it would be nice to get some fresh air."

She gave Perciville a look.

"Lead the way," he said.

Before they crossed the threshold from the cosy interior and into the refreshingly cool, moonlit outdoors, a fleeting thought of concern crossed Fjona's mind.

"What about him?" she asked Jat, looking over to the sleeping oaf.

"Don't worry about Gruno, he's something of an *honory* resident of The Tipsy Mercer. I like to consider him our sleepy caretaker. He'll be up in an hour or two, clean up anything I may have missed, and go back to bed on one of the benches over there, ready for a day of the same tomorrow."

It wasn't exactly nothing to worry about; after all, Gruno's life seemed so sad. The same routine, day after day: wake, drink, sleep. Then again, who was Fjona to judge? Her routine wasn't all that different. The same village, the same chores, day in, day out. Perhaps she, a humble villager from Wychwold, shared something intrinsically close with the lonely old elf whose appearance alone sang 'I've given up'. They were both trapped.

She shook herself out of her stupor, thanked Jat for his hospitality and accompanied Perciville to a wooden bench, looking out over the Near Sea. The rain had settled by now and a gentle breeze floated through the copse of trees that surrounded them. It carried with it a singed fragrance from the courtyard. Evidently the effigy had been burned at some point during the festivities.

Fjona was quick to resume her interrogation. "So where are you heading next?"

"Why so many questions?"

"I find you mysterious. I've never so much as heard of magic, let alone someone who can actually do it."

A brief look of scorn crossed Perciville's face, but he quickly fashioned it into a smile.

"Magic is doing tricks: sleight of hand, coins behind the ear. Sages refer to what we do as *the art of manipulation*. It is so much more than magic. We toy with the particles that surround us, bend them to our will to conjure and transform."

On that note, he glanced around to make sure that nobody was watching and whipped the bottle of port out from beneath his robe. He then grabbed his staff which had been quietly leaning against the bench behind them.

"How did you do that?" Fjona asked, surprised that she again had failed to notice it.

Perciville smiled. "It's a shielding spell. I cast it on the staff itself so that it wouldn't draw unwanted attention. Not invisible, simply unnoticeable."

Fjona considered this. "But if you're so desperate to not draw attention, why not cast such a spell upon yourself?"

"I have done in the past but it becomes very challenging ordering a drink. Plus being totally ignored is a dire condition. I found myself going loopy," he replied before going very quiet and using the staff to conjure two diminutive, elegant port glasses on the bench between them. "I like to think I have some level of grace beyond drinking directly out of the bottle."

Perciville poured out the alluring liquid into the two glasses then lifted his to make a toast.

"To unexpected company," he said, clinking the glass against Fjona's.

"To unexpected company," she replied before taking a hearty sip.

They were both quiet, listening to the waves crashing against the white cliffs. Even the revellers and musicians in the plaza sounded as though they'd disappeared to bed.

"So what is it like living here in Marrow Myre?" Now it was Perciville's turn to ask the questions.

"It's brilliant!" Fjona said sincerely, though her tone soon shifted into sarcasm. "I get woken up at the break of dawn by a screaming chorus of birds, share my breakfast with dozens of villagers whose names I hardly know, spend the daylight hours cleaning up goat droppings and fixing fences, then lie in bed unable to sleep because the sun has barely set before everyone turns in for the night." She lifted her glass again and forced a smile. "Cheers."

Perciville grinned. "Cheers," he said, and their glasses rang like miniature bells.

"In truth, it's not really that bad here, though I do feel like my life is racing ahead of me and I've only seen the same few places," Fjona admitted.

Another peaceful silence hung between them.

"Can *I* travel with you?" she asked.

It was a simple and honest question, not just the port telling her to trust this man but a more primal desire, deep inside her, longing to accompany Perciville, at least for a while.

Perciville seemed to consider her request. "I couldn't take you away from your friends, and what about your family? You must have family. What would they say?"

"Todie and Evelyn would understand, I'm sure, and my parents are travelling anyway. I can be back before they even get home. Todie can look after the goats while you and I nip across onto the mainland for a couple of weeks," Fjona replied, confident that her argument was strong enough to convince the sage.

To Perciville's credit, he really did spend some time mulling this over. "I'm sorry, Fjona, but I travel alone. Besides, you'd spend one day with me before getting fed up and begging me to bring you home again!"

"I promise, I'm tenacious. If it comes to it, I'll force myself to not get fed up with you," she pleaded, but it was all in vain.

Perciville just shook his head. "Believe me, you can find better company with whom to visit the Arvum."

Somehow Fjona sensed that Perciville was talking to himself. She felt deflated but decided not to push the point further. Disappointed, she petulantly stood with the intention of finding her friends and squeezing into bed with them, but Perciville was quick to react.

"Please, stay. I know you wish you could come along with me but in time you will realise that you made the right decision. Be that as it may, we have the best part of a bottle of exquisite port here and it wouldn't be right to see it go to waste."

Although Fjona was fairly certain that Perciville could make the bottle disappear and conjure up a fresh one at will, she appreciated the sentiment that he wanted to share this particular batch with her, and retook her place on the bench alongside him without the need to say anything. Perciville poured out another glass each and they remained in place, nursing their drinks in contemplative quiet.

The moon was beginning its descent and the first kiss of early morning sunshine could be seen on the horizon as if the sun itself were reaching out from the depths of the sea.

Perciville caught Fjona shivering from the corner of his eye. Perhaps because he didn't want to break the silence, or perhaps because he was afraid of sounding patronising, he wordlessly took his staff and conjured a fire on a patch of grass before them. It only singed the tips of the surrounding weeds without spreading further and, though the fire was small, the heat seemed to wrap around them like a blanket.

Fjona poured out the last of the port. "Thank you, Perciville."

"I was feeling a little chilly myself," he replied.

"No, not just for the fire. For a new perspective. Until tonight I was living a contented, simple life in a tiny Myrish village. I want to get away more, maybe visit the whole island. Todie invited me to visit the Great Forest of Aulden. Perhaps that could be a start..."

"Well, I'm certainly glad that you can take something positive from our brief encounter," he said warmly.

The cosy heat from the fire was beginning to make both Fjona and Perciville feel increasingly lethargic, not helped by the last drops of Autumn Elf Old Port which soon left the two strangers comfortably catatonic on the wooden bench. It wasn't long before they were cuddled up against one another, the messy curls of Fjona's head resting dreamlessly on Perciville's pointed shoulders.

It was the perfect setting in which to welcome an abrupt change of heart.

CHAPTER 11

COLLIDING METEORS

At first Perciville wasn't sure whether he was awake or dreaming lucidly. His brain felt like it was sloshing around in a pool of water, throbbing evenly against the inside of his skull. This was a sensation he had become all too well acquainted with first thing in the morning.

His skin felt clammy from the heat of the fire which was still burning under the spell, and his lips were sticky and dry, with only the aid of his sleeve to remediate it.

The sun was rising now and fully visible in the distance of the Near Sea behind a curtain of wispy clouds, though it wasn't the burgeoning light that had summoned Perciville from a heavy slumber. He had been disturbed by a deep-rooted and primal instinct; a premonition that within his very being told him to be alert.

Fjona's head suddenly felt very heavy and Perciville, with painstaking care, gently lifted it up, shuffled off the end of the bench, and lay her back down without so much as a peep. He lifted her legs up onto the bench too, and would have conjured a blanket for her to cuddle up under had the fire not proven to be so effective.

Now Perciville turned his attention to the next subject on his mind. "Why am I awake?" he thought.

He scanned his immediate surroundings to ascertain whether his instincts had alerted him to the presence of a predatory animal or unwanted, unsavoury company but, besides an orange fox sniffing around the tavern, there was nothing at all, and something told Perciville that it wasn't due to the fox that he was awake.

Then he saw it. High up in the northern sky, a subtle but brilliant meteor raced southwards offering a flickering red glow as it soared across the Arvum. It was no bigger than the nearest star though certainly far brighter. It tore through the atmosphere, burning a fiery streak through the crust of the sky like a fatal wound across a torso. Then he glanced southwards to see a blue meteor, following the opposite trajectory along the exact same alignment as its northern cousin. The sky had never seemed so enormous until that moment and the prospect of two cosmic bodies coming together was so close to impossible that Perciville knew this pertained to a greater meaning.

He stared at the flying objects as, moment by moment, they sped closer together. His heart ached with a feverish anxiety, terrified not for the consequences of the two meteors making impact, but for a sickening feeling that everything was about to change.

He clenched his eyes shut at a desperate attempt to reject what was surely unfolding before them but, when he finally released them, the two meteors were still there.

Closer and closer they got, stretching across the sky, tailed by a ribbon of red and blue light. For a fraction of a moment, it seemed that they were going to pass by one another and continue their separate journeys beyond their own horizons. As if they could offer a gentle nod to one another like two friends meeting on a narrow street, then proceed to wherever it was they were heading. Though that was not the case.

Perciville instinctively tensed as the two meteors collided into one another with incomprehensible, planetary shattering force, and was surprised when he couldn't feel the ground beneath him shake under the impact. He thought he could hear discordant bells jingling in the distance, could almost feel them vibrating beneath his skin.

The sky then seemed to return to normal except for where Perciville could just make out a dark cavity at the point of the meteors' collision. He watched unwaveringly until, finally, a single green light appeared in their place and one meteor, tracing a new direction, turned eastward towards the sun. He stared, mesmerised by it as it fell beyond the distant horizon as if it had toppled over the edge of the sky.

The air felt still and only the sounds of the ocean and the first few wallowbirds of the morning could be heard.

Perciville stood, transfixed, hairs pricked up along his spine. He was a well-travelled sage, after all, and wore a proverbial coat of badges that illustrated his worldly experience. What he had just witnessed – two meteors merging together and sailing away on a new path – was not merely a natural phenomenon. It was a sign. A cosmic message sent to all whose eyes it had been intended for.

He was pacing back and forth now as he fought to interpret

what it could mean, though in truth he already knew. In actual fact, Perciville was considering as many alternatives to his gut feeling as possible, in the hopes that he was wrong. Because, if he were right, then he may receive the greatest gift of his existence though not without the greatest cost. What made the situation all the more challenging was that the great cost had, by Perciville's estimations, already begun and the great gift was near impossible to touch.

Then his mouth creased into a sly smile. Had anyone else seen him they may have mistaken the look for one of cruel greed. Perciville turned his darkening eyes on Fjona and recalculated her proposition.

With hands clutching his staff, he stamped it on the ground like a giant pestle. A gusty wind tore through the trees and the fire blinked out leaving no clues that it had ever existed. For a fraction of a second the wallowbirds seemed to be singing a macabre, minor tune though this may only have been audible to Perciville.

Fjona's evergreen eyes flickered open and she carefully sat up on the bench. A few seconds passed as she groggily glanced around her. She rubbed her eyes before looking up to find Perciville smiling fondly at her.

"Good morning my *derine*," he said with a voice like honey.

Fjona returned his smile. "Good morning, Perciville Harper."

His full name, spoken aloud by someone else for the first time in recent memory. It felt strange to his ears like a different language, though that's not to say he didn't like it.

Before Fjona had even a chance to stand up, Perciville

spoke. "I've changed my mind."

These words didn't seem to register with Fjona at first. She remained seated, staring blankly at Perciville, making him feel anxious that she had completely forgotten their conversation from the previous night.

"What do you mean?" Fjona eventually replied.

"I mean, Fjona, that I would very much like the pleasure of your company, should you still be interested."

Fjona's jaw dropped, a look of bewilderment and scepticism passing across her face.

"Why? Why the change of heart?"

Perciville shrugged. "I slept on it."

Fjona didn't even offer him the respect of questioning his response. She merely glared at him until Perciville started to feel uncomfortable.

"Okay fine," he said, taking a step closer to her and casting his eyes upwards, as if trying to pull the words from the back of his head. "I saw something, but it's difficult to explain. In truth I don't fully understand it myself and there's a chance that I could be humiliatingly wrong. Though, that being said, if it happens that I am right then the implications could be catastrophic." He paused and looked down at Fjona, who was staring blankly back at him. "I'm serious, Fjona! I don't even have the vocabulary right now to describe to you just how severe the consequences could be if what I think is going to happen, is what is going to happen."

Fjona was becoming increasingly perplexed by Perciville's frantic explanation, though she thought it best to entertain the idea that, just perhaps, he was telling the truth.

"Okay. So if you are correct about this *thing* that you saw, what do want with me?"

Perciville looked intently at Fjona, his eyes conveying a dangerous concoction of sincerity and wonderment.

"I want to make you a sage," he said.

CHAPTER 12

THE ARCHIVUS

There were only a few folk roaming the Upper Gate as Oolia passed the two Home Guard sentries at the door and briskly descended the steps from the Sultan's palace.

The guards wore long blue coats in the shade of lapis lazuli with the symbol of the giant embroidered on the right side of their chest. Atop their heads they donned tall steel helmets, which presumably took a lot of discipline to not remove in the suffocating heat. A narrow bladed shortsword was strapped into a scabbard at their hips, though they stood with a silver-tipped lance in their outer hands. One could only imagine the state of their feet in the heavy leather boots at the end of a twelve-hour rotation.

Oolia hurried past a spring elf, who was heading up to the palace, and followed the edge of the sparkling pool of water to a square courtyard along one side of the Upper Gate.

A white iron fence demarcated the enclosure, behind which stood a row of trees with fist-sized plums bursting through the leaves. This slice of the city was completely incongruous, not just for the thriving trees, but for the luscious lawns of dewy grass and the hum of furry bees, busily distributing pollen amongst the wildflowers. The garden was fed by a network of streams that cascaded into a pond between two meticulously maintained flower beds.

In the centre of the grove stood the Archivus, a captivating cylindrical edifice supported by a ring of limestone pillars and adorned with statues of historical scholars. It had several stories, each distinguished by tall, arched windows, and a copper domed roof with a small bell chamber on top. Flocks of plump white doves would roost inside the chamber and glide back down to the leafy plumage of surrounding trees, though they would never venture beyond the threshold of the courtyard.

Although Oolia had been permitted into the Upper Gate for nearly thirty years, twenty of which she had served the Sultan, opportunities to visit the Archivus had been scarce. It was an impressive and beautiful place but an unwritten etiquette discouraged visitors from attending without a purpose besides that of education. This was an etiquette that folk from across the Arvum respected, not merely those from Panamaya City.

Oolia followed a stone path that twisted and turned between the blossoming flora, and crossed a stream by a narrow, wooden bridge. The door to the Archivus was wide open and she was relieved to step into the cool shade within.

She entered into a foyer with a low ceiling that obstructed the view of the main library behind it. Immediately before her was a curved mahogany desk, behind which sat two elderly tipids, each with hooked noses and varying degrees of thinning grey hair.

The first stopped Oolia in her tracks without even looking up from the disproportionately large book in which he was absorbed.

"And you are...?" the tipid asked.

The second tipid shot her head up to inspect the visitor. She pulled a monocle up to one eye and peered through it with furrowed brows.

Oolia was taken aback. Although her notoriety was a fraction of the Sultan's, most of those with access to the Upper Gate ordinarily recognised her as his steward. Besides, it can only have been a few years since she had last visited the Archivus.

"Are you deaf?" the first tipid asked in a condescending tone.

"What is your name?" added the second as she sat up as far as her hunched back would allow.

"My name is Oolia Khamun, Steward to the Sultan," Oolia replied to two bemused faces.

"What did she say, Lappili?" said the first tipid, scratching his grey, wrinkled head in confusion. His fingers were long and spindly with stretched, arthritic knuckles.

Before the second tipid could answer, Oolia spoke up again. "I am the Sultan's steward," she began slowly, carefully enunciating each syllable. "My name is Oolia Khamun and I am here by request of the Sultan to speak with one of your proprietors."

By her profession she had developed a high tolerance for patience but now it was beginning to dry up. She flicked her eyes between the two diminutive secretaries but neither showed any sign of comprehension.

Just as Oolia was about to lose her temper, she was saved by a fellow summer elf who also sought admittance to the library.

"You need not waste your time with these two," he said. "Lappili and Desmée are living far beyond their years. They can hardly hear a word you say, though their minds are sharp enough to locate near every one of the books shelved here."

Oolia looked up at the elf. He was big by all accounts. Tall, broad at the shoulders and large around the waist. His eyes were as light as silver and his hair was a tangled net of red twine that hung as low as his thick chest. He wore a loose-fitting, white cotton robe that just came down to his ankles, and his pointed ears were decorated with an eclectic arrangement of rings and gems.

"Isiah Fethen, Proprietor of Intellect in Botany and Horticulture." He proffered a giant, callused hand.

Oolia gladly shook it, her own hand completely engulfed in the summer elf's palm. "I am—"

"The Steward to the Sultan, of course," Isiah finished. "Oolia Khamun, I gather?" He walked gaily over to the desk and said idly, "She's with me."

Desmée seemed to ignore him, still engrossed in a chunky leatherbound tome, while Lappili waved them through, though not without a scrutinous expression on her wrinkled face.

Isiah made his way around the desk with enormous strides and it took more than a little effort for Oolia to keep up behind him.

Although she had visited the Archivus in the past, it never failed to amaze her each time she stepped into the main library. For one thing, the sheer scale of the room was entrancing, even from the perspective of someone who spent every day in the Sultan's palace, and there was something holy about the way the warm light from the sun burst through large windows up above the eaves that lit up the columns of methodically stacked bookshelves. The high ceiling was supported by a series of tall, elegant pillars, and there were several mezzanine floors that could be reached by a network of crisscrossing staircases.

It was near-unsettlingly quiet in the vast space with only the sounds of the footsteps of academics echoing from the heavily polished floor, until Isiah said, "So what beckons you to the Archivus?"

"I wish to speak with a proprietor with a knowledge of dreams and prophecies."

"For the Sultan?"

Oolia was careful to reply. She didn't want rumours of the Sultan's state of mind to spread across the city.

"For the Sultan's fascinations, is all."

Isiah shrugged. "Well, I don't know of anyone who has study in dreams, but let me introduce you to Proprietor Sialah Bouwer. She is an expert in the Ancients and may be able to lead you in the right direction."

He guided her up a stairwell to one side which snaked up to a floor above the main library. It was lit by several porthole-like windows that looked out over the city and into the desert beyond. Although Oolia may have stopped to admire the views at any other time, she was desperate to keep up with the pace of her chaperone.

At the top, they came out into a wide windowless corridor with a low ceiling and dozens of doors on either side.

It seemed to contradict the grandeur of the library below in all respects: gloomy, cramped and dusty.

"These are the proprietors' chambers," Isiah explained. "Mine is the third door on the left, should you care to pay me a visit. My door is always open to those who are interested in discovering more about the gardens and flora that cover the Arvum. As for your needs today, Sialah Bouwer can be found in the second chamber from the end on the right-hand side."

With that, the large summer elf continued to his door. Before he went inside, he added, "I hope you find what you are looking for."

"Thank you, Proprietor Fethen. You have been of great help today," Oolia replied.

Isiah smiled with his enormous mouth and disappeared inside.

The floorboards creaked, even under Oolia's slight weight, as she furthered down the corridor to Sialah Bouwer's chamber.

She knocked tentatively on the door and awaited a response. Oolia stood patiently in the gloom of the musty passageway, but no sound came from the other side.

She persevered, her small hand rattling against the wood and echoing down the barren corridor. "Hello? Proprietor Bouwer?" she called out into the silence. "I am here on behalf of the Sultan."

There was still no reply.

She knocked again, this time more purposefully. "Sialah Bouwer?"

This time, a resigned voice came from within. "Yes, yes, fine. Come in."

Taking a deep breath, Oolia pushed open the door and stepped into a wide, open space. It was starkly different to the corridor: illuminated in a golden sunlight from great windows, every table surface stacked with all manner of reading material. The floor was an ocean of plush carpet, in the middle of which sat Sialah Bouwer who was perched over her desk, immersed in literature, reading through thick-lensed spectacles.

Unusual relics and strange apparatus were distributed about the room, some on top of tables but others scattered about the floor. Oolia couldn't help but stare at them, trying to figure out what she was looking at. There were old fragments of pot, stone tools, scraps of metal.

"Funny," Sialah spoke, "you weren't mute while you were hammering at my door and calling out my name."

She was facing away from the door and Oolia found herself replying to the back of the proprietor's silvery hair. It had been tied up neatly with a strip of red ribbon, fashioned into the rough shape of a rose.

"Proprietor Bouwer, forgive my interruption. My name is Oolia Khamun, the—"

"Steward to the Sultan, yes. Continue..."

It was now that Oolia finally lost her patience. Why was it so difficult to communicate with people in this place? Her frustration had been coursing through her body since she'd met the curators and now it was ready to erupt before the Proprietor of Intellect.

"Look," she said, "I am here on behalf of our Divine

Excellency, Sultan Ayermune Dahller Sé. If you value your position here at the Archivus, not least your life, then I suggest that you take my presence more seriously. You may even have the courtesy to relieve yourself from your work and turn to acknowledge me." The steward exhaled gently from the relief of getting that off her chest.

At first, Sialah Bouwer seemed to completely ignore Oolia's request. Her head remained stooped, fixed on the pages in front of her. Then she yielded. She pushed herself back on her seat and stood steadily, turning gently on her toes to face Oolia. The proprietor towered over the summer elf. She herself had paler skin, though still tanned in a rust-coloured shade, the epitome of an autumn elf from the Free Capital of Havensend. She wore a sleeveless cotton shirt and thin, loose-fitting breeches: clothes suitable for those who were still acclimatising to the oppressive heat of the desert.

Her dark brown eyes were magnified through her spectacles and resembled those of a fruit fly.

"Thank you, Oolia, for your concern over my security here at the Archivus but I am governed by the Warden of Intellect whose principal focus is to the pursuit of knowledge and not that of assuaging the Sultan. If you or he take issue with my lack of obedience, well, then you may take it up with Daemund Newblood, for he is the only person to whom I report."

She gestured to the door and returned to her desk.

Oolia was stunned into silence. Very rarely had she played her role with the Sultan for her own gain but, when she had done, it had always worked.

Sialah Bouwer was a tough nut to crack, but Oolia was well

trained in appeasing difficult people.

"Proprietor, I understand, truly, and I wish only that I could leave you to your studies, but the Sultan is in need of counsel and I have been advised that you can help. I ask only that you hear my plea and offer whatever wisdom you can, after which I shall endeavour to never disturb you again."

Sialah Bouwer sighed.

"Very well, you may have but a moment of my precious time."

Oolia did not hesitate. "The Sultan is suffering intensely vivid dreams—"

The proprietor sighed again, already clearly disinterested in the topic, though her blatant attitude would not dissuade Oolia who was grateful enough to have a least one set of ears to talk to.

"The dreams are always the same. He tells me he is standing at the steps of the palace, looking out over the city and down into the forum. It is bustling with people from all over the Arvum, children among them, happily going about their business: playing games, trading, enjoying the fruits of this city. Then things begin to take a turn. My Sultan tells me that he looks down at the Panamayan spring and it is all but dried up. He says that he kneels beside it, begging for help but that nobody can hear him. The sky turns dark, though it had been as bright as the Pentari sun on the highest hour of the solstice and, when he looks back down into the spring, he sees himself, lying dead at the bottom, vultures already circling above him to tear through his corpse. He reaches out as if to hold on to his life, but then the ground begins to shake violently, and a great trough shears through the middle of the Upper Gate. From the depths of the chasm emerges an enormous hand, as big as the entire palace, he tells me. Then, finally, just before he is shaken from this nightmare, in the dream I, Oolia, say these same, simple words: 'he is awake'. My Sultan has had this very same dream, every night for the past few weeks, each time feeling more real than the night before. Please, Proprietor, is there anything you can tell me?"

Sialah Bouwer remained still for a moment as if weighing up the details of the dream in her incredible mind. "I have a thought," she said.

Oolia's face lit up with optimism.

"I think that the Sultan has a brilliant imagination and is under a lot of stress."

This conclusion sent a wave a disappointment through the steward and her shoulders slumped forward in resignation.

"However, I can theorise two possibilities which may explain these events. Firstly, as I am sure you know, the Panamayan spring is by no means a natural feature of the mountain." The proprietor paused abruptly when Oolia's eyes widened. "Or perhaps not," Sialah added, releasing a long sigh. "I'd have thought someone of your calibre would at least be educated enough to know her own city."

Oolia bit her tongue, conscious not to say something that may lead to her quick dismissal from the Archivus.

The proprietor continued. "Beneath the palace exists an ancient well, long since dried up and serving as a vessel by which the Sultan may communicate with the Sleeping Giant. When the well could no longer supply the Panamayan people, they were forced to trek for miles across the Pentari Desert to transport water from the aqueducts at the Precipitous Mountains to the city. That was until, before the collapse of the Sagedom, a visiting sage conjured the spring, proclaiming that it would provide water to the city for three hundred years as a gift to the Sultan of the time. It stands to reason then that the sage's spell is soon to be lifted and the spring is about to dry up. It may just be that the Sultan's dreams are based on this very premonition."

Oolia considered this for a moment. If the Sultan knew that the spring had been created three centuries ago then would he not have shared that knowledge with her?

"Thank you, Proprietor Bouwer. What of your second theory?" she asked, casting aside her doubts.

"Throughout my studies I have researched much into the ancient mythologies of the Arvum and there is much written about the mountain upon which we live: the Sleeping Giant. However, to extrapolate truth from such legends could be considered unacademic. My peers would laugh me out of the door were I to postulate meaning behind the fables of old. That being said, one of my finest students is a budding anthropologist and mythologist, and I should recommend that you seek her out. San Kendi has a rare enthusiasm for deciphering the past and quite the acumen for unravelling the truth. I can show you her dwelling on a map, should you choose to speak with her."

"I see no reason why not," Oolia replied eagerly.

"You will have to venture into the Lower Gate, however."

Oolia suddenly felt less enthused. Nevertheless any leads in pursuit of the Sultan's happiness would be foolish to decline.

Sialah Bouwer unravelled a map of the city that was hidden away at the back of a drawer and circled around a hovel with a quill and ink.

"Kaikura Kendi has a brilliant mind. I hope that she can aid you on your quest."

"I cannot thank you enough, Proprietor Bouwer," Oolia replied, gladly accepting the map.

"Say no more. Really. We are done here."

Sialah again gestured to the door and recommenced her reading.

Not wanting to push her luck any further, Oolia quietly retreated and closed the door behind her, the map clutched tightly under her arm.

She hurried back along the corridor and, so distracted by her thoughts of conspiracy and premonitions, nearly knocked a passing scholar down the stairs.

"Forgive me, please, I am so sorry," Oolia said, startled by the unexpected encounter.

The scholar was wearing a long white robe with a gold trim. It was exquisite and rivalled the wardrobe of the Sultan.

He replied, with a soft stammer, "N-nonsense, the fault was most certainly mine. For years I have practically sp-sprinted up these staircases!"

The scholar had a handsome face with rounded ears and a rosy, snub nose. His hair was a soft shade of greying brown, cut relatively short, and around his mouth he kept a very well-maintained beard. Most reassuring was the kindness that he carried in his warm eyes as he smiled down at Oolia.

"But there's a lesson to be learned. Ignorant is the fool who thinks his d-daily habits bear no consequence. May the Four Good Gods be in your favour," he said simply and continued in the opposite direction.

Oolia stared, mesmerised, if not by the authoritative way in which he held himself, then by the allure of his striking attire, as he disappeared through the door at the furthest end of the corridor, opposite to where she stood.

At the bottom of the stairs, Oolia was cautious to avoid finding herself on the receiving end of a one-sided conversation with the two elderly curators. Fortunately Desmée had fallen asleep and was drooling into his book, but Lappili was more assertive and, though she didn't say anything, watched every step that Oolia took as she made for the exit.

Outside, Oolia strolled over to one of the bridges that crossed over the spring. She found herself really noticing it for the first time in her life and appreciating it for all that it provided to the people of Panamaya City. For hundreds of years it had quietly served them, saving them from dehydration or a long trek across the desert, without anyone really paying it much attention. The water was still high and the mid-afternoon sun made it shimmer like a precious stone, yet not a single passer-by seemed to notice it.

"Perhaps," Oolia wondered, "they will when it has all but gone."

She decided it best to check in with the Sultan before seeking out the scholar to ask whether he might arrange for a couple of Home Guards to escort her to the Lower Gate and ensure her safe passage.

She passed the sentries at the entrance to the palace and cut through the grand entrance hall, up two flights of lavish stairs and directly to the audience chamber where she abruptly stopped in her tracks.

The door was slightly ajar and Oolia could hear voices coming from behind it. Perhaps before today she would have politely knocked or returned later on but, in spite of her best intentions, Oolia found herself eavesdropping on the single most powerful person in this part of the Arvum.

"...you are revered as if you were our own king," a voice she did not recognise said. As soft as a feather, perfectly enunciated, and most definitely female.

"And my army?" the Sultan replied, almost childishly.

The other voice groaned enticingly. "Feared and venerated in equal measure. I know not a single spring elf who doesn't agree that Panamaya City is the true and native capital. If that were the case then tell me, what would that make you, Ayermune?"

Ayermune! Who in the Arvum would dare to address the Sultan by his name? Oolia pondered, her pricked-up ears practically poking around the door.

"*Their* Sultan," he replied.

"Their *god*!" the other voice corrected, followed by heavenly sweet laughter.

The Sultan laughed too, though his was gravelly and sticky, which made Oolia wince.

When the laughter died down, the mysterious guest said, "I have enjoyed my visit to the palace. To be permitted to bask in your presence is an honour."

"I assure you, the honour is most certainly mine."

Then followed the unmistakable sound of a kiss.

If on the lips then who was the Sultan's unsolicited companion? If on the cheek then perhaps an old friend? Or else the hand but then to whom would the Sultan bow down for?

Oolia shuddered. She had never known the Sultan to insinuate superiority in anyone other than himself. Something gave her a horrible, twisted feeling in her stomach.

"I fear I must take my leave, Ayermune, but I will be sure to pay you another visit the next time I am in the city," the guest said.

"And when might you expect to return?"

There was a pause before the guest replied. "It may not be for another few weeks but I assure you, you will know when I am back."

She spoke so cleanly, so almost kindly, that Oolia was surprised at herself for distrusting every word that practically sang from her lips.

"Until next we meet." the Sultan said, followed by another kiss.

To the sound of bright footsteps echoing from inside the audience chamber. Oolia began to panic. To be caught listening in on the Sultan had, in years gone by, resulted in punishment by death. She tiptoed away from the audience chamber as fast as she could and proceeded down the stairs, though the moment her feet met the bottom, she heard a voice behind her.

"Ah, you must be the Sultan's intrepid steward."

She was a spring elf, vaguely familiar to Oolia and most certainly the voice from the Sultan's conversations. She was very pretty, even Oolia could admit that. The spring elf adjusted her orange dress and retied her long pine-coloured hair before gracefully descending the flight of stairs.

There was little choice for Oolia but to tread carefully and not show her festering mistrust.

"I am indeed," she replied. "I have just got back this very minute from running an errand in the Upper Gate for the Sultan." Oolia hoped that by providing more detail she wasn't becoming increasingly conspicuous.

"So I gather," the spring elf replied with a smile so bright it could attract moths. "Well I best be on my way. Toodle pip!" As they passed, the spring elf waited and added, "Steward..."

Oolia paused and turned to see the elf gazing up at her with a stern expression on her otherwise flawless face.

"Where do the fleas live when the dog has died?"

Oolia was too taken aback to reply and the spring elf disappeared down the stairs.

When the strength had returned to her legs of jelly, she forced herself up, clinging to the banister, repeating the spring elf's words over and over in her head.

What did she mean? Was the Sultan the dog and Oolia merely a flea, depending on him to sustain her? After all, where would she go if something were to happen to him?

By the time she had reached the audience chamber, Oolia had managed to compose herself enough to walk straight in through the, now, wide open doors.

"Oolia! You have returned," Ayermune said enthusiastically.

He was sitting at the table, indulging in a large glass of white wine.

Oolia noticed a second glass on the table that was mostly gone.

"I trust you have good news for me."

It took a great deal of discipline to hold her tongue and to not interrogate her superior. Oolia would like to have asked, 'Who was that strange elf you had visiting just now?' or 'What are you up to behind my back?', but instead, she said, "I spoke to Proprietor Sialah Bouwer who had two insights that may explain the nature of your dreams."

The Sultan raised his eyebrows and stared expectantly at his steward.

"Were you aware that the spring was created by a sage?" Oolia asked tentatively.

The Sultan's stare quickly changed to a scowl. "Sages?" he barked back at her. "Don't you disrespect the mighty power of the Sleeping Giant with talk of sages!" His eyes were a canvas of fire, burning with an angry flame. "The summer elves discovered this mountain and this mountain serves the summer elves. No sage can outwit the needs of our people." He hammered the wine glass on the table, liquid bubbling over the edge of the rim.

Oolia waited for the Sultan to stop raging before patiently adding, "Sages or not, Sialah Bouwer believes that your dreams may relate to a premonition about the spring drying up. I would urge—"

"Premonition?" he retorted. "How might I have a premonition over some crackpot idea that I've never before considered. Use your brain, Oolia."

That one stung, but Oolia knew better than to retaliate. "You are of course right, Divine Excellency, and I shall say little more on the matter, only that you may wish to convene with the architect to discuss reinstating the aqueducts at the Precipitous Mountains."

She breathed a long, tortured breath. Whatever the Sultan may decide to do, Oolia had at least delivered everything she needed to.

For whatever reason, the Sultan didn't snap back at her this time. He screwed up his face in concentration and tapped his crooked fingers on the table.

Eventually, he replied, "Aqueducts mean resources, and resources mean power. Very well, I shall speak with San Baerita to see what can be done. What of the second insight, or is that likely to disappoint me further?"

There was no going back. Oolia had proffered an alternative suggestion and now she had to follow through.

"There is a renowned scholar who resides in the Lower Gate. An expert in deciphering dreams. If perhaps you could provide me with a Home Guard or two to accompany me, I can bring the scholar to you and she will help resolve your troubles."

His fingers started to drum again on the hardwood of the table before he resignedly replied, "You may take Darazith and Terin. I'm sure they'd appreciate stretching their legs down to the Lower Gate. But make this expedition worth my while."

Oolia nodded. "Thank you, Your Divine Excellency."

"Then be gone," the Sultan added firmly.

As she made for the door, Oolia hesitated. A thought niggled at the threads of her mind and she simply couldn't let it go.

She turned back to the Sultan and asked, "Did the minstrel not play for you this afternoon?"

The Sultan waved a hand to her. "That overpaid bard failed to show. I've been here alone, bored out of my mind and waiting upon your return."

Sialah Bouwer rubbed her eyes. She had been staring at the pages of a textbook for so long that she was beginning to feel dazed. With a heavy hand, she swept the book aside and heard it thump against the soft carpet beneath her.

Feeling guilty for her brash behaviour, she leaned over to pick it up. As she did, something caught her eye. It was the cover of a book that she felt she'd looked upon hundreds of times before, yet had never really seen. It was twenty or so books deep in a pile of old dusty tomes that she had recovered from the Ancient and Protected Materials section of the library only two days ago. The red leather cover was faded and embossed with the words *The Compendium of Sages* in gold leaf down the spine. Sialah was surprised at herself for never having spotted it before but, for whatever the reason, she was seeing it now.

She carefully extracted it from the tower of old books and set it back down on her desk, then mechanically opened it up to the contents page.

Her eyes scanned the list of chapters: *Yilsommen, The First Sage, The Tree of Birth, The Progressive Nature of Wands to Staffs...*

One chapter in particular caught her eye and she flicked through the thin pages to locate it. Sialah could barely believe what she was reading, considering the conversations she had had with the steward only earlier that day.

Her heart was pounding, blood racing to her brain – a signal that she required more energy to focus her mind. What were the chances that, today of all days, she should stumble across the chapter of a book that chronologised the formation of The Sleeping Giant?

Not the legend but the cold hard truth.

"Impossible," Sialah said to herself as she absorbed the ancient text before her. "*Sil'yhab forlein.*"

CHAPTER 13

AN UNTIMELY INTERRUPTION

Purple ink dribbled onto the parchment leaving a mingling of splotches across the page. In previous decades, ink was a much more valuable commodity and a scholar may have been chided for wasting even just a few precious drops. More recently, with increased trade coming into the city, the cost of a small jar of ink was much more affordable, not that Kaikura Kendi would want to be wasteful.

She was leaning over her table, busily, though neatly, scribing her thoughts pertaining to the use of magic in the ancient world.

By the sixth dynasty, she wrote, *the reputation of the Sagedom had expanded beyond its seat at the Rock of Caeznor and the southern regions of the Arvum, and its influence now reached the island of Bouanda in the far north. One may therefore argue that it is during the reign of Sagen Master Raelin Thon that the Sagedom was really established as a unified government.*

Kaikura placed the quill in its stand and leaned back in her chair, processing all she was learning.

"This begs the question of how its influence spread," she pondered aloud. "Was the Sagedom forced on the people of the Arvum or were they willing to assimilate?"

She tapped the bridge of her nose in quiet contemplation.

In moments like this, Kaikura would ordinarily talk it through with Bobassa even though he couldn't reply in a coherent way, but he was busy roaming the neighbourhood in search of vermin to satiate his primal instincts. The summer elf would just have to make do with her mind and a number of interesting, though often overwhelming, texts.

Just as she was about to open a different book entitled *An Anthology of the Arvum by Gerrin Aschwin,* muffled voices caught Kaikura's attention. She turned her head up to the door, training her ears to the chattering beyond but was unable to discern any actual words.

There were heavy footsteps, at least two pairs, walking atop the roof, causing wispy flakes of dust to float from the ceiling and onto the floor around her.

Kaikura gently pushed back on her chair and, with the grace of a sandkat, made for a sharp spear that was attached by a small length of rope to a hook on the wall. It was more of a relic than a weapon, an ancient item that she had acquired from a fellow scholar at the Archivus. Its long faded wooden handle was heavily worn and coated in splinters like a cactus, but for a rope grip that Kaikura had implemented to make it possible to hold. At its tip was a sharp pointed flint blade that had been expertly knapped on either side to form a spearhead that was equal parts beautiful and lethal.

For the most part the spear had remained as part of the wall décor, save for a few occasions when it had been useful to deter thieves.

Kaikura watched as the hatch door was flung open and an enormous moon-shaped head peered into her humble sanctuary. The moon head wore a steel helmet which appeared to only just fit over his fat skull, and his face had a sunburst complexion: most definitely Grugan.

"She be here!" he shouted to his companion on the roof.

"Thank you, Darazith, that will be all. If you would..." replied another voice in a slightly frantic tone.

The Grugan's big head disappeared from the entranceway and was replaced by a summer elf with white hair tied up in buns.

"Please forgive our intrusion. I insisted that we should knock but my guard here can get a little carried away."

The elf looked down at Kaikura who was clutching her spear in two hands and pointing it towards the top of the ladder.

"I can see that you don't get much company," she continued. "Mind if we come in?"

Kaikura mumbled a response but, even if she'd been clearer, it was unlikely to have made a difference. Before she knew it, both the summer elf and the Grugan were descending the ladder into her home. The Grugan was dressed in a long blue coat which made him instantly recognisable as a member of the Home Guard. He was proceeded by a second guard, a tall and muscular summer elf with a perfectly clean-shaven face and a sternness to his brow. Both guards carried longswords at their hips and Kaikura noticed the gleam of a knife blade, just visible on the inside of the second guard's boot.

She felt anxious. Confrontation was not exactly her strong suit, especially when the opposition were the authorities.

With a dry, throaty voice, Kaikura asked, "How may I serve you?"

"I am Oolia Khamun, Steward to the Sultan."

Kaikura felt a wave of nerves wash through her like a strong drink. "And you came here because...?" she asked, her voice shaking as much as her hands.

Oolia put her own hands out in a reassuring manner. "Please, you have no reason to be afraid. I come only to ask for your help."

The Grugan stood obediently beside Oolia while the summer guard distractedly leafed through the pages of a book on the table. It pained Kaikura so much to see somebody unappreciatively peel through the pages of an ancient text that she instinctively pulled the book away from the guard and slammed it shut. Even her usual pristine manners could be cast aside when the preservation of a book was at stake.

"Terin, leave her stuff alone," Oolia scolded and shot the summer guard a sharp look.

He raised his eyebrows before stepping to the other side of the steward with a quiet huff.

The steward turned back to the slightly dishevelled scholar. "I understand that you are San Kaikura Kendi, a member of the Archivus. I was hoping that your research may be of some use to the Sultan."

"Oh I sincerely doubt that. My studies focus on the ancient

peoples and mythologies of the Arvum. How can I possibly be of any use?"

"You were personally selected for the role," said Oolia.

"The Sultan requested me?" Kaikura replied, dumbfounded that the Panamayan leader should even know her name.

"Not quite. I first spoke with your mentor, Proprietor Bouwer. She spoke highly of you and advised I pay a visit."

"Sialah Bouwer recommended me?"

This caught Kaikura's attention. She was an excellent student at the Archivus and got on very well with her proprietor, but for her to have been hand selected to assist the Sultan showed just how much her research was respected.

"What does the Sultan want with me?"

"I think it's best that he explains himself. I should urge you to entertain his Excellency and, if you are indeed able to help, then perhaps a significant donation may be made towards your research."

Another enticing prospect. The Archivus provided Kaikura with enough money with which to live but it could only go so far. A significant donation may help pay for a chaperone to guide her beyond the desert to explore the wider world and visit the places that she could only ever afford to read about.

Before anyone could speak, a loud screeching cry echoed down from the open hatch. The summer guard jumped and was quick to draw his longsword, turning on the balls of his feet as he did. He pointed the blade in the direction of Bobassa who was glaring down at this party from the top of the ladder, sharp teeth bared and a venomous look in his bronze eyes.

The Grugan was a little slower to react but soon he too had

unsheathed his sword, while Oolia stepped back behind her guards.

"Keep back, you vile critter," Terin called, his pulsing muscular arm outstretched behind his sword.

The sandkat didn't take kindly to this threat and leaped down onto the bedroom floor to get closer to the uninvited guests.

"Bobassa is a perfect companion, I will have you know, and most certainly not a vile critter!" Kaikura said before approaching her pet. "Bobassa, it's all right. They mean me no harm." She smiled fully, catching Bobassa's hungry eyes. "We're safe, Bobassa."

The sandkat softened a little though he still stared menacingly at the two guards, saliva bubbling around his dark lips.

"Come any closer and this will go straight through you!" Terin said, a fierce look in his eyes.

"I should advise you to lower your sword. Bobassa's been known to rip the flesh from the face of a thief or two, weapon or not."

On deft paws, the scaly feline inched closer to the edge of the floor, now glaring at Terin and his longsword.

"Lower your blade, I urge you!" Kaikura called.

"Keep back, beast!" Terin said, now waving his sword in the face of Bobassa.

Darazith snarled before reluctantly sheathing his longsword. This seemed to satisfy the sandkat further though he was not finished with the summer guard. He leaned on his forepaws as if ready to pounce.

"That's enough, Terin! Do as Kaikura says, lower your weapon," Oolia now interjected, but it was said in vain.

Terin jabbed the point of the sword towards Bobassa in the hopes of scaring him away but it only antagonised him. Before the guard could react, the sandkat was sailing through the air in a controlled arc above his sword. It landed on top of Terin's helmet and wrapped its two tails around his neck.

The soldier gasped for air, dropping his sword so that he could use his hands to tear the tail away from his throat but Bobassa's grip was too tight.

"H-el-p," he managed to squeeze out through constricted airways.

The other three were beginning to panic too, not least Kaikura, who was afraid word of this may reach the ears of the Sultan and Bobassa could find himself at risk of execution, the usual punishment for harming a member of the Home Guard.

"Bobassa! Get off him this minute!"

The sandkat loosened its grip and looked over at Kaikura.

"He's dropped his sword, there's no threat anymore. Please, come back over to me," she added with composure.

It was enough to get through to Bobassa, who flopped from the helmet and bounded over to Kaikura, brushing up against her legs.

Oolia released a long exhale. "Well that could have ended a lot worse."

"A lot worse? I was seconds from strangulation by that foul beast!" Terin cried, holding his neck and taking deep, controlled breaths. "I should have the Sultan hear of this! He will have that thing killed for harming his personal guard!"

The Grugan grunted in agreement.

"*You* provoked *him*!" said Kaikura.

"I was protecting—" Terin began, but was cut off by the frustrated scholar.

"Who? Me, Bobassa's friend? Who has lived with him for several years without so much as a scratch!"

"A creature like that should not be permitted in the city. We have enough trouble with elven violence without beasts like this one wasting our time and resources."

"Stop calling him a beast!"

"It's no better than a dalachite!"

"That's enough, the both of you," Oolia finally intervened.

Terin opened his mouth to speak but Oolia held up a finger before he could get a sound out.

"Terin is correct that the Sultan may not take kindly to this, should we decide to say anything."

Kaikura didn't like where this was heading.

"But I suppose if you were willing to offer your knowledge to his Excellency, then perhaps we can keep this minor incidence between us. After all, nobody was really hurt."

"Did you not see it around my neck?"

"I said that's enough, Terin!"

The abashed guard looked to the floor.

Kaikura conceded, realising she had little choice in the matter. "Very well. Take me to the Sultan. Let's see if I can help."

CHAPTER 14

THE EIGHT AFFLICTIONS

Fjona was dumbfounded. "I'm sorry, you're going to have to repeat yourself... you want to make me a sage?"

Perciville nodded. "Indeed."

"You mean you are going to use your... *manipulation*, to create my very own sage to do my bidding?" She stood up and paced back and forth, a fresh morning breeze kissing the back of her pale neck.

He seemed a little taken aback. "No. I mean that I would like to teach you how to harness your energy to manipulate the—"

"Yes, I realise that. I was being facetious," Fjona interrupted. It was a little too much for her to comprehend this early in the day. "And you are being deadly serious?"

A brief nod.

"How?"

Perciville was quiet as he ruminated over this seemingly innocuous question. "Well, we start by crossing onto the mainland and locating, what we sages know as, The Tree of Birth. Should we find it, and I know where to look, then we will quickly discover whether or not you have the moral capacity to be a sage."

When Fjona's only response was a confused and vacant expression, Perciville said simply, "You get a wand."

Fjona's eyebrows lifted. "I get my own wand?"

Another nod. "Yes."

"But I thought sages used staffs?"

"Well eventually we do, but every sage has to start with a wand." He laughed lightly. "I mean, did your mother teach you to cook by showing you how to boil an egg, or by getting you to poach a whole salmon?" He paused for a moment before correcting himself. "Actually, this is Marrow Myre. You were probably skinning salmon the day you were born!"

Fjona's vacant expression changed to a tight glare. "Point taken," she replied. "Whatever the case, I dare say it would be unwise for me to join you. I have a home to take care of, chores to do. Besides, even if that weren't the case, my parents would be horrified when they get home to find me missing. I don't suppose you could make me a sage in, say... two weeks?"

Fjona's nervous joviality was met only by the sage's suddenly darkening tone.

"Miss Sarsen, being enveloped by the light of such a beautiful sunrise as this, it is near impossible to imagine the horrors that I believe, strongly believe, are inevitably to unfold." His shocking, pale eyes narrowed. "This is more than just a premonition, Fjona. This is the most foul of atrocities that the Arvum could ever witness and, with your help, I may just be able to stop it."

Fjona was finally paying attention now, her simmering

intrigue beginning to spill over.

"People will die, cities will fall. The fabric of the world we know of today could be very different if you and I do not intervene. Fjona, if you are to become a sage it will consume the rest of your life but...!" His brilliant eyes lit up and his mouth opened into the most wonderful of smiles. "What a life you will have! In discovering the art of manipulation, you will find yourself gazing into the very soul of the world. Fjona, you must realise how this is a rare opportunity, not just for yourself, but for the Arvum, as no new sage has been born for centuries." He became very solemn again. "But first, Fjona, we need to prevent the fruition of what has come to be known as..." Perciville could barely find the strength to say it. He leaned heavily on his staff for support, though he still swayed gently.

"As...?" asked Fjona.

The sage gave a deep sigh. "The Eight Afflictions – and make no mistake, they are far more horrifying than even the name suggests."

Something changed for Fjona in that moment. She felt the sincerity with which Perciville spoke and the weight behind the words he shared. His skin had taken on a cold pallor and she half expected him to throw up.

She quietly considered Perciville's offer. "How do I know I can trust you? I mean, I've known you for as long as a single night. There are people in Wychwold who I've known for my entire life and I wouldn't trust them to tie my shoelaces, let alone protect me on the mainland."

"Well..." Perciville began as Fjona optimistically waited for a few words of wisdom to reassure her. "You can't," he said, matter-of-factly.

"Oh," she replied, her voice dropping as heavily as her hope.

The sage placed a gentle hand on her shoulder. "What I mean, is that I could spiel a string of reasons as to why you can trust me but what good would that do? Trust takes time and we haven't yet had the virtue of that, but come with me and I assure you that before we even cross to the mainland you will have at least an inkling as to whether or not it is wise to accompany me."

Fjona remained quiet, pensive.

"Or else," Perciville continued, "I shall seek the company of somebody else. Sure, they may not have your brazenness and passion, but so long as they are willing to carry a wand, it matters little to me."

His eyes twinkled with cheekiness, and Fjona couldn't help but return a smile.

Then the sage shrugged. "You can stay here in the safety of Marrow Myre with your two friends and patiently await your parents' return. Get back to mucking out stables or knitting jumpers or whatever other thrills this place has to offer. Then perhaps, once I've saved the Arvum from the resurgence of the Eight Afflictions, I might pay you a visit and regale the whole, wonderful story over another bottle of port!"

The truth of Perciville's words stung deeply inside Fjona and her heart ached with a mixture of guilt and longing. For how long had she dreamed of leaving Wychwold? For how long had she fantasised about seeing the rest of the world? Now, standing before her was a man, strange though he might appear, giving her the chance to live everything she had ever hoped of. Her parents, after all, had packed their bags and gone on an adventure of their own. Why shouldn't she?

When she eventually spoke, Fjona's voice was so soft that it may have been lost in the wind. "I'll do it," she said, then she abruptly shook her head, curly hairs bouncing around like a field of springs. "No, I can't, I'm sorry."

She expected Perciville to appear crestfallen and, for a moment, maybe he was, but his disappointment was subtle if it existed at all and he stood motionless, eyes fixated on her.

Fjona buried her head in her hands. "Or perhaps I *should* accompany you. Marrow Myre will continue on regardless. I might as well live a little..."

Before Perciville could interject, Fjona was on her feet and pacing back and forth behind the bench in a dizzying frenzy.

"Argh but I can't just leave my friends and my home, and who knows when I'd return, and what if we get into trouble or become separated and I get lost, or attacked by bears or..."

Fjona was starting to hyperventilate and her stream of anxiety was making her feel lightheaded.

"Look, forget I ever asked," Perciville finally managed to say. "Really, I take no offence. Your place is here and there's no shame in that. I realise now that it is an awful lot to ask of a..." He gestured at Fjona with a lazy hand.

"Of a what?" she shot back, hands on hips. "A *woman*?"

Perciville's shoulders slumped with frustration. "Of a Myrish folk," he said sincerely. "Your people aren't as adventurous as they used to be, and I do not begrudge them for it, but time really is precious and if you are unwilling to accompany me then I need to find someone who is."

A silence, but for the waking wallowbirds, followed and Fjona and Perciville merely stared at one another in a perfect stalemate. The wallowbirds, a brand-new tune but the same old routine.

With a defeated grin, Perciville said, "It really was a pleasure to meet you, Miss Sarsen. When I have saved the world, I will be sure to swing by and let you know how it went."

As he walked past her, Fjona felt a great, engulfing pit of shame and disappointment well up inside. Her head was still spinning with ambivalence, but she had made her decision to stay and that was final.

So when the words, "Wait, I will come with you," spilled out of Fjona's lips, she was as surprised as Perciville.

The sage paused a few paces away from her, gently shaking his head.

"You don't have to do this to yourself, Fjona, you have a perfect life here."

"Except I don't," she replied, finally feeling the sweet taste of resolution. "I don't have a perfect life here. Far from it, in fact. I really do intend to accompany you. Please."

When Perciville turned to face her, his eyes had lit up and he beamed at her like the morning sun.

"But I have a few conditions," Fjona said, raising a finger to stop Perciville from speaking. "I want to know everything. I am not a fan of surprises and if I ask you a question then you must answer me honestly, every time."

"You have my word," he replied, the colour returning to his face.

"And whatever dangers may befall, you must always have my back."

"That goes without saying."

"And know that if this is all some ruse and you are just trying to goad me back to the mainland to be sold as a slave to some elven warlord, then no level of magic can protect you from my wrath."

"I very much believe that to be true. Is that all?"

Fjona looked away and stroked her chin. "Yes, I think that's about it. Do you promise to remain true to my conditions?"

Perciville knelt before her, holding his staff upright and bowing his head. It made Fjona feel a little uneasy but she allowed him to make his peace.

He tilted his head up to her and said, "Fjona Sarsen, I Perciville Harper promise to abide by your wishes. I offer you honesty, protection and respect. May all the sages who came before, and all the sages who come after, bear witness to this mantle."

As he stood, he brushed away the dirt from his knee.

"A simple *yes* would have sufficed," Fjona said, still a little uncomfortable.

The sage smirked boyishly and replied, "I'm sure that it would, but to pledge a sagen oath carries a little more reverence, do you not agree? Now, Miss Sarsen, I have proven my commitment and we have quite the journey ahead of us. I would insist that we proceed in pursuit of the Tree of Birth immediately and make the most of the day we have ahead of us."

He spoke now with a sense of urgency and Fjona was very

much prepared to comply, at least on this occasion.

"Absolutely," she replied with her brilliant, disarming smile.

"Excelle—"

"But first I must tell Todie and Evelyn." She was about to head back over to The Tipsy Mercer when Perciville pulled her back by her arm.

"Wait. What? Come now, we simply do not have the blessing of time. Your friendship with them is a trifle of the significance compared to what our mission entails."

"My friendship with them is what got me here in the first place," she replied feistily. "I grew up with Todie and have known Evelyn for most of my life. They deserve to know where I'm going."

The sage released a heavy sigh, perhaps for the first time acknowledging the immensity of what he was asking of Fjona and seeing how much she was prepared to give up.

"Very well, say your goodbyes, but do be quick for we've a long day ahead of us."

They parted ways and Fjona headed back around to the entrance to the tavern.

She had barely closed the door behind her when Jat entered from beyond the bar, rubbing the sleep out of his eyes.

"Morning greets you," he said with more gusto than Fjona would have expected from anyone this early in the morning. "Heading out to catch the sunrise?"

A pang of guilt weighed on Fjona as she remembered Jat's request that she lock up after coming back inside, a request she had very much failed to fulfil.

"I thought I might get a glimpse of the view, though I

realised I should let the other two know where I am or they may wake up concerned."

"Very wise," he replied with a smile before tending to Gruno who was passed out on one of the benches, clutching a bottle of liquor in one hand that was spilling on the floor around him.

Fjona left him to it and made her way upstairs to a narrow corridor, barely lit by the modest light that could reach it. There were six rooms in total: three to her left, two to her right and one at the furthest end, though for the life of her, she could not remember which room Evelyn and Todie were staying in. She had little option but to try them all, tentatively opening the door to Room One.

A musty aroma of stale beer filtered out of the door as Fjona glanced inside, hopeful to see her two friends but instead being severely disappointed.

"Eeh!" a corpulent spring elf cheered at her from a slouched position in an armchair beside the window.

He had long, but thinning, brown hair and was drinking out of an old shoe, though what exactly Fjona could not tell. Most strikingly, however, was that he was completely naked from the waist down and his admittedly sizeable member hung freely like the branch of a weeping willow.

"'bout time you got here," the well-endowed elf slurred through drunken sticky teeth. "You'll have to sort me 'ere, I'm too pissed to get up."

Fjona looked elsewhere around the room. It was all she could do to avoid staring directly at the elf's cumbersome appendage.

"Hush now," a weary voice said from beneath the sheets of a bed, pressed up against one wall.

"No hush, just fuss," the elf replied.

"Keep it down," came another voice from a different bed. Or perhaps the same bed, it was very hard to tell.

More voices began to call out, offering their displeasure at the horny elf and Fjona decided to slip out before a riot ensued.

Room Two was locked and Room Three was just as bad as the first. She walked in to find what she thought were two Myrish locals engaged in extramarital relations, only for a spring elf to pop up from beneath the sheets, and definitely a fourth pair of feet sticking out from beneath the covers.

If nothing else, she hoped that this wasn't Evelyn's room. How would she look her friend in the eye after seeing that?

Finally Fjona came to Room Four and quietly opened the door to find her two friends cuddled up in a single bed in the middle. Clearly their modest finances had been sufficient enough to afford a private quarter, and she felt a sense of adoration as Evelyn and Todie slept deeply, bathed in a stream of light coming in from the window.

On the bedside table was a small sheaf of parchment and a leaking ink bottle. Evelyn had left a note for Fjona. It was barely legible but could just be made out to read:

Fjona, my derine.

I offer my sincerest thanks for sharing with me a night of such wonders. If, upon seeking night rest, you find little space within the bed, then take it upon yourself to remove Todie.

Fair wishes and fair slumber, Evelyn

P.S. Remove Evelyn instead! Todie

Another wave of guilt suddenly hit Fjona. How could she possibly leave her friends behind? Perhaps she could convince Perciville to invite them along, though somehow she suspected not. Maybe Evelyn, he seemed to have a fascination with helvens, but Todie?

The allure of adventure was too much for Fjona and she dared not squander the opportunity. If she were to wake them, they most certainly would strive to talk her out of it.

They seemed so peaceful together in bed; Evelyn's long, silver hair draped over Todie's shoulder. Maybe their life together depended on Fjona's absence, she reasoned.

In the end, Fjona made a decision. She took the quill and dipped it in the pool of ink. Beneath Evelyn's message she wrote:

Evelyn and Todie,

I hope you can forgive me for leaving you this letter but I couldn't bring myself to wake you.

Please do not be afraid for me. I have decided to accompany Perciville, the man we met in the tavern last night, to the mainland.

He says there is a threat coming to us all and that I can help him.

This may sound peculiar to you both but he intends to make me a sage! I didn't even know such a thing existed and yet...

He has proven that he will keep me safe.

I ask only that you respect my decision.

Truly your friend,
Fjona

P.S. Todie – please keep an eye on the goats and, if I'm not back before my parents return, then come up with something clever to explain my absence. We'll visit the Great Forest of Aulden when I get back.

It was hard to write but Fjona knew that it was all for the best. She left the note where she had found it and used the ink jar as a paperweight in case somebody opened the window.

"I'll miss you both, dearly," she said in little more than a whisper.

Evelyn moved as if she were waking, but instead she rolled over on to her side, resting her head on her hands.

On tiptoes, Fjona exited the room, gently closing the door behind her. Butterflies were dancing to a medley of guilt, anxiety and excitement inside of her as she snuck back downstairs and reconvened with Perciville outside.

"Did they take it well?" he asked casually and greatly lacking in sincerity.

Fjona shrugged. "Not sure. I suppose I'll find out when I come home."

The sage scrunched his face up.

"I left them a note. Couldn't bring myself to wake them up and, besides, they'd only argue with me and delay us further."

"Very well," Perciville said. "For where we are heading, the most direct route is to head west across the island to a point called Aserae's Lip. If memory serves, there's an old boy who can ferry us across to the mainland Arvum and directly to the forest where the Tree of Birth lives. You wouldn't happen to know where we can procure a couple of horses?"

Fjona shook her head. "Port Widow is notorious for not having many horses to hire out, only places to board your own overnight, since most visitors come and go by sea."

She considered suggesting they take Shagwell and the palomino but decided it was bad enough ditching her friends, without taking their only ride home.

"There is a town due east, though. Swirleybucket is bound to have horses that we could borrow."

"Swirleybucket?" Perciville asked with more than a hint of derision. "Of course," he added to himself. "How long will it take to walk there?"

"If we follow the river then maybe half a day."

The sage sighed, clutching his staff in a firm grip. "We'd better make haste, then."

CHAPTER 15

SANTHÉ AND THE ROCK OF CAEZNOR

They set off away from The Tipsy Mercer, through the plaza and back along the winding streets of Port Widow, leaving the remnants of Lullatide in their wake. Before they knew it, they were out of the town and crossing through the crop and pasture that sustained the locals; all the while Fjona bombarded Perciville with question after question surrounding sages and what she should expect.

"Are there others like you?" she asked.

"There's no-one else quite like me!"

"You know what I mean. Are there any other sages?"

Perciville had to think about this one for a second. "Truth be told, I've no idea. There were many of us, once. Perhaps close to a few hundred at the peak of the Sagedom, though that was long before my time. If I had to guess, maybe a dozen remain, though we scarcely make contact."

"What's the Sagedom?" asked Fjona.

Perciville chuckled. "Are you being facetious again?"

"No, I'm serious!"

"What did they teach you when you were growing up? That

the world is run by fairies?" He paused, then added, "Actually, it may have been once..."

They clambered over a wooden fence that marked the edge of the field and joined a dirt path.

"Which way?" Perciville asked.

Fjona surveyed the area. Ahead of them was a small farmstead with a modest herd of hairy black cows grazing in the meadow.

"Left would lead us to the coast so, I suppose, if we are to join the river, then we must go right."

"You suppose? I thought you knew where we are headed?"

"In principle, yes, but I've never been out to this part of the island before. I've seen a map, though, and I have a fairly good sense of direction. If we continue along this path, it should take us straight to the River of Aulden and we can follow it down to the village in no time."

Perciville shrugged. Fjona knew as well as he did that there was no use in arguing, it would only cost more time.

"Right it is," he replied, inviting Fjona to lead the way.

Along the path they continued, banked by corn as tall as a spring elf to the east, and rolling hills speckled with woodland to the west.

It was peacefully quiet, just the sound of the wind rustling through the crop and the occasional call of the cattle grazing in the neighbouring pasture.

"You were telling me about the Sagedom," Fjona reminded Perciville while she blinked dust out of her eyes.

"Ah, yes, the Sagedom! I am quite astounded that you have never heard of it. It's hard to know where to begin..." He trailed off and furrowed his brow as if figuring out where to start. "The world is many millennia older than even the Arvum and in all that time it has laid the grounds for generations of different folk who have lived, died, and breathed the very same air. Some scholars speak of far ancient civilisations: innovators of great technologies but blind to any knowledge of the art of manipulation. An ancient world wiped from the history books and long since forgotten until your lot, the Myrish, came about. Then, moving forwards, for the past fifty thousand years, give or take, and until..." He went quiet again as he made calculations using his fingers. "... two hundred and seventy-four years ago, the Arvum was governed by a council of sages; people like me, as you put it. A Sagen Master would hold the seat at the Rock of Caeznor, from where they ensured prosperity and peace for all the races across the continent. During the sixth dynasty, the Sagen Master expanded the influence of the sages and unified the Arvum which lasted until the events that led to its collapse nearly three centuries ago."

Perciville swept a low-hanging branch out of his way as they continued along the path.

A tidal wave of questions flooded Fjona's brain and she felt so overwhelmed trying to decide what to ask that she fell silent.

Eventually, just as they reached the shade cast by a row of apple trees, she asked, "What happened three hundred years ago?"

"Two hundred and seventy-four," Perciville corrected, "and it's rather complicated. However, in lieu of keeping my word, I will share with you now a brief synopsis, but be reassured that I will explain in full when you understand enough of the sages to fully comprehend the demise of the Sagedom."

Fjona looked at him, perplexed, and nearly tripped over a stray root from one of the trees.

"If you insist," she said, trusting that he would eventually reveal the whole story.

Just as Perciville was about to embellish, the two travellers came upon the river. This far west, the River of Aulden was nearly at its widest point, about the width of six modest houses placed side by side. The water was a clear green-blue and flowed rapidly, swelling around pointed boulders that jutted out of the surface, forming a small archipelago of rocky teeth. A stone path had been laid along the south bank for tradesfolk who dared not carry their wares along the river for fear of losing their vessel to one of the many rocks.

Fjona led the way, following the path upstream through a small area of woodland.

"When a sage is responsible for the death of somebody whom they truly love, they become consumed by a force that eventually manifests into evil," Perciville began. "It was for that reason that a turned-sage conspired to overthrow the last Sagen Master, Herak Siadonis, and bring anguish to the Arvum in the form of the Eight Afflictions. Faithless men, those who supported the sages and opposed the turned-sage, would become tormented; faithless women would be sacrificed to their offspring. The Sleeping Giant would awaken, and the Tree of Birth should wither and die, to make way for the Tree of Reckoning. The seeds of war would be sown, famine would ensue, Sirens would beckon the unwitting to death, and the Arvum would plunge into endless night."

They were both pensive as these words hung in the air. Only their feet scuffing against the stone, the rushing of the water, and the occasional salmon leaping in the river could be heard. Fjona could feel her heart knocking against her ribs.

Perciville continued. "The only way to prevent these atrocities was to dissolve the Sagedom, but Herak refused. He didn't want to submit to the turned-sage, nor bring an end to an institution which had existed for thousands of years, an institution that he swore to protect. The Sagen Master believed that he could defeat the turned-sage, but his power was no match. Years of experience, a wealth of knowledge and every good sage on his side failed to outwit the deviousness and malice that the turned-sage had harnessed. However, there was one other who could collapse the Sagedom, Herak's only daughter, Santhé. She was the heiress to the Rock of Caeznor, not because she was Herak's daughter but because she was the next most powerful and virtuous sage across the Arvum. You must understand that succession to the seat at Caeznor is not hereditary, though it does often run in families, and only when the title is handed to a sage of a different family does the dynasty end. Her father objected, of course, and it was left to me to stand in his way, but Santhé did the only thing that she could. She absorbed the Eight Afflictions and used her power to dismantle the Rock of Caeznor, thus dissolving the Sagedom. Nobody knows what happened to the turned-sage, they seemed to vanish from the rubble, along with the afflictions which had already begun to take effect."

"Wait, what do you mean *you* stood in Herak's way?" Fjona asked. "You said these events took place nearly three centuries ago."

Perciville nodded. "The life of a sage is far longer than anyone else across the Arvum, and the stronger a sage becomes, the longer their life may be. After a while you begin to lose count but would it surprise you if I said not only was I present at the collapse of the Sagedom, but I was about one hundred and twenty years old at the time?"

Fjona's jaw nearly fell from her face. She studied the sage as they continued along the path. He appeared a few years older than her, perhaps in his thirties, but for him to be nearly four centuries old was inconceivable. His skin was wrinkled a little about the eyes but otherwise Perciville had a very tidy complexion, and his hair was thick and vibrantly brown. In fact he looked decades younger than her parents. Decades younger even than her late grandparents had.

"Are you pulling my leg?" she asked.

"Not even pulling a toe. I joined the sages when I was younger even than you are and I might expect to live for another five hundred years, provided I don't get killed along the way," he said, nonchalantly, as if death were as a simple as riding a horse.

Thoughts bombarded Fjona's head. How much danger was she putting herself in by joining this stranger on a quest to a foreign land?

In the end Fjona settled on the only question that she felt Perciville could actually answer.

"So what happened to Santhé?" she asked as they left the woods and passed into a shallow valley basin with gentle, grassy hills on either side.

"As you can imagine," Perciville replied simply, a fleeting

sad expression across his pale face. "Herak survived the conflict but passed away several months later, and the remaining sages went their separate ways, broken by the collapse of Caeznor. I, as you know, travelled about the Arvum for a long time trying to make sense of all that had happened, and found a new way of life—"

"Drifting from tavern to tavern?" Fjona said, lightening the mood.

Perciville smiled. "Yes, something like that."

"Back at Port Widow you said you need my help in order to prevent the Eight Afflictions from coming to fruition. Does that mean Santhé wasn't able to completely absorb them?"

"I can't say for certain but I do not doubt they are back. If you leave milk in a jar, eventually it will go off and the smell will get out," he replied, though Fjona wasn't sure she fully understood.

They continued further along the river until they came to a confluence. To the right, the river flowed down from the dew-glistening hills, back past the way they had come, and out to the sea. To the left, it meandered downhill to a small settlement at the bottom of a scree-strewn ridge.

"Swirleybucket," said Fjona, gesturing to the distant town.

"Let's not waste another moment," Perciville replied, sounding more chipper than he had been so far that morning.

He focused his energy and a purple light splayed from the head of his staff, wrapping around its long wooden shaft. Perciville released it and the staff hovered in the air, then gently swooped behind his back where it remained, separated from his spine by about a finger-length.

Fjona stared in awe. "That was impressive," she said.

"*Attachment* spell. Very useful if you need both hands or want a break from carrying it," Perciville replied, beginning the descent to the town.

"Why did you wait until now?"

"I was using it as a compass," he replied. "Not that I didn't trust your directions," he added quickly, "but I thought it wise to have some bearing on where we were headed."

Fjona rolled her eyes and said, "Typical bloody men!"

The path followed all the way down to Swirleybucket, with several bridges crossing over the same river as it weaved into the town.

It was very similar to Wychwold, with humble roundhouses and lofts, flower gardens and allotments, animal paddocks and coops. Even the people shared a likeness to those with whom Fjona had grown up and she was certain that Todie had an aunt or two who lived here.

Swirleybucket was a more populated town than Wychwold and was roughly laid out in a ring around a small lake from which it got its namesake. Crisp, clear water lapped gently against the banks where several fist-sized toads chirped boldly at one another as if in competition.

The two newcomers had barely crossed the timber entranceway when they were accosted by an elderly local, dressed in a cotton vest, suede jacket, and tattered threadbare breeches with soiled knees. His feet were bare and marred from a cocktail of dirt and insect bites, and in his hand he carried a rusty spade as if it were a spear.

"Keep back," he said, pointing the spade unsteadily at Perciville.

"We mean no harm," Fjona replied, gesturing with her hands for the man to lower his tool, but instead he directed it at her.

A bead of sweat trickled down from his nest of curly white hair and over his bulbous nose.

Perciville and Fjona exchanged a bemused glance.

"Look, we really don't have time for this," Perciville said as he reached a hand behind his back for his staff, but Fjona was quick to intervene.

"Please," she said in a hushed voice, "he's a little old man." She turned to the self-proclaimed gatekeeper. "Sir, my name is Fjona Sarsen and this is my" – she looked over at the frustrated sage – "*assistant,* Perciville Harper."

A juicy vein began to throb on Perciville's forehead, but he remained quiet.

"What's your name?" Fjona asked the old man.

"That is little of your concern," he growled back at her, "now be gone, this is no place for unwanted guests."

He jabbed the spade at Fjona and she jolted back a step.

"We gave you a chance," Perciville said and he grabbed his staff. He pointed it at the old man and a bright green light billowed out of the staff's head.

The old man jabbed with the spade again but it suddenly flopped down at the end like a long, flaccid noodle. In fact, the whole tool was hanging limply in the old man's hand and, as he attempted to poke it towards Fjona, it simply swung back and forth like a misled pendulum.

"Shall we?" Perciville asked as he and Fjona stepped around the old man who, unable to match their pace, proceeded to yell a series of expletives at them and gestured rudely with his fingers.

"What a grumpy old mule," Fjona muttered as they wandered along a short avenue between the houses and out towards the lake.

Perciville simply shrugged.

It was the early hours of the afternoon and the sun was desperately trying to pull apart the clouds; a gloomy haze hung over the landscape. Despite this, the residents of Swirleybucket were outside, joyfully tending to their gardens and chatting to their neighbours. One or two of them looked over at the visitors but, for the most part, Fjona and Perciville walked through the centre of town within a veil of anonymity. It was apparent that visitors were more familiar to the locals than the spade-wielding concierge had inferred.

Another major difference between Wychwold and Swirleybucket was commerce. In Wychwold, perhaps owing to its small population, the residents shared what they had between one another, occasionally trading for more varied goods with the neighbouring villages. Swirleybucket, however, relied on an organised form of bartering, allowing the whole community to trade easily with one another. A dairy farmer, for example, may have exchanged a bucket of goat's milk for a loaf of rye bread from the baker and a couple of eggs from the fowl farm; the seamstress may have exchanged a pair of new breeches for some milk provided by the dairy farmer and a pair of leather shoes from the cobbler; and the cleric may have received a pair of breeches, a jar of milk and a block of hard cheese in return for a blessing by the Four Good Gods.

The Paddolgolian Brothers' General Store, a family business of many generations, was the centre of trade in Swirleybucket, and occupied a handsome plot right beside the lake. It was an impressive two-tiered elliptical structure, considerably larger than the homes that surrounded it and had its own stables in the grounds behind.

The shop was decorated with vibrant bunting, long swathes of ribbon, and was fronted by shelves of freshly harvested vegetables. Half a dozen or so customers were outside perusing the products that were displayed by the entranceway, enthralled by mundane yapping.

"Let's make this quick," Perciville said, heading to the door of the substantial building. "We go in, find the owner, arrange a couple of horses and—" he cut himself short as he pushed through the door and stepped into an enormous throng of people, busily tearing through stalls packed high with produce.

To make matters more chaotic, the same folk were tugging along carts of their own wares to exchange, or shepherding live animals to sell. To the tune of bartering, stamping, bleating and yelling, it seemed to be louder here than the music was at Port Widow, and the mix of smells was unbearable with fresh fish, mature cheese and cattle droppings all mingling under the same roof. It beggared belief as to why they hadn't simply moved the market outside, though the locals seemed oblivious to the oppressive environment.

A deep mezzanine floor ran around the perimeter of the building and Fjona could just see to the level above. There appeared to be far fewer people upstairs, somehow spared from the maelstrom below.

"May the Afflictions take me now," Perciville cursed, paling at the sight of the crowd before him.

Fjona, meanwhile, was completely enthralled. "This is remarkable," she said, gazing around the packed space.

It reminded her of breakfast at Wychwold: chaotic from the outside but perfectly synchronised in the middle. The thought made her stomach growl and Fjona realised that she had missed at least the last two meals, unless she counted port and ale as sustenance.

"Are you in or out?" came a stern voice from behind as an older gentlemen pushed past them and entered the frenzy. He was followed by a young girl who was dragging two goats by rope tied about their necks.

Fjona could sense Perciville seething.

"Not a fan of big crowds?" she asked him, though it was something of a rhetorical question.

Perciville took a deep sigh. "Big crowds, small crowds. Just most people in general."

Fjona nearly asked, 'Why are you like this?', but decided not to probe him. Instead she suggested he waited outside and leave it to her to acquire the horses.

The sage was only too willing to accept her offer.

"Wait a second," he said, fishing out his purse which was buried deep inside his robe, "take a handful of coins." He tipped out a palmful of *bassals*.

Fjona shook her head. "They won't be any good here. I've heard of the Paddolgolian Brothers' Shop. We need something to trade," she said, feeling a little disappointed to have come this far without the forethought to have provided anything to exchange.

Perciville didn't hesitate. He scooped the coins back into the purse, then wielded his staff which had been hovering inconspicuously behind his back.

"Keep watch. There was a time when being caught selling conjured goods may have resulted in death, though I daresay nobody will be wise to it now."

They headed to a quiet nook between the store and a tall oak tree to provide a little cover while Perciville trained his energy through the staff to produce, for the second time since landing in Marrow Myre, a bottle of Autumn Elf Old Port in a slender crystal bottle, secured by a plump red cork.

"Is that the only spell you know?" Fjona asked in a mocking tone.

Perciville smirked as he lifted the bottle up from the ground. The nearly viscous liquid sloshed about inside the bottle leaving streaks of port up against the glass.

"Artisanal conjuring is amongst the most challenging form of manipulation. Make no mistake, it took me years to perfect this recipe alone. Factor in the decades it required to have the skills necessary to even try to conjure this bottle..." He tailed off as he handed it over to Fjona. "It's very valuable across the Arvum so it should certainly cover the cost of a couple of horses."

Just as Fjona turned to make for the store's entrance, Perciville grabbed her wrist with his spare hand.

"Be sensible, Miss Sarsen. We'd be wise not to draw attention to ourselves."

Fjona instinctively shook his hand off. "Don't fret, Harper. I'll be in and out before you know it."

She turned gracefully on her heel, clutching the lucrative inebriant in her hands, the tail of her cotton shirt lofting in the breeze behind her.

Attempting to reject a quiet voice telling him that everything was about to go wrong, the deceptively ancient sage conjured a fist-sized wooden ball, leaned his staff against the tree, and flopped down onto his backside.

He began to toss the ball from hand to hand, all the while trying to figure out the best course of action following the arrival on the mainland. It was useful spending the time to plan the next stage of their journey as it helped repress the guilt he was feeling having already broken his promise to Fjona.

CHAPTER 16

THE DREAM TRANSLATOR

The Upper Gate was far from unfamiliar ground for Kaikura who had visited the Archivus nearly every day since her enrolment, but never before had she been permitted to enter the Sultan's palace.

It was a consensual agreement that Bobassa should not accompany them though he did keep a watchful eye over Kaikura until they had passed through the forum. From the top of the dividing wall, he watched the three summer elves and the Grugan ascend the steps to the palace and pass the two Home Guards at the door.

Inside Kaikura stared in amazement as she was led into the vast open entrance hall. Her feet tapped on an expansive white marble surface, in the middle of which was a bronze mural depicting the Arvum with Panamaya City more or less at the heart. Surrounding the continent was a glimmering cerulean ocean.

Either side, two wide staircases curved up to a mezzanine floor which was bordered by a series of tall, elegant arches that formed a balustrade around the room.

"Thank you, Guards, for your assistance. You are dismissed," Oolia said to Terin and Darazith.

They bowed curtly before passing over the mural and disappearing through a door to one side of the hall.

Oolia then turned to Kaikura. "The Sultan will be in the dining chamber at this hour. Come, come," she said succinctly, leading the scholar through to a door at the far end of the entrance hall. The steward continued to chat genially as they swiftly navigated through a maze of corridors, passing Home Guards and humble servants at nearly every turn. "The Sultan is very particular about with whom he shares his meals. Ordinarily he eats alone and, if in a good mood, will leave the leftovers to his staff. In a... lesser mood, shall we say, he has been known to leave his scraps for the camels. Although he is expecting you, do not presume his hospitality. Eat only if he invites you to, drink only if he insists; he doesn't take kindly to guests helping themselves to his food. After we enter the chamber, I will introduce you before the Sultan permits you to make your case—"

"My case?" Kaikura interrupted, her stomach suddenly feeling like a lead weight was swinging inside of it.

"Yes, your case as to how you are qualified to aid his Divine Excellency over his turmoil."

"But I'm not!" Kaikura stopped defiantly in her tracks.

"Keep moving, you won't want to turn up late," Oolia said without so much as a fleeting look over her shoulder.

Kaikura followed.

"After you introduce yourself, the Sultan will either invite you to take a seat at his table..." She went quiet as they pulled up before a frosted glass door at the end of a long hallway.

"Or?" asked the scholar.

"It's probably best not to think about it," Oolia replied, opening the door before Kaikura had a chance to argue.

The dining chamber was a long open room at the rear of the palace which boasted panoramic views of the Pentari Desert through enormous windows on three sides. A minstrel, clad in green velvet, was performing a solemn piece of music on a reedaphone, a curved instrument crafted out of nurtured pinewood by exquisite hands. It offered a rich warm timbre that flowed in waves of sweeping melodies. The sound was like nothing Kaikura had ever heard before. It was so bold that she could feel it vibrating through her very bones as she watched the performer's fingers race up and down the keyholes of the reedaphone's spine, while he bent his body to manipulate the air that he breathed through the mouthpiece.

Ayermune Dahller Sé was sitting at the furthest end of a great table that occupied the middle of the room. It was brimming with platters of fresh exotic fruits, slices of pork that glistened in their own fat, and cheeses made from the viscous milk of the Pentari camels.

One servant boy was pouring the Sultan a glass of red wine from a crystal carafe while another plucked purple grapes from a vine and plopped them into a small ceramic bowl.

"Your Divine Excellency," Oolia said with a polite bow of her head.

"Oolia," the Sultan replied, looking up from his plate. He paid no attention to Kaikura, as if she were but another member of his nameless staff.

"I would like to introduce you to San Kaikura Kendi, a renowned scholar of the Archivus and an expert in deciphering dreams."

The lead weight inside Kaikura's stomach dropped heavily and only a long, controlled breath was enough to prevent her from vomiting

She tried to look past the steely amber eyes of the Sultan that felt as if they were seeing right through her. It was as if he were weighing up whether or not she was worth his time based solely on her appearance.

After an agonisingly awkward period, he eventually said, "Please..."

He gestured with oily fingers for Kaikura to speak.

She exchanged a nervous look with Oolia who nodded for her to proceed.

After another deep breath she gave a gentle bow, as the steward had done. "My Sultan, I understand that you have been suffering from troubling dreams. I believe that I can assist you with my advanced knowledge in anthropology and mythology."

Ayermune clenched his jaw.

"And dream translation," she quickly added after a subtle nudge in the ribs from Oolia's right elbow.

The Sultan appeared to loosen up a little.

"Your Divine Excellency, please accept my offer of counsel." Kaikura bowed again and remained with her head down to avoid making uncomfortable eye contact with the most powerful man in the city.

The sound of a chair scraping against the polished stone

floor grabbed her attention and she looked up to see one of the servant boys lay a place for her at the table.

"Very well, San Kendi. Please join me," Ayermune beckoned.

Kaikura glanced at Oolia who smiled reassuringly at her and, on shaky legs, made for the seat adjacent to the Sultan. Just as her nerves were beginning to settle, he spoke again.

"This conversation is of an intimate nature. You may all leave."

The reedaphone player stopped abruptly on a fierce note in its upper register and did not hesitate in vacating the chamber along with the servants. Even Oolia, who may have expected to have been invited to remain, knew to respect the Sultan's wishes and politely made for the door. They left with a shuffle, and only the sound of their shoes squeaking on the stone floor resonated around the cavernous room.

When the door was shut firmly behind them, the Sultan addressed Kaikura.

"Thank you for taking the time out of your research to tend to my troubles. I trust that you can help me."

Usually posed as a question, Kaikura sensed that this was more of a demand than a request. Her throat suddenly felt as dry as sandpaper. She decided just to smile and nod gently to save the embarrassment of croaking a response.

"So how does one go about a dream interpretation?" Ayermune asked casually as he took a sip from a crystal chalice.

A direct question. Kaikura had no choice but to reply.

"Well..." she began, the cogs of her brain rapidly spinning in the hopes of fishing out some buried knowledge of the matter. "If first you could begin by regaling the nature of your dreams? After which I will proceed to decipher them using my palette of experience and understanding..." She was conscious of her own voice in the echoing space; aware that she was just waffling.

Without a word the Sultan rose from the table and Kaikura instantly feared that her ruse had been sussed and a brutal punishment was imminent.

Instead, the Sultan simply said, "Please..."

He invited the scholar to join him by the west window that looked out over the city and the desert that faded into dust on the horizon. From here they could see the vast trench of the canal carving through the landscape like a torn seam of a doublet.

"Each time it begins the same, staring down at the forum and watching the citizens roaming around, bartering and coercing, but just as I feel content with the wealth of my city, I look down before the palace to find that the spring is nothing but an empty pit, barely even a drop of water to satisfy a roach. The sun disappears; thick, black clouds enshroud me. When they clear, I find that I am staring at my own limp body, sallow and lifeless at the bottom of the dead spring."

The Sultan was quiet for a moment, his jaw clenched with seeming anger; or perhaps fear, Kaikura wondered. It was impossible to tell if the Sultan had finished speaking or not. Was he expecting Kaikura to reply? She opened her mouth to speak, then thought better of it. The Sultan would invite her to speak, would he not? Then again, perhaps his quietness was her invitation...

The uncertainty was agonising for Kaikura but, just as she was about to break the suffocating silence, the Sultan continued.

"From the bank of the spring, I futilely attempt to reach out for my rotting corpse but, as I do so, the hand of the giant breaks through the ground and tears apart the Upper Gate." He turned to Kaikura and stared, a shadow of solemnity cast across his features. "'He is awake'. Those same three words, every night. I speak them to my steward, Oolia." Another troubled breath; a deep sigh of regret. The Sultan's anguish could be felt with every word that he spoke.

Kaikura was so enraptured by the poignant details of the dream that, for a heartbeat, she forgot herself and spoke without invitation.

"This is certainly most peculiar but I am sure I can—"

"I am not done," Ayermune interrupted, turning his gaze to Kaikura with a harsh stony expression. "If I may continue, for the past couple of nights, at least, there has been something of a development but I am too ashamed to tell Oolia. After the hand reaches out of a great chasm that splinters through the city, a hooded man approaches me. He stands before the spring, wielding a wooden staff and points it at my lifeless body. Before my eyes, my corpse transforms into Oolia and it is now she who is dead at the bottom of the empty pool, not me. San Kendi, tell me what this means. Am I to sacrifice my steward to save my own life?"

Kaikura remained contemplative, looking out to the construction and watching a division of Noble Guards keeping sentry over the workers. How she yearned to be outside, breathing in the hot Pentari air, away from the problems of the elite.

"How long have you been suffering from these dreams?"

"In their full form, I would say a few weeks, though I've had snippets of these visions for several months," Ayermune replied.

Visions. This word seemed to ring a bell in the scholar's mind.

Kaikura remembered an extract from an old book and she hungrily clung to it. "There was a philosopher from the 8th dynasty. Bayerina the Apostle, she came to be known, as she believed that she could communicate with the ancient gods. Bayerina was quoted as saying that 'all visions are but dreams, not all dreams are but visions'. For decades she studied the minds of the spring elves where she lived and learned that one may experience the same dream over a few nights and that nothing may come of it. However, when one had the same dream for several weeks, the spring elves would notice particular events transpiring in reality. A different scale to your own, Your Divine Excellency, for Bayerina writes of good harvests and long periods of drought."

The Sultan interjected brashly, "Yes all very good but what has that to do with *my* dreams?"

"Well, Bayerina the Apostle concluded that visions are not prophesies but rather premonitions derived from the world around us. For example, the spring elves might have sensed the oncoming of a drought because of a lack of rain and this played into their subconsciousness. What I speculate is perhaps there are real world events that are playing on your own mind and which are manifesting in your dreams."

The Sultan stood brooding for a moment before, in a flourish of elegant cloth, he turned and stomped back towards the table.

"Tell me, scholar, is it possible to have a premonition about something you'd never previously heard of?"

Kaikura could feel the sweat on her palms. The Sultan's questions were slipping further and further away from her field of study and she wasn't sure how many more she could attempt to answer.

"A premonition developed without real-world stimuli could feasibly occur," Kaikura responded. "However that would rely on exterior intervention such as gods, or prophets, or—"

"Sages?" asked the Sultan.

Kaikura nodded. "Or perhaps indeed the sages. Although the vast majority of sages have died out, if not all; it is possible that their legacy might have a prolonged impact on your state of mind, particularly considering your elite position."

The Sultan was pacing around the dining chamber, agitated enough to make Kaikura feel a little bit dizzy. He suddenly stopped in front of her, peering down as if he were the giant itself.

"San Kendi, forgive my blasphemy but do you think it possible that the Panamayan spring was in fact conjured by a sage?"

"I... umm... I..." Kaikura stuttered, unable to form a response. The notion that the spring might have been the creation of a sage was entirely preposterous, and yet...

"Have you swallowed your tongue, peasant?" the Sultan yelled, hammering his fist on the table. "Is the spring destined to dry up?"

Timidly the scholar replied, "I've never heard of such a claim. We all know of the tales of the Sleeping Giant but nobody really believes that the mountain, and thus the spring, was created by a sage. The summer elves have worshipped the mountain and the spring for as long as they have lived here, or so I understand. If it were to transpire that the spring had been conjured then that may undermine all summer elven beliefs."

"My sentiment exactly, except now a shadow of doubt has been cast before me and I can't seem to dispel it. Oolia has warned me that had a sage created the spring the enchantment may be fading, and the city will be plunged into drought. There are ancient aqueducts, previously built by the Kelner elves who lived too far from the city. Tell me, scholar, if I were to reinstate them and start shipping freshwater along the new canal, might I be relieved of my slumbered plague?"

There it was – the overarching question. Festering dreams feeding on the hidden fears of the Sultan, now begging for a solution. To say yes might deliver false hope, but to say no may invite further interrogation. Somehow Kaikura felt that ambivalence would beckon worse consequences.

Desperate to be freed from the Sultan's domineering presence, Kaikura opted for the simplest solution and prayed inwardly that her theory might just be correct.

"I believe you must be right," she said, then as a hasty caveat added, "on the presumption that the spring, conjured or not, will imminently drain, then drawing in water from a fresh source may – will – put your mind at ease." Kaikura found herself speaking more than intended and, before she knew it, the words just slipped out of her mouth. "Alternatively, your dreams might relate to some greater catastrophe."

The Sultan twisted his narrow neck towards her like a vulture. "Enlighten me."

A voice inside Kaikura screamed at her for speaking more than was necessary but she'd allowed no option other than to share what was on her mind. "Perhaps your dreams are foreshadowing the awakening of the Sleeping Giant."

The silence that followed was quieter than death. Kaikura gazed up nervously at the Sultan's stern, furious face. His jaw was clamped shut and his teeth were grinding. She noticed his fists clenching and relaxing and clenching, and she was certain the Sultan was moments from throttling her. She could feel her blood pulsing in her ears and a weakness in her knees as if she might collapse before him.

Then the Sultan's lips started to curl up towards his eyes, and his shoulders slumped forwards, trembling.

Before Kaikura knew it, the Sultan was in a fit of laughter.

"San Kendi, thank you!" he said, grabbing her arm to stop from keeling over. "Your fine humour, as much as your thorough counsel, has provided me some peace of mind. The narrative is quite straightforward, as you have revealed to me. The *natural* Panamayan spring is slowly drying up and my astute eye has noticed it. I shall see to the restoration of the aqueducts, have my workers complete the canal, and before I know it my dreams will be free of the harrowing images I have been suffering."

Not precisely the narrative Kaikura had suggested but in an effort to avoid contradicting the Sultan, she merely bowed her head politely without saying a word.

"Know that you have been of exceptional help. You are dismissed." Ayermune returned to his chalice of wine at the table and took a seat, leaving Kaikura feeling somewhat awkward standing alone by the windows.

Relieved that she could finally leave, she hurriedly made for the door and stepped out into the corridor where Oolia was waiting patiently.

"Still with us, then?" the steward asked with a smile.

"Just about. I believe he was satisfied with my response. I only hope he doesn't pass the blame on to me if things don't go as planned."

Oolia nodded in agreement. "Allow me to show you out," she offered.

Kaikura gladly accepted and was led back through the winding corridors, wrapped up in her own thoughts about the spring, the giant, and the canal, while Oolia talked inanely about the décor of the palace and pointed out which artists created which paintings.

"Do you need the guards to escort you back to the Lower Gate?" the steward asked at the steps of the palace.

Kaikura shook her head dismissively. "That's okay, I have my own chaperone," she said, catching Bobassa's gaze from on top of the wall on the far side of the Upper Gate.

"He'll probably be more useful if you find yourself in trouble," Oolia agreed before making her excuses and returning to the cool shade of the palace.

The events from the day led to a very restless night for Kaikura who found herself tossing and turning irritably on her hard bed. Somehow the images that the Sultan had described from his own dreams were now replaying in her mind. She imagined herself standing on the palace balcony, looking down at the Sultan as he mourned the death of his loyal steward, slumped at the bottom of a pit. In the next scene, it was Kaikura who was staring up out of the cold spring and gasping for air, only to see the Sultan looking down at her with a bemused look as if they had never met before.

Despite thrashing about on the bed and kicking the sheets away from her, Bobassa was fast asleep at her feet, whimpering softly as he breathed.

By the early hours, when the morning light was just beginning to peek through the ceiling, Kaikura gave up on sleep.

Careful not to disturb Bobassa, she quietly rose and descended the ladder to the main room. The sandkat had been known to react badly to being unexpectedly woken and she thought it best to let him doze a while longer. She quietly prepared a cup of tea, pouring out the water before the kettle was ready to whistle, and proceeded to examine the spines of the books stacked beneath the table.

Not that she knew exactly what she was looking for. Kaikura was hoping that the words *sage* or *conjured spring* would scream at her but instead she was presented with niche books about ancient cultures, languages and practices, the majority of which discussed places elsewhere across the continent.

She decided that a trip to the Archivus later in the morning would be necessary if she were to dig deeper into the nature of the spring. For the time being she would have to nurse her hunger for knowledge by delving into a book about the early island elves of Bouanda who founded the Carved City and, for centuries, became the wealthiest inhabitants of the Arvum.

Kaikura had a fascination in all kindred species across the world but her elven cousins of Sallisai'Mae were particularly enticing. Culturally, they were worlds apart, at least from what she had read. For one thing the divide in wealth was far less acute than in Panamaya City where the elite lived off the hard earnings of the poor who themselves were fortunate if they could scrounge together a meal by the end of the week. Not to mention the folk who lived beyond the Lower Gate, outside the walls of the city itself; to be of so low a status that access into Panamaya was a rare and often short-lived treat.

In Sallisai'Mae, the island elves seemed to share their wealth. There was a monarch, of course, though Kaikura couldn't even be sure if the current leader was a king or queen. The most recent account she could find referred to Queen Selbya, Bearer of Fortune, Lady of Bouanda. However, the book itself was written nearly fifty years ago when the queen was a few years shy of five hundred, and it was likely that she had been succeeded since then.

For Kaikura, the opportunity to visit such a mystical city was inconceivable – in fact, a dream of her own.

As she flicked through the pages of the book before her,

her thoughts tracked back to the offer of funding towards her research by Oolia Khamun. If her advice to the Sultan paid dividends then perhaps she really could afford to visit the Carved City.

This thought of pleasing the Sultan only furthered her desire to read up on the spring and Kaikura decided that really there was no need to delay visiting the Archivus.

She gently closed her book but, as she was about to stand, noticed that she had indeed awoken the sandkat, despite her best efforts.

"I'm sorry, Bobassa," she said, getting to her feet and looking up at the bedroom floor.

Bobassa looked confused. Ordinarily Kaikura would expect him to be whining in dissatisfaction having been disturbed, but instead he appeared to be trying to figure something out. He was like a mathematician mulling over a difficult equation, though with more whiskers.

"What's up?" Kaikura asked though the sandkat was busy tilting his head and rotating his long ears as if to decipher a sound.

Kaikura listened out too, though she could hear nothing save for a few desert cicadas chirping in the streets outside.

Then Bobassa leaped down from the floor and onto the table, seemingly mesmerised by the cup of tea which Kaikura had barely sipped.

"What in all the Arvum has got into you?" she asked, now equally as confused as her companion.

"Hsss..." the sandkat replied, his sparkling bronze eyes transfixed on the cup in front of him. He flailed his two tails to get Kaikura's attention, though he needn't have bothered as she too was already staring at the small cup.

The burgundy liquid was rippling gently as though someone was banging on the table.

"That's strange..." was all Kaikura could say, reaching out for it, though her hand had barely come close when she felt the ground beneath her begin to vibrate. It was incredibly gentle, borderline unnoticeable, but most definitely happening. Had she been asleep, Kaikura didn't doubt that even she would have slept through it.

"Can you feel that, Bobassa?" she asked, anxious that she may be going crazy.

The sandkat purred in affirmation and hopped down onto the floor. He lay on his side and stretched his body out as if testing the extent of the shakes.

The pans and utensils which hung on the kitchen wall clanged together quietly like a windchime and a fresh sprinkling of dust drifted down from the ceiling. Even the ancient flint-tipped spear swayed a little on its hook.

Outside, the cicadas had gone quiet as if they too were concerned, trying to work out what was happening.

The vibrations lasted no more than half a minute and, afterwards, Kaikura felt as shaken as the ground itself.

Her brilliant mind was racing through a jungle of incoherent thoughts, rapidly trying to piece together every semblance of knowledge she had in order to make sense of this event.

Was it localised to her house, or had the whole city felt it? Was there an enormous caravan of wagons passing along the street with enough force to make it shake, or perhaps the

Sleeping Giant was snoring?

All these considerations and more were enough to make her feel dizzy but, eventually, Kaikura snapped out of it and made up her mind.

"Come on, Bobassa. We'd better get a move on," she said to the sandkat, who was happily lapping up her tea. She grabbed her satchel and made for the ladder.

There was something strange going on in Panamaya City and Kaikura knew she had to get to the bottom of it.

CHAPTER 17

THE OTHER DENVILLIER

Immaculately dressed in a fine black doublet and cream-coloured breeches nestled into sturdy leather boots. Swept-back sandy hair, as thick as wool, that rested on broad shoulders, and piercing blue eyes like the Near Sea on a clear day. Tall but not gangly, muscular but not constrained, devilishly charming but never enough to be considered smarmy.

A lot could be said about Benjamin Denvillier but what was truly and utterly undeniable was that he was a very handsome spring elf.

He walked purposefully, back straight and head up, along the crowded street that skirted the cliffs of Rosensted. Somehow, even the salty breeze of the Near Sea did little to distress his hair as he followed the cobbled promenade and cut between the fishmongers and grocers.

It was a blissful morning and Benjamin could hardly wipe the smile off his chiselled and perfectly shaven face as the sun radiated upon him in a near-heavenly glow. Over his shoulders, he carried a tanned leather satchel that jangled with glass while he navigated the walkway.

As he passed a small courtyard, a young child called for his attention.

"Mr Denvillier!" the girl cried, her face so freckled that, from a short distance, her skin tone seemed several shades deeper than it actually was.

She needn't say any more. Benjamin was immediately attentive to the young girl and he dipped towards the courtyard with a boyish grin.

"Ahh, Miss Rosette, I trust your mother is well?" he said to the girl with an air of grace and formality that made her giggle. "Are you perhaps inviting me to take a turn?" Benjamin glanced up behind the freckled girl to her two ragtag friends, who were playing on the grass.

"Conquest for the Arvum," stated one of the boys, who must have been half the girl's age and was dressed in a pair of torn shorts and a sullied shirt.

"Do you know it?" the girl asked.

Benjamin smiled, his perfect teeth glistening like a row of marble pillars. "Know it? Why, young madame, I practically invented it!"

The children giggled at his response and the young girl gripped his hand and showed him the course.

"Here," she said, pointing to a small pyramid of stones nearest to her, "is Havensend!"

"The Free Capital," said a skinny boy with grazes on his knees and a big purple bruise on his elbow.

"It's the closest to the line but the hardest to topple," interjected the youngest boy.

Then the girl stepped around it to a heap of earth and said,

"This one is *Panimaya* City…"

"I believe you mean *Panamaya* City," Benjamin corrected her, to which she slapped herself playfully on her forehead and proceeded to repeat the name over.

Benjamin took it upon himself to explain the others. "Rosensted," he said, pointing to two standing stones with a miniature lintel over the top, "Elkensen," he wagged his finger at a pyramid of sticks, "and Sallisai'Mae," he concluded, gently poking the standing sticks at the furthest end of the arena.

The rules of Conquest for the Arvum were simple and Benjamin had often partaken in a game when he was accosted by excited children in the courtyard.

Each player ruled one of the cities or towns who fought in the Arvum War, then took turns throwing pebbles at each other's from the same place. Although one may engage in diplomatic negotiations, amongst the children this scarcely happened and the rules would often be scrapped in the way of heated arguments. Much like in the real war.

"You can rule Rosensted," the girl said to Benjamin, thrusting a handful of pebbles into his palm.

So the game began, pebbles chaotically discarded across the arena with the relaxed dexterity and precision of a child. Mostly, they missed or came close to their targets, though the skinny boy did manage to knock a few stones from the pyramid of Havensend, but not enough for the younger boy to be eliminated from the game.

When it came around to Benjamin's turn, the children begged him to unleash his force on one another's pile, but he had long decided which one he would target.

He steeled his gaze, raised his arm, and projected a pebble at the heap of earth with pinpoint accuracy.

"Oh no!" the girl wailed as the earth tumbled down to a sad heap in the middle of the playing arena.

"Sorry, young madame, but as I said..." he winked at her with a fatherly expression "... I practically invented this game."

Just before the young girl erupted in a tantrum, Benjamin offered her his remaining pebbles and bid them farewell. As he left the courtyard, he could hear the adamant objections of the two boys who felt severely unfairly treated, and glanced back to see the youngest kick Sallisai'Mae into a heap.

Benjamin couldn't help but chuckle at their childish frivolities as he swung back into the crowded market and continued his way along the promenade.

He stopped by the florist stall, purchasing a vibrant bunch of locally picked lilies, then to the baker's where even he couldn't resist the sweet fragrance of a seeded loaf.

"Mr Denvillier," the baker said with a bewildered smile as more coins than the bread was worth trickled into his skinny purse. "Thank you. Sincerely."

"It's the least you deserve, Horace," Benjamin replied, tucking the bread into his satchel before ducking back into the market, this time crossing towards the main town.

He chose a narrow, slightly sinister, alleyway which was little more than a crack between two rows of leaning houses. Here, just as it opened up into a tight junction, he stopped by a low door, before which stood a scantily clad spring elf.

Her dress was clean but sparse, stopping just below her knees and barely containing her generously proportioned breasts, though Benjamin knew from experience that her brassiere was somewhat padded out.

Her face was pretty, despite the heavy bags beneath her eyes, the deepening wrinkles around her mouth, and her overall complexion, which was as grey as the street on which she stood.

"I've not seen you for a while, Mr Denvillier," the elf said, adjusting herself so that her breasts appeared somehow bigger.

She was about to turn to open the door but Benjamin instead offered her the bunch of lilies. "Not today, I'm afraid," he said, "but I thought these might bring you some joy."

His gesture was received with raised eyebrows and a frown as he thrust the bouquet into her arms.

"Flowers?" she asked with scrutiny.

"So you're familiar?" Benjamin replied sardonically.

"Your custom would have been preferable."

"My custom, or just my coin?"

She looked him up and down, then smiled wickedly at him. "For most of my patrons I would prefer the coin, but for you, dear..." She ran her hand up along his arm, across his collarbone, then swiftly down his chest, his abdomen and pelvis, before clutching his crotch. "Huh?" she exclaimed, confusion spreading across her face.

"I'm afraid I'm already spent," Benjamin replied, retreating from her warm and sweaty grasp, "but enjoy the flowers!"

He really was in a tremendously good mood and practically skipped down the alleyway. At the far end, he fell out onto a road that banked the marina, then followed it around, relishing in the fresh ocean breeze.

Before long, he came to the rear door of a tavern and let

himself in. He ran up the bare, wooden stairs, crossed the corridor and threw open the door at the far end.

Inside, bathing in a golden hue, were two naked female spring elves, intimately caressing and kissing one another. They each had long manes of glossy hair: one richly black, the other a soft brown.

They were kneeling on the bedsheets, their slender oily bodies writhing and pulsing to their own synchronised rhythm.

Benjamin found himself staring at the two elves for more than a moment, biting his lip with sheer pleasure.

When one of the elves clocked him by the door, she smiled wryly and started to giggle. Then, she beckoned him over with a long teasing finger.

Without a word, Benjamin floated towards them, pushing them gently apart so that he could participate in their kissing.

"What took you so long?" one of the elves asked in a hushed, sensual whisper.

"Errands," Benjamin replied, then reached into his satchel and extracted two glass bottles of white wine. He pushed the bottles into each of their hands. "Pour me a glass. I shan't be a minute." He then vacated the bedroom with the collected demeanour of a king.

Without even closing the door behind him, he quickly descended the stairs, entered through a heavy iron door below, and bounded down another flight of stairs into a dank basement beneath the tavern.

He continued his way along another corridor and burst open the chamber door.

Similarly to the bedroom, he was greeted by a naked elf,

though this one was far less pleasant to look at. For one thing, his skin was raw with streaks of whip marks, burns and gashes; his eyes were bulging and puffy, and his hair was matted with his own blood that seeped out of the wounds across his frail body.

His hands were bound to the arms of a chair with leather straps, and his legs were spread apart so there was no hiding his tiny shrivelled member.

Blood drooled from his lips, and his head hung low as if he simply hadn't the strength to look up at the two bandits towering above him.

"Any luck?" Benjamin asked, resting his foot on the chair between the elf's legs.

One of the bandits, a summer elf wielding an iron mace, replied gruffly, "Says he wants to join the covenant."

Benjamin raised his eyebrows. "Is that so?" He kicked the chair and the tortured elf jolted upright, trembling with fear. "You wish to join us?" Benjamin asked, sternly.

The elf started to nod frantically.

"You spied on us for at least two months, lingered outside our chamber at night, made advances on our youngest member." He gestured to a female elf who was several years away from adulthood. "And wish now to join us?"

"P-please, Mr Denvillier! You are my sa-salvation!"

Benjamin looked contemplatively at the devastated elf, then conceded. "Very well. Harlan?"

He looked over to the young elf who, without a word, retrieved a wooden staff that had been leaning against the wall and handed it to Benjamin.

The tortured elf looked at the staff with confusion and horror.

"Let's see if you've got what it takes," Benjamin said simply, then pointed the staff at the elf's chest.

A terrifying, erratic white light erupted from the head, piercing the elf's chest and illuminating the otherwise dulled chamber. The elf screamed hoarsely as his body writhed on the chair. He screamed until his lungs were empty and there was no air left in his wasted, broken body.

When the light faded, the tortured elf made not even a whimper. He hung limply forward, as Benjamin had found him but now with, somehow, less animation.

His chest glowed with a faint white pulse, though that too didn't last long and soon faded into nothing.

Benjamin kicked the chair again with the heel of his boot but, this time, there was no reaction.

"Shame," he said, "I had bigger hopes for him."

With a shrug, he handed the staff back to Harlan, dug his hand into his satchel, extracted his loaf of bread, and ripped off a chunk, popping it into his mouth.

"Chuck him in the Near Sea," he instructed after swallowing down the bread. "I'd do it myself but I need to get back upstairs."

With that, he disappeared back out of the chamber.

CHAPTER 18

THE PADDOLGOLIAN BROTHERS

The Paddolgolian Brothers' General Store was heaving like an ant's nest beneath a heavy boot. Fjona knew not where to start. She timidly stepped into the fray and found herself being jostled about by a swarm of frantic customers, too wrapped up in their own business to pay her any attention.

"Last cob c' corn," one farmer called from a stall buried deep in the crowd.

"Goat's milk?" cried another.

Quite how anybody could keep tabs on who was exchanging what for what was beyond baffling.

"Do you know who I can speak to about—" Fjona began, having made eye contact with a kindly looking woman.

"Sorry my *derine*," was all the woman said, before Fjona had even finished her sentence.

The woman disappeared back into the crowd, a crusty loaf of bread under one arm and dragging her freckly son along by the other.

"Excuse me," Fjona tried again, this time to an older gentleman who was carrying a small crate of vegetables.

He walked straight past her as if she were nothing but a wilting flower.

It was no good. Nobody seemed to have the time nor care to help her out.

She looked up to the floor above and noticed again just how quiet it was upstairs. She wondered that if perhaps she could find the stairs, whether there may be somebody on the floor above who might just be able to help her.

Gripping the bottle of port tighter than ever, she braced herself and charged into the crowd. She ducked away from an elbow or two, then skimmed behind the back of a large pair of shoulders before stepping near-gracefully around a moving cart stacked with bottles of milk. It was suffocating to be enveloped by so many people, not least from the stench of sweat and animal droppings so pungent that she could almost taste it in the back of her throat.

The hubbub of chatter became increasingly deafening, and keeping her eyes on the back wall of the shop was all Fjona could do to avoid becoming disorientated.

She cut through the waves of customers and landed at the far side of the store, out of breath but feeling somewhat relieved.

Here, she looked up to see an elegant staircase leading up to the top floor, at the foot of which was an immaculately well-dressed man sporting a meticulously groomed moustache and proudly wearing a tall black hat. The man's double-breasted coat was a crisp, deep burgundy and hung stiffly down to his knees. He was the epitome of eccentric and Fjona felt almost too embarrassed to speak to him.

Thankfully for Fjona, the man spoke first.

"My, my!" he exclaimed, with an unusual lilt to his voice. "I should hardly have expected anyone with such bravado to survive the mass of shoppers!"

Fjona's eyes widened. For a moment, she imagined that she were in a play by the way the man addressed her.

"I was hoping that maybe you could help me out?" she asked.

The man smiled from cheek to cheek, though not with his eyes. "I daresay that I might, as one of the proud owners of this establishment."

He gestured around the room with an unsettling grin on his face, similar to that of a clown though without any make-up. Fjona wasn't sure whether she should compliment the shop or simply applaud. She settled for the former.

"It's a wonderful place," she said with enough conviction that the man turned his somewhat disturbing smile to her.

"Rori Paddolgolian, a pleasure to meet your acquaintance," he said, tipping his hat to Fjona and revealing a head of neat russet hair. "My brother, Jorge, and I are the current owners."

He leaned in far too closely to Fjona's ear; she could feel his hot breath on her neck.

"Though in truth we have nine older sisters who should like to have taken it on from our late father. Ah, but tradition is tradition, after all!"

Rori clapped his hands together so firmly that it made Fjona jump, before looking out over the crowd again.

"Anyway, my *derine*! Why are you here and not fighting for the last scrap of food? The first sign of a bad harvest and they all go doolally as if Kalzeth had forsaken us!" A morose look passed across his face but was quickly replaced by his salesman smile.

"A bad harvest?" Fjona asked, feeling unexpectedly anxious.

"Good grief, barely! A few rotten potatoes and a couple of bad sheaves of wheat, I should wonder but, alas, the townsfolk are beside themselves."

Fjona remembered Perciville's urgency to get what they needed and leave as soon as possible.

"Mr Paddolgolian, I was wondering if you might know whether I could exchange this for a couple of horses?"

The shopkeeper's bright eyes widened as Fjona proffered the crystal bottle of port.

"By the Four Good Gods, is that what I think it is?" Rori murmured, utterly stupefied.

His reaction caught Fjona by surprise. Perciville had said that it was valuable but she had never imagined it could render the chattiest man alive, speechless.

Rori snatched it from her hands and examined it closely as if he were appraising a precious artefact. "This is far too exquisite to trade downstairs! I must insist that you exchange it with the House up in the gallery! Please..." He gestured to the staircase behind them.

Fjona was hesitant. "I'm afraid I don't quite understand," she said, pushing her hair over one ear. "Is there no stable hand who I could exchange with?"

"Come, come," Rori replied, ignoring Fjona's question, "I shall explain."

He began to ascend the stairs leaving Fjona no choice but

to follow him.

As they climbed the shopkeeper continued. "Downstairs is open to the locals to trade their day-to-day goods with one another, though scarcely as chaotic as today I might add. However, on occasion, somebody such as yourself may enter my store with something of a more elite calibre. It would be remiss of me to decline the opportunity to acquire such a fine item as this for myself – Jorge!" he exclaimed at the top of the stairs, drawing the attention of his brother who was in conversation with a couple whose attire exuded wealth.

He abruptly, though politely, concluded his discussion and headed over to Fjona and Rori.

The mezzanine floor ran a ring around the shop and was occupied by an array of large stalls, each held by an employee of the Paddolgolian brothers, though from the top of the stairs, Fjona wasn't able to see what they were selling.

There were only a couple of dozen customers up here, a far cry from the numbers crowded downstairs, and the rancid fragrance of animal faeces and sweat seemed not to travel so high as the House trading floor.

"Jorge, please treat our guest with the highest degree of respect. Miss..." He rotated his head like an owl and stared at Fjona in a way that implied 'and your name is?'.

"Sarsen," she replied, stunned by the shopkeeper's sheer gaze. "Fjona Sarsen," she added, "and I really mean to cause no fuss. Only that I might—"

Jorge Paddolgolian put a cool finger on her soft pink lips and said, in a voice indistinguishable from his brother, "Ah-ah! I shan't hear another utterance of deprecation." He looked over to his brother. "What value has Miss Sarsen exchanged?"

Rori lifted the bottle. "Whatever she needs."

Jorge's bushy eyebrows rose beneath his mop of red-brown hair and his bearded jaw hung open. "Well I never," he said. "Where in Marrow Myre did you obtain this?"

A hot flush flared through Fjona as Perciville's warning about *conjured goods* echoed inside her head. Flustered, she replied with the first excuse that came to her.

"It was a reward for directing a traveller back to Port Widow."

It was vague, but she imagined the Paddolgolian brothers had heard it all before.

In any case, it seemed to satisfy Jorge who bowed shallowly to Fjona and said with a resolute smile, "Let's see how we may be of service."

About time, Fjona thought, desperately hoping that Perciville wasn't cursing her name over the delay. She could imagine him impatiently pacing back and forth outside, desperate to be back on the road and eventually giving up and leaving on his own.

Rori excused himself and returned downstairs, while Jorge led Fjona to the stalls around the gallery.

Jorge was a fraction taller than his brother. Broader too, so that his own coat seemed a little snug on his frame. His gingery beard was neatly clipped and, though his mannerisms were mostly similar to Rori's, he lacked some of his brother's eccentricities.

As his feet tapped firmly on the polished floor, Jorge Paddolgolian asked, "Are you looking for anything in particular?"

Fjona was one tangential conversation away from wringing his neck until his blue eyes popped out, and released a heavy sigh, resentful of the fact that this whole ordeal had gone on much too long.

Resigned, she replied, "I need only a couple of horses so that my travelling companion and I can get across to Aserae's Lip and cross over to the mainland. Time really is of the essence so if we could perhaps return to the stables then I would really appreciate it."

"The mainland?" Jorge said, screwing up his face into a bemused expression. "Whyever are you going there?"

Now there was a question for Fjona. Why was she going to the mainland? Solely to assist Perciville on a strange and unlikely quest? Did she really believe that far-fetched and fantastical story of sages and curses that he had relayed to her? Was she accompanying a hero on a journey to help save the world, or simply a madman in a tavern who dreamed of bigger things?

However vague and unbelievable Perciville's tales were, something had resonated with her. Something unusual going on in the world, and she could feel it too. Quite how to explain that to a stranger in a shop was a difficult enterprise of its own.

In the end, she answered with more truth than any other question that the Paddolgolian brothers had sent her way.

"I love Marrow Myre, really I do, but I have recently become discontented with my life here. I wish to see the rest of the Arvum, meet the elves and folk who live there, and explore what the rest of the world has to offer. Really, Mr Paddolgolian, I just need a horse or two, please."

Jorge appeared to ponder this. "Why of course Miss Sarsen, whatever we can do for you. Unfortunately we can only loan you a couple of steeds as we have too few to sell. As for the rest of your journey, I can only presume that you are fully equipped for the environs across the border? Fresh clothes and blankets, lanterns and sustenance? Have you a satchel to contain it all and a canvas with which to make a tent? Hmm? The bottle of port which you wish to exchange is a most highly sought and precious commodity here in Marrow Myre and it would be ill service of me to sell you short of what it is worth. If you require just the horses then I shall assuredly provide you with just those, but do not hesitate to speak up should you need anything more."

A bell suddenly rang in Fjona's head and a fleeting wind of doubt prevailed within her. She felt foolish for failing to consider anything else that she may have needed on her travels, slightly blaming Perciville for her naivety. She had absolutely nothing but the clothes she was wearing, though at least those included a decent pair of boots. Jorge Paddolgolian was right, though. Fjona had no change of clothes or anything to keep her warm at night should she find herself separated from Perciville and his staff. Even that, she had only so much faith in. So far he had conjured a fire and a bottle of port, employed it as a compass and enchanted it to hover behind his back. What if that was the extent of his ability? No magic, or *manipulation* as he had put it, but merely a few party tricks and some clever sleight of hand.

A pit in her stomach began to fill with dread and Fjona, for the first time, felt anxious about what she had agreed to.

Nonetheless, she truly did want to get off Marrow Myre, at least for a bit, and Perciville could offer her that.

"Let's have a browse," she said. "I may need one or two things after all."

It transpired that Perciville had not been agitatedly awaiting Fjona outside at all. Instead, the respite from their lengthy journey and from answering a barrage of questions had enabled him to quietly figure out a plan for when they arrived on the mainland. Acquiring a wand for Fjona was just the first step on a very tall ladder from which many of the rungs were missing, and it was enough to make Perciville feel light-headed when he mentally weighed up how much they needed to do against the impending deadline.

He bit his finger, leaving sharp impressions in his flesh, as he contemplated an insurmountable number of objectives, while clutching the little wooden ball tightly in his other hand. It was only when Fjona emerged from the stables behind the shop that he was awoken from his stupor.

When he looked up at her atop a grey-blue steed, it took him a moment to process what he was seeing. Her grotty undershirt had been replaced with a fresh one which was so clean, one may have mistaken Fjona for someone who valued good laundry. She had evidently opted to maintain the burgundy cap and neckerchief, and now wore Evelyn's pine-coloured shirt unfastened.

In addition to Fjona's appearance, Perciville glowered at

two large satchels attached to either side of the muscular horse. The bags were bulging and the sage could only wonder what unnecessary paraphernalia they contained.

"What is all this?" he ejaculated, and not in a good way.

A wave of embarrassment washed through Fjona, but she replied with enough confidence in her voice to not let it show. "The horses you requested as well as a few provisions to last us for a while on the mainland."

Perciville clenched his jaw and rested his head between his forefinger and thumb. "We do not need—"

He cut himself short as a squat, aged woman appeared from behind the shop, leading two additional horses, and pulled up closely behind Fjona. The woman wore a tartan shawl around her scrawny body, ragged shorts and a heavy pair of leather boots. Her forehead was creased like ridges of sand at low tide and her hair was a silver bird's nest, held loosely in place by a length of black ribbon.

Perciville was beside himself. "Who...?" he uttered in a voice shaking with frustration.

"Relax, Perciville!" Fjona assured, hopping off her horse gracefully and gently placing a hand on its neck. "They could only loan us these horses so Moki here is going to accompany us to Aserae's Lip so that she can bring our rides back with her. She shan't be a nuisance at all. Apparently, she hasn't said a word in forty years." Fjona exchanged a cautious glance with their new riding companion.

Moki stared back vacuously as if her head were an empty bowl balancing on her sinewy neck.

"We don't need provisions!" Perciville objected. "What we

need is to carry as little with us as possible so not to slow us down. I can conjure—"

"Look, Harper," Fjona interrupted, "if you want my help then you are going to have to accept the baggage that comes with me. I don't know yet how much I can trust you and that staff of yours but if we are to become separated on the mainland, I need to know that I can look after myself, okay?"

She dug a hand into the satchel nearest her and fished out two warm pastries, filled with sweet apples and cinnamon.

"And it's been too long since I last had something to eat. I imagine you must be feeling hungry too," she added, the satiating fragrance drifting towards Perciville's pointed nose.

The sage took a resigned breath and stood, realising that arguing would be futile, only delaying them longer.

"Very well, but don't be surprised if you end up leaving the baggage under a tree because it's too much to carry," he said, shrugging and accepting one of the pastries without a word of gratitude.

The party of three trotted off along the path that led westward out of Swirleybucket, just as a light rain began to fall.

Perciville and Fjona rode alongside one another while Moki held back a good twenty paces, the distance between them as much socially as physically.

As they left the town, it was Perciville who posed most of the questions, probing Fjona for details of what else she had procured from the store, but Fjona soon returned to her curiosities as the fields opened up and they could follow the river again.

"Why don't you use his name?"

Perciville furrowed his brow. "What?"

"The turned-sage," Fjona replied. "Before you only referred to him as the *turned-sage* and never by his name. Why not? Who is he?"

Perciville smiled sheepishly and let out short breath, almost like a laugh. "Ah, well that is a very good question."

"Come on, Harper, please don't say 'I will tell you when you are ready'," Fjona said, mocking his voice. "I want to know."

"Well, it's complicated, but I can try to elucidate, though it may beckon yet more questions." He glanced back to ensure that Moki was out of earshot and continued. "In truth, nobody really knows who the turned-sage is, and you have made the gross assumption that they are a man. In reality, there are three contenders, two of whom are women."

"How can nobody know who the person trying to kill them is?"

"If you permit me just a moment's space without your relentless pestering then perhaps I can explain!"

Perciville raised his eyebrows and shot Fjona a look. She dipped her head, mouthing 'okay' as she did so.

"As I mentioned before, it is when a good sage is responsible for the death of somebody whom they love that their powers manifest into evil and they turn. When previously they may have sought to heal, soon they seek to cause pain. When they may have sought to build cities, now they desire to tear them down. It becomes impulsive, so the texts say, like an itch that could be scratched only by causing suffering. In the many thousands of years of sages, there have been few examples of turned-sages and most, if not all of those, are mythologies based on theories and ideas. Whatever the case, it was only the turned-sage of three centuries ago that led to anything as devastating as the demise of the Sagedom."

The rain was beginning to pick up now and the sky was swathed in a blanket of thick grey cloud. If not for a canopy of tree cover, the three travellers would have been drenched through to their skin.

"For hundreds of years, there had circulated rumours of an ancient monument hidden somewhere across the Arvum, within which contained a relic that would amplify the beholder's staff immeasurably. A totem, supposedly created by an ancient sage that could transcend the art of manipulation. So powerful that it was rumoured to be guarded by the fiercest of beings known as Gaeya'san: a deadly ethereal entity that suffocates the air around you before you even know that it is there. But, these three sages were very cunning and believed they could find a way to defeat them and get to the relic. Now this is where the story gets a little bit vaguer. I simply do not know what happened inside the monument, nor whether the three sages managed to surpass the Gaeya'san, but whatever the case, only one of them made it back out alive."

Perciville could almost hear Fjona's heart pounding against her chest as she listened to his tale.

"That one, as I am sure you have figured out, is the turned-sage, the harbinger of the Eight Afflictions and the end of the Sagedom. As for who they are, well, I suppose we should start with Nimyedd. She was the eldest of the three and perhaps the most experienced. An autumn elf with red hair as fiery as her temper, though very generous should you have got to know her. Very ambitious and, had she retrieved the relic, then a likely successor to the Sagen Master, though in my opinion, she is the least likely of the three to have turned, for reasons that will be clear in a moment. See, then there was Gilwen, a spring elf and a very attractive one at that. She was physically very strong and incredibly intelligent. Kind, thoughtful, and would certainly have brought a lot of good to the Arvum had she reached the relic I don't wonder. It's quite possible that she is the turned-sage, though I can't say for certain. Only that it would stand to reason that the turned-sage is Gilwen or her husband, the third candidate."

Perciville took a deep breath. The three horses had now passed through the woodland and were back into rolling hills, though at least now the rain had subsided and was only spitting again.

"Ferod. He was a good man, mostly, though even as a sage he could have cruel tendencies. It was his lust for power that he even went searching for the relic, knowing full well that his skills were too lacking to succeed, and wanting only to leapfrog his peers. Maybe Ferod isn't the turned-sage but something tells me that he is, I don't know. He was completely unprepared for such a dangerous mission but was goaded both by his wife, Gilwen, and by his resolute sibling rivalry."

"Ferod had a sibling?" Fjona asked, looking over at Perciville whose face bore a sternness that she hadn't seen before.

"Yes," Perciville replied. "Me."

CHAPTER 19

ASERAE'S LIP

The horses had climbed to the top of a ridge, from which Fjona and Perciville could just about spot the western edge of Marrow Myre. To the north, they could see the Whistling Lake, glistening in a speck of light that leaked between the clouds, and further to the west, the Dire Cliffs that dropped down into the murky swamp that was the Myre of Maw.

Fjona felt a pang of guilt as she faced the south, her humble home of Wychwold somewhere in a thicket of trees, and the Infant Mountains among which her parents too were having an adventure of their own.

Had the allure of Perciville's tale not enticed her so, she may have been tempted to bid him farewell and make for home, away from the uncertainties that awaited beyond Aserae's Lip.

Though how could she? Perciville was just getting to the good bit...

"Your brother is the turned-sage?" Fjona asked incredulously as they kicked their heels into their horses and made their way along the ridge, Mcki now tight on their hooves.

"I can't say for certain and it has plagued my mind for

centuries but I fear that it may be the case. In truth, it matters little to me. Would I prefer Ferod to be the turned-sage or to be dead? I've had a long time to process that and still I haven't come to a conclusion."

Fjona tried to imagine herself in Perciville's shoes but it was an impossible situation. For the first time, she felt sorry for this man and was beginning to understand his cynicism.

"I'm sorry." It was all she could say, though Perciville didn't reply.

Fjona broke the silence again with another question that had been hounding her.

"How dangerous is this mission going to be?"

The sage's lips curled up into an incongruously reassuring smile. "Extremely," he replied but quickly added, "though your role will be minimal and I will protect you when you are unable to do so yourself. Once we have you a wand, it will take time to train you up. Teach you a few spells, show you the ropes, so to speak. We will then travel south to Rosensted where I am hoping to recruit an old friend of mine called Bosmar Fodd. He has a certain set of skills that I anticipate will be useful for tracking down a weapon that I believe is the only way to stop the Eight Afflictions. The only danger that may befall you will be at the end, and I will be by your side should you need me, though by then you will be well prepared."

Fjona looked perplexed. "You have a friend?"

It was said with complete sincerity and no cruelty intended. This was a man, after all, who travelled alone and got tired of people whom he had only met the day before. For him to have someone whom he considered a friend seemed more preposterous to Fjona now than tales of curses and a magic-wielding sub-culture.

"Friend. Acquaintance. Somebody I have known for a long time and who should be able to assist me – us, I suppose."

Less than a friend, it seemed. That made more sense to Fjona.

"So what *is* my role?" she asked simply, wanting to understand exactly where she fitted into this puzzle.

The ground beneath them was becoming rockier and they were forced to navigate around the scrag. They would soon be at the edge of a hill where they could descend down to the open plains that would lead close to Aserae's Lip.

"There is a weapon, or a vessel" – Perciville was struggling for words, trying to figure out how to explain – "a box! Somewhere in the Arvum, a box that if opened can rid the world of the Eight Afflictions. The snag is that, in order to prevent the turned-sage from accessing it themselves and using it to enhance the curse, Sagen Master Herak Siadonis sealed it so that only a demi-sage can open it: a sage in training, essentially. Developed enough to wield a crook, but not a full staff, do you understand?"

Fjona shrugged. "I think so. You need me to open the box to stop the Eight Afflictions because you yourself are too experienced to do so?"

"Bingo!" Perciville replied, with his trademark smile.

"And a crook is...?"

"Somewhere between a wand and a staff," the sage said matter-of-factly.

Fjona's head was swimming with information as she

desperately attempted to digest Perciville's explanation.

Then she asked the next question that had been playing on her mind. "You said at Port Widow that you saw something that made you believe the Eight Afflictions are back," she began, to which Perciville hummed in agreement. "Well, what exactly did you see? Are you certain it means the Eight Afflictions have returned?"

"Admittedly, I had my doubts at the time, but in reality those doubts were just denial. When Herak sealed away the box, he manipulated an enchantment that would alert the sages if the Eight Afflictions ever were to bleed back into the Arvum. It was only on his deathbed that he revealed to me what that enchantment was. 'When meteors collide, so it will be that the Eight Afflictions have returned'. That is what the Sagen Master said to me, and that is what I saw last night. Actual signatures of the curse I am yet to have spotted, but I most definitely saw Herak Siadonis' warning. Whether or not there are other sages out there who may have seen it too, I cannot say. All I can say is that having witnessed the colliding meteors myself, I have a moral duty to act."

At the bottom of the ridge, Moki had caught up with them. She grunted from the back of her throat and nodded vaguely, trying to convey some message to her companions though neither Fjona nor Perciville could figure out what.

Before they could ask, Moki whipped her horse with a leather riding crop and galloped across the grassy plains in the direction of Aserae's Lip.

"I guess she wants us to get a move on," Perciville said, as he and Fjona kicked their heels and raced off in Moki's wake.

With the wind impeding their hearing, they galloped westward without conversation, while swirling dark clouds threatened to storm above them. The grass was slippery with dew that had persisted since morning but the horses made no complaint and bounded in the direction of the Farway Forest, the final landmark before the cliffs that separated Marrow Myre from the rest of the Arvum.

Fjona had never felt so alive as a cutting breeze pressed against her ribs and her undershirt clung to her slender frame. Feeling her cap shaking loose, she quickly whipped it from her head and stuffed it under one arm allowing her messy brown hair to billow in the air around her.

The horses startled a family of deer who were grazing in the plains and they swiftly leaped back towards the woodland in search of shelter.

It had been many years since Fjona had raced on a horse like this and she couldn't help but yell in ecstasy. The last time must have been when she and Evelyn had been sent off as young teenagers to hunt rabbits for their dinner, and they had goaded one another to ride faster and faster through the nearby valleys. That was as good as an adventure had got for Fjona in Marrow Myre.

Before long, Perciville and Fjona pulled up in front of the Farway Forest where Moki was awaiting them, her own steed tucking into mushrooms nestled between the roots of a chestnut tree.

Perciville steered his horse around her but Moki stuck out her riding crop in front of him and grunted again.

"What now?" he asked, irritably.

Moki simply thrust the crop further in front of the sage, groaned and shook her head.

"You can make noises with your throat; why can't you say actual words?"

"Play nice, Harper. I think she wants to leave us here and take the horses back. Maybe she's concerned about the weather or that it's too difficult to ride through here."

"Or she can't be bothered to go any further," Perciville muttered to himself, as he slid off the saddle. "Come on then, it's not too far from here. Probably."

Reluctantly, Perciville took one of the satchels and, in the same way that he had attached his staff to his back, carried the bag behind him without it weighing on his shoulders.

"Can you not attach this satchel to my back?" Fjona asked as she removed it from the other side of her horse.

"I told you it would be a hindrance," Perciville replied smugly, "though sadly not. The *attachment* spell serves only the beholder."

Moki tied the horses together with a length of rope, clambered into her saddle, and began the journey back across the plains, just as the skies opened and fat raindrops flumped onto the ground.

Sheltered a little by the trees, Fjona extracted a hooded cape of fine cloth from her satchel and replaced Evelyn's shirt with it, before putting the bag over her shoulders.

"There's one in your bag too, if you want it," she suggested to Perciville.

"I'll be fine," he replied, though he did pull the high collar of his robe tighter around his neck.

Compared to the Myre of Maw, the Farway Forest was a much more pleasant experience for Perciville. Though the trees were just as confined, the air was less stagnant and much easier to breathe, and besides for a few wallowbirds and wood pigeons, he never got the feeling that they were being watched.

The rain was getting heavier and a murkiness hung between the branches. The mossy ground was becoming slippery and Fjona had to use the trunks to keep herself from falling over.

Perciville did wonder whether the satchel slung over Fjona's back was causing her to lose balance, but he had to admit, to her credit, she made no complaints. He, meanwhile, was using his staff to keep him on his feet. Its head shimmered with a faint blue-green glow as he leaned on it, tilting it forwards slightly for navigation.

"Answer me this, Miss Sarsen," Perciville said, ducking under a drooping branch, the leaves soggy from the rain, "why is it that you are so willing to get off this island? Not least with a stranger."

He posed the question tactfully, hoping to satisfy his curiosity without spooking Fjona and casting doubt in her mind.

Fjona swept a branch out of her way and stepped over a tree stump. "At first it was the promise of adventure, the chance to visit the mainland. Since a child, my parents – my whole village even – have ingrained in me that there is nothing else in the Arvum besides Marrow Myre I need bother with. The other children and I were taught to fish and hunt, chop wood, cook, and help build houses. My parents were particularly generous with their teaching, showing me how to defend myself against a predator, though bears are really only known in the Parish of Yore. They taught me to start fires with flint, repair clothes with a needle and thread, even how to navigate with the stars, though I've had little practice with that. My point is, children of Wychwold are made to be self-sufficient. I have always had an interest in the wider world but never a chance to see it for myself, but with my parents going off on a spiritual journey and then me meeting mainland folk in Port Widow, it reignited my dreams to see what else is out there."

The rumbling of fast flowing water could be heard beyond the trees. Aserae's Lip was close.

"Then when I met you," Fjona continued, "and saw your mag... *manipulation*, it reinforced the fact that there is so much more out there. How could anyone refuse the opportunity to visit the mainland, not least with a sage, and with the invitation to learn it yourself? What really sealed the deal was the way you talked of the Eight Afflictions." Her tone darkened a little, a hushed flavour of sincerity in her voice. "I can't put my finger on it but I was already feeling a sense of unease before I even met you. It's been brewing for a few weeks but yesterday it became ever more tangible. I'm not sure what it is, but when you told me that something evil is lurking around us, it suddenly resonated with me. It made sense to me. Your stories may sound crackpot crazy at times, but I believe them."

"And it has nothing to do with your friends?" Perciville asked.

A terse and frigid wind caught Fjona by the neck and she held tightly on to the scruff of her hood to keep herself warm.

"Todie and Evelyn? No, why should it? They are curious too, but have no inclination to leave Marrow Myre. Todie is our new village cleric, after all, and is destined to serve the Four Good Gods, and Evelyn is content assisting her father on the vineyard. They have each other. They will barely even notice that I'm missing..." She trailed off just as they passed the final line of trees that brought them to the edge of an immensely tall cliff.

Here they stood at a chasm, the two of them separated by rapid, gurgling water that echoed up the cliff faces and flowed with such ferocity that Perciville could feel the ground beneath him murmuring. If one were to have found themselves battling for their life in the powerful waters below, they may just avoid drowning, only to be strewn against the jagged rocks peering out of the rushing current and shatter their skull.

The thought alone made him shudder.

"So what next?" Fjona called above the torrent of the increasingly heavy rain and thrashing waters below, almost wanting Perciville to declare Aserae's Lip too dangerous to cross and call off the whole expedition.

A rotting signpost read *Ferryman's Crossing* with an arrow pointing down a flight of precarious steps, cut into the cliff, and down to a wooden raft which rocked dangerously in the current.

"I don't fancy that," Fjona added, nodding down to the timber ferry, barely floating above the water.

Perciville didn't speak. Instead, he stood close to the sheer edge and leaned his dark oaken staff before him. His face was a stern and focused canvas, his pale eyes squinting and mysterious. With the rain hammering around him and wind gathering about his robe, the sage carried an ominous air.

Fjona watched with a look of wonderment as a silvery green light spilled from the end of Perciville's staff and the first few rungs of a suspension bridge began to appear before him. Two timber posts materialised in the ground either side of the sage and a tapestry of interweaving ropes formed either side of the bridge to provide a handrail.

Just before Fjona could comment, praising Perciville for his skill and intuition, the manipulation seemed to dry up and the bridge stopped appearing, only extending across Aserae's Lip by a fraction of the distance. Despite not reaching the opposite side, it hung in position as if it were connected all the way across.

The sage released a heavy sigh.

"What happened?" Fjona asked.

"Since the Sagedom was dissolved, my abilities have become increasingly dampened. I have the skill and the knowledge but I'm lacking the strength to fully execute it." He dipped his head a little and avoided making eye contact with Fjona. "It's worse still when I've been overindulging in a tavern or failed to sleep for a few nights, but I thought I'd have my usual ability today..."

Fjona felt disappointed, if not a little relieved. "Well, I guess that's that then."

"What do you mean?" the sage replied.

Fjona chuckled nervously. "We can't possibly go on that raft, we'll get ourselves killed!"

"I agree," Perciville said, raising his voice just enough to be heard over the wind, rain and rushing water.

"So we can't get across to the mainland..." Fjona stated, in an enquiring tone.

With a smirk, Perciville replied, "I see no reason why not."

With a flare of his robe, he gaily bounded for the partly extant bridge. The sage held tentatively on to the rope and took a fair step across the wooden rungs. As soon as his foot had landed a pace inward from the cliff edge, the first rung, closest to dry land, faded in that same silvery-blue light and a new one appeared several rungs ahead of Perciville.

Fjona's eyes glistened with astonishment and, despite her better senses warning her to keep back from the sheer drop, she headed over to the edge of the bridge.

To demonstrate the brilliance of his creation, Perciville jumped back and forth causing rungs at either end to disappear and reappear with every move.

"This is brilliant!" Fjona said, and only for a sudden gust of oceanward wind did the bridge rock abruptly, forcing Perciville to stop fooling around.

"Perhaps we should take a little more care as we cross over," he said, wandering back towards Fjona so that the first rung could materialise again and she could join him.

A torrent of emotion, heavier even than the rain, embraced Fjona as she cautiously stepped onto that first rung, tightly gripping the ropes in each hand. Her body filled with a tincture of excitement, anxiety and unadulterated fear, but a supernatural bridge was too much for her to turn away from now.

She could feel the timbers creaking as she walked, and she was careful to keep her chin up so as to avoid looking down at the thunderous rapids, battering the cliffs far beneath her.

They crossed at a steady pace, as if the fate of the Arvum wasn't in their hands, but had Perciville walked faster than Fjona, then the rung beneath her would eventually disappear and he would be in need of a new travelling companion.

Fjona's attention turned to a sudden flock of birds erupting from the trees behind her, and she and Perciville stopped in their tracks to look back.

"What was that?" she asked, anxiously scanning the treeline.

"No idea."

He prepared to take another step but Fjona stopped him.

"Just wait," she said, as if they weren't suspended two hundred feet above certain death.

"Are you kidding me?" Perciville replied through gritted teeth.

An extended rebuke was cut short when Shagwell came careening out of the trees and charging towards Fjona, skidding on his clumpy hooves a short distance from the edge of the cliff.

"What even is that?" the sage asked.

But before Fjona could reply, Todie came dashing out of the trees, angrily calling Shagwell's name. He was completely soaked through and his clothes were caked in mud.

"Fjona!" he cried above the roaring river and rain, stopping short of his diminutive horse. "Fjona!"

He stared in awe at the incomplete bridge, a look both terrified and amazed. Fjona knew that, as a cleric, it defied everything Todie knew of the world.

"Todie?" Fjona called back. "What are you doing here?"

"What am I *doing* here? Evelyn and I have been searching for you since morning after reading your note. She's gone back to Wychwold in the hopes that you'd just got fed up and gone home. We've been worried beyond ourselves, praying that this was all some big joke, but it isn't, is it? You really think this guy is going to make you a – what was it? A... *sage?*"

"Pfft, some guy?" Perciville muttered, taking a further step along the bridge.

Fjona pulled him back as the rungs behind her began to vanish. "I completely believe that Perciville is going to make me a sage," she yelled back over the empty space between them. "You don't understand, Todie. I need to do this! I need to get away from here for a while."

"Is this about me and Evelyn?"

There was a pause. Fjona hadn't expected Todie to throw that ball at her. She wanted to reply 'no, of course not', but something inside prevented it.

Instead she said, "You need to let me do this, Todie. Please..."

Todie shook his head, heavy drops of rain exploding from his darkening hair. "I can't leave you, Fjona. You don't know this man, you don't know the Arvum, you are going to get yourself hurt!" The words fell out of his mouth in one blurry sentence. "You belong in Marrow Myre, not on the mainland. This is your home. There's nothing more out there for you. This is all you are!"

Todie's face dropped as if he knew he had spoken out of turn the moment the words had passed his cold lips.

"This is all I am?" Fjona repeated, her eyes wide and her jaw hanging open. "And what exactly is that? A farmer's daughter? A fence-building, hay-bailing, fish-catching loner? Well forget it, Todie. Maybe you think that of me, and maybe you think I don't belong on the mainland, but I certainly don't belong in Marrow Myre. Come on, Perciville, you see my potential."

With that, she turned on the spot and Perciville took another cautious step, the gap between Fjona and Marrow Myre increasing as the bridge crept ever closer to the mainland.

A tear rolled down Todie's rosy cheek.

"Fjona, wait!"

She paused again. This time, Perciville felt her reluctance and he waited with her.

"I can't let the same fate that befell my father and Rodmear befall you. I can't allow myself to lose you."

"It seems that you already have," Fjona replied scornfully, her eyes narrow with contempt.

Todie seemed almost afraid to look at her. "Fjona, I—" he began, but the wind caught in his throat and he stopped short.

Instead, Todie resignedly dug deep into the pocket of his jerkin and extracted his grandmother's rose-shaped amulet.

"Take this," he said. "I wish it to bring you good fortune when you need it most."

With a heavy heart and a determined face, he threw the

prized, sentimental gift towards the bridge, then collapsed onto the wet mud as he watched it sail inches away from Fjona and plummet towards the river below.

Fjona nearly cried for him too, but saw a green light encapsulate the small object and watched, mesmerised, as it drifted back up towards her.

"What in..." she started to say, then turned to see Perciville pointing his staff over the edge of the bridge, an unmoved expression on his face.

The amulet rose elegantly through the wind and dropped down neatly into Fjona's cupped hands. She examined it briefly, traced her finger over the etchings and glass core, then stuffed it safely in the pocket of her trousers.

"Goodbye, Todie. I will see you when I get back."

Todie watched on in amazement, sullied, broken and in despair, though relieved that his token of good faith had arrived safely with Fjona, although not without the help of the sage.

"Thank you, Perciville," he said in a voice barely loud enough for him to hear.

He continued to stare from the cliff edge as his dearest friend crossed over to the mainland, not even looking behind her when she got to the other side.

CHAPTER 20

THE FOURTH WEST DIVISION

The six steeds, with their six white-coated riders, looked out over the scorched sand, away from the Sleeping Giant. Although camels were preferred for long voyages across the desert, Pentari horses provided quick travel for short distances in the region closest to the mountain.

It had taken Lais Stone a barrelful of patience and tenacity to persuade the labourers to return to work but eventually they had wielded their tools, continued late into the night to excavate the immense trench, and had now been toiling away again since the early hours of the morning. The trench was stepped on either side and a series of mechanical pulley systems had been erected to carry the spoil away to the top of the construction where dozens of Kelnish workmen were dumping it along the edge to form a steep mound on either side.

Two of the rangers, both summer elves, sat astride their horses on each bank, serving as sentries as they scanned the desert wasteland.

Callis Holden, Stone's second in command, had a dour face

as he surveyed the horizon for further signs of bandits. He was a useful asset to the Fourth West Division, internally referred to as *the muscle.* Holden towered over most summer elves and had been known to look down on one or two Grugans, though even he rarely matched them in strength. His thick beard was perfectly shaped and the left side of his face bore a pale tattoo of a swirling rune, the signet of his family.

Lisbelle Bracker, on the far heap, contrasted Holden in most respects. She was timid and slender, though not the least bit in personality. Bracker was known to have a harsh tongue and was never afraid to speak her mind. On expeditions into the desert to hunt dalachites, ferocious sand-dwelling beasts that were notorious for ransacking the outposts and making bonemeal for the vultures, Bracker would make easy sport of the culling. The cutlass at her hip was stained faintly blue, the colour of dalachite blood, despite the regular cleaning and polishing of the blade. Her head was cleanly shaven and her long thin ears were weighed down by a plethora of rings and studs, many of which she had acquired unfairly when growing up on the streets of Panamaya.

Patrolling the length of the construction at the foot of the heaps were adopted siblings Fayne and Cedarman.

One may have been forgiven for not believing that Fayne was an island elf since a lifetime under the Pentari sun had darkened her skin and stolen the shimmer from her hair. Only the paleness of her eyes and a Bouandan lilt in her voice gave away her true heritage, not to mention her inherent dexterity which had earned her the bow she carried on her back as well as the cutlass on her hip.

Her brother, on the other hand, was a summer elf by all accounts: skin like rich coffee and long black hair as stringy as his muscles. They had grown up together, enlisted together, and fought to be kept together in the same unit. The same tenacity with which they had survived in the city had led to the canvas of burn scars that Cedarman bore on his arms – a permanent reminder that blind perseverance can carry a burden of its own.

Recruitment into the Noble Guard had often upheld the tales of chivalry and patriotism from generations gone by when being a soldier meant accompanying an army out to war. There was a time, not all that long ago, when the opposing armies throughout the Arvum were tens of thousands strong, all in the pursuit of claiming the land for themselves.

When the six troops of the Fourth West Division signed up to the Noble Guard, Panamaya's entire army had been an exclusive club. While the Rear Guard was ten thousand strong, the Noble and Home Guards were capped at just five hundred troops as part of a diplomatic agreement. One may have been misled into believing that the punishing recruitment programme, a process that suffered more fatalities than were ever reported, would amount to something more fulfilling than patrolling one allocated segment of desert, chaperoning wealthy visitors to the city, or, in recent weeks, simply staring out over the horizon on the off chance that they may see a bandit appear through the hazy sands.

The cost of wearing the fine uniform, handcrafted by the Sultan's personal tailor, was long, monotonous days, scanning a desolate landscape with only the encroaching threat of bandits to provide a means of self-worth.

Lais Stone sat atop her corporal red-brown horse at the top of the construction, alongside Ranger Elian Sole.

The ranger was younger than Stone but, being Marrowborn, appeared many years her senior. He was of an average build albeit with long, fibrous muscles, and his dark, tanned features were wrinkled from long exposure to the sun. Beneath his helmet was a head of thinning black hair, specked with greys that had started to appear at an exponential rate.

"Why now?" Lais muttered to herself.

"Corporal?" the ranger replied.

"Why now? Canal's been under construction for years yet bandits attack only yesterday. That not strike you as odd?"

Sole quietly pondered this as Lais continued.

"I get there's historical frictions with Havensend and Elkensen but now seems a strange time to sabotage the project..." Lais trailed off as the gears in her head attempted to make sense of the situation.

"'The worst is yet to come' That's what the bandits said. Whoever they work for, they must have something bigger planned," said the ranger.

"That's a good point, Sole. Who *are* they working for?" Lais pondered, over the clattering of tools and construction chatter from down in the trench.

"I guess that's for General Kheller to find out?"

"He took counsel with the Sultan yesterday, but I've heard nothing from it," Lais said with a tilt of her head.

The corporal watched, deep in her thoughts, as Cedarman and Fayne passed one another and continued their patrol along the length of the trench. Then, simultaneously, Bracker and Holden raised their arms to signal the approach of travellers in their field of vision. The desert horizon was buried in a cloud of dust and they could only see the silhouettes of figures far along the trench.

"Probably Captain Lahsilli returning from a hunt," Elian suggested.

"Probably, but I'm going to check in with Holden anyway," Lais replied. "Keep an eye on the workers until I return."

The ranger placed a hand over his chest and dipped his head respectfully as Lais Stone trotted over to the southern heap and ascended to the sentry on top.

"What can you see?" she asked with an abrupt sense of urgency.

"Looks like six – no – seven riders on horseback, northside of the trench, moving quickly towards us from the west," Callis Holden replied in a hearty voice that was as rich and deep as a pot of hot cocoa.

The corporal focused her gaze. "Seven riders. Could be the captain and his Guard," she said.

"They're travelling surprisingly quickly, Corporal," the ranger pointed out. "Perhaps they're in trouble?"

He was right. In the time they had been speaking, the riders had covered considerable ground, even for Pentari horses.

"Corporal!" Becker yelled from the opposite heap, but Lais already knew what she was about to say.

"Those aren't horses," Holden said, speaking aloud what Lais was thinking.

The incoming riders split apart revealing twice as many as

Ranger Holden had reported.

Lais blew her war horn to alert her division. "With me," she instructed to Holden and rapidly descended to the bottom of the heap where the other rangers assembled.

Cedarman had his cutlass in hand, Fayne ready with her bow.

"I've never seen a camel move so fast," Elian Sole murmured as he too unsheathed his cutlass and pulled his horse up alongside his comrades.

The five rangers stood in a triangle behind Corporal Stone.

"Any sign of hostility, we charge. We cannot allow the same losses as before," Lais instructed, glancing from ranger to ranger. "Am I clear?"

"Forgive me, Corporal Stone, but is this wise?" Callis Holden asked, forever the voice of reason. "If we leave our post, if we get this wrong, you might find yourself in breach of your oath."

"And what do you propose, Ranger Holden? We wait for them to get close enough to cause more damage?" Stone shot back. "I don't care about bureaucracy, I care about doing my due diligence."

"Holden's right," Elian piped up. "If we engage them in combat and they break our defence, the repercussions could be dire. Should we not hold our line and await reinforcements? Lahsilli will seek any excuse to have you court martialled."

Lais considered him for a moment then shook her head. "I'm your corporal and you do as I command. If we wait any longer, we risk more of the workers' lives."

There was a pause while the rangers contemplated whether

or not to further their arguments.

"I'm behind you," Holden reluctantly agreed.

Lais kicked her heels and began cantering towards the riders, her five rangers in tow.

"Rotten, dirty bandits," Bracker hissed under her breath.

Then the sun glinted off a raised sword from the lead charger and Lais Stone conceded to Bracker's assumption.

"For the Sultan!" Stone cried and charged towards the intruders, her own sword held high above her.

"For the Sultan!" the rangers echoed and shot off behind her, dust kicking up in their wake.

So hungry for action and indoctrinated by tales of grandeur were the Noble Guard that the disadvantage in numbers didn't even play on their minds.

Perhaps it should have.

The plains of sand between the Fourth West and the bandits closed in fast and, for the first time, Lais could see what they were up against.

Fourteen unnaturally muscular and ferocious camels, travelling at a remarkably fast pace. Nothing like the docile breed which civilians used to cross the desert.

Grey foam frothed at their prominent mouths, their eyes, steely and focused.

Upon each camel rode either one or two bandits, fully clad so their eyes were only just visible in a slit between their dusty headscarves. They wore ragged shirts, armoured by disparate pieces of leather and iron, and their arms were protected by lightweight gauntlets.

Suddenly the doubt that Lais had rejected so far began to

seep into her mind, but there was no turning back.

The bandits sang an eerily warbling battle cry as they raised their array of weapons: swords, axes, stone slings, torches and bows. Two of the bandits carried morning stars: a spiked iron ball that attached to a wooden handle by a length of chain. They swung them about their heads with near-careless ferocity.

All the Fourth West could do was brace themselves as the two bands collided. Lais attacked first, taking a swipe at the bandit leader's waist but they were quick to parry her blade with their own. She steered away from one of the morning stars and came dangerously close to the end of an axe, avoiding it only by ducking her head at the last minute.

Fayne peeled away from the division to create space to fire an arrow. With deft fingers, she nocked the arrow, briefly released the reins of her horse, aimed and fired. The shaft spiralled through the air and struck one of the bandits in their leather armour but it was too well-padded to cause any harm. They plucked the arrow out of their armour and discarded it like an old piece of meat.

An opposing arrow shot towards Fayne, but she was able to duck safely clear, pulling away from the melee.

Meanwhile Lais had met swords with two further bandits and managed to slice through the side of one of the camels, causing it to fall onto its haunches and toppling the rider off onto the blood-soaked sand. Moments later, she deflected the onslaught of a sword with her shield as she steered deeper into the rampaging camels.

Callis Holden had a little more success as he swiped at two of the axemen, splitting apart one of their gauntlets. The blade had cut through the leather and a fountain of deep red blood sprayed out between the seams. He cut the other bandit's wrist which erupted in a shower of blood: a wound, most likely fatal though the ranger couldn't be sure if it would be. They swiftly retreated, collecting the grounded bandit whose camel was bleeding out in front of him and groaning in distress.

Elian Sole was only able to slice through one of the archer's bows but they were quick to retaliate and stabbed the loose arrow into his shoulder.

"Mother…!" Sole cried in pain, knowing that attempting to pull it out himself would only make it more agonising.

Instead he sucked in his breath, and frantically swiped at the oncoming riders with his sword, though he failed to land a hit. The ball of a morning star caught him on his helmet sending a shockwave of vibrations down his spine. Disorientated and dizzy, he found himself inadvertently leaning his horse to one side and away from the fray.

Bracker and Cedarman were equally cunning and aimed for the legs of the camels, able to disable one of them each but missing the riders themselves, one of whom held a small throwing axe. They tossed it in the direction of Cedarman, and the wooden shaft caught him on the back of the head, causing him to lose balance and collapse from his horse, face down in the sand.

"You have no idea who you are up against," the axeman said, standing over the ranger. "*Sil'yhab forlein!*" he called, elevating the weapon above his head and preparing the execution.

Just as he swung the rusted iron down, an arrow from Fayne caught him in the throat and he dropped the axe into the baking sand.

Blood gurgled up inside his mouth and the bandit issued a guttural, pained howl before falling next to Cedarman.

The unsaddled ranger rolled on to his front, winded from the fall. Fayne came over to assist him but he rejected the offer.

"No, they need you," her adopted brother insisted. "I'll be fine."

He was met by a succinct nod of the head and the Fourth West archer turned back towards the riders.

By now, the two bands of riders had passed through one another and the remaining bandits had a clear run towards the construction.

"Come on!" the corporal yelled, rallying the four rangers who were still on their horses.

They began the charge back towards the camels but the distance was too far to catch up. Fayne fired a number of hopeful arrows only one of which came close, but even then it failed to make contact.

Of the remaining bandits, three of them held stone slings and were each coupled up with a torchbearer. The ammunition had been coated in oil and the torchbearers were carefully igniting the pellets and placing them in the slings. The slingers then pelted the fiery rocks at the construction site, taking out three of the mechanical pulleys and hitting several of the workers. The casualties would likely have been much higher had not a number of the Kelner elves evacuated the trench when the conflict had begun.

Fuelled by oil, the flames spread contagiously, engulfing the wooden scaffolding, ladders and tools. Some of the workers, those who didn't perish in the flames, were trapped on the steps and more than a few braved broken limbs as they leaped back down to safety.

The workers at the top of the construction, those who were closest to the marauders, were stabbing their mattocks and shovels at the riders but this served as more of a deterrent than an attack.

The last remaining archer managed to loose one arrow that pierced the eye of a worker. White goo dripped down his bloodied face and congealed in his tangly beard. The sight made another Kelner elf vomit.

"*Sil'yhab forlein,*" the lead bandit called in a deep, feminine voice as the camels pulled up alongside the trench, and the stone slingers pelted more firestones at the pulleys. "If you fail to cease this construction then you will wake the Sleeping Giant. You have been warned. Else, we will continue to tear it down ourselves."

She kicked her heels into the side of the camel as two additional divisions of the Noble Guard came rattling around from the southern side of the trench, led by the black horse of a captain.

Lais Stone and her riders, with the exception of Cedarman who was only now just getting back on his horse, had finally caught up with the bandits and now the three divisions were in chase behind the bandits.

The added weight of an extra rider on the camels slowed them down enough for the Noble Guard to close the gap.

Without command from the captain, several archers tried their luck at range, piercing two of the retreating bandits, though failing to knock them from their camels.

"We need to get close enough to draw swords," the captain commanded. "They are wearing too much leather to beat them by arrow."

They had chased the bandits towards the North Division, the mountain of the Sleeping Giant looming quietly behind them. Before long, they would be outside of Panamayan territory and on rough sands where the camels would have an unparalleled advantage.

Rolling dunes were appearing on the horizon and already the ground beneath them was becoming softer.

"Watch out!" Lais called as a barrage of fiery stone bullets were slung backwards from their aggressors. She instinctively pulled her horse away, costing her precious distance from the bandits.

Two of the Noble Guard horses came close to collision with one another in an attempt to evade the attack, bringing them to an abrupt halt.

Another took an arrow in the shoulder, forcing them out of their saddle, and was nearly trampled by his comrades.

The monstrous camels made easy work of the first dune as the bandits ascended without breaking their stride.

Stones continued to hail down at the Noble Guard who were left immobilised at the bottom.

The captain cursed to himself. "Fall back. It's all over."

"They're still in range, we can follow them," Lais argued, but it was no use.

"Corporal Stone, you have wasted enough effort already without needlessly chasing camels across the desert," the captain responded, turning back towards the city.

"Wasted effort? Had it not been for us they'd have slaughtered all the workers!"

Now safely away from the slingers, the captain removed his helmet. Beneath it was the rugged, stern face of Captain Beric Lahsilli. His wavy, ochre hair was unusual for a summer elf, though he wore it well, and above his lip he kept a meticulously groomed moustache.

It wasn't an unattractive face and Lais may have found herself disarmed by his looks had she not found Captain Lahsilli to be such an insolent, self-aggrandising turd.

"You're quite right, Stone. You did prevent the bandits from killing *all* the workers. Just a few, but hey, they're only Kelnish slaves," Lahsilli mocked cruelly as they rode side by side.

"That's not what I said," Lais replied but the captain paid no attention to her defence.

"Yes, yes, just a few more dead workers on your hands, not to mention the destruction of their equipment and the injury to two of your own soldiers. Unless I'm mistaken...?"

"That wasn't her fault," came a voice from behind them.

The captain and the corporal turned their heads to find that Elian Sole, the arrow still wedged in his shoulder, had come over to find out what the discussion was about.

"Is that how you address your commanding officer?" Lahsilli asked.

"Forgive me, my Captain, I was just—"

"Sole, head back with the others. Get your wound sorted out; this doesn't concern you," said a stone-faced Lais.

"But—"

"Now!" Her voice was firm and forceful, and turned the heads of several other riders who were close by.

The ranger dipped his head abashedly, then led his horse towards his companions.

"Such authority," the captain said sarcastically.

Frustration boiled up inside Lais; tightening her jaw was all she could do to contain it.

"I mean, you are a member of the esteemed Noble Guard of the Sultan and not some backstreet militia," he snarled at her. "Here you are, clad in tempered steel and chains, armed with the finest of blades, crafted by the hands of the greatest blacksmiths in the Arvum, blessed with decades of invaluable, life-asserting training, and where do I find you? Being outwitted by a band of nobodies, barely covered in scraps of leather with a mismatched array of iron and fire! Your inexcusable, egotistical desire for glory has resulted in abysmal failure and has humiliated, not only yourself and your division, but the authority whose emblem you so proudly wear on your coat. Suffice to say I will be telling the general of your failures, Stone. Had he my sense he would suspend you today. Had he the Sultan's sense he would retire you from duty and lead you behind the stables like a lame horse!"

"My failures?" Lais shot back at him. "My division were outnumbered two to one, and I don't know what they've been feeding their camels but they were like nothing I've ever seen before. In any case, the Sultan knew of the bandit attacks yesterday. He and the general should have prepared us better, allocated more soldiers, perhaps from the Rear Guard, and not left six of us to our own devices. Training, weapons and armour will only go so far when your numbers are halved. We did the best we possibly could have done under the circumstances."

Captain Lahsilli chuckled. "That's your story then?"

"That's what happened, so yes."

"So it's the Sultan's error?"

Lais's mouth opened but no words came out. Military failings may result in dismissal but undermining the Sultan could be punishable by death.

"I didn't think as much," Lahsilli said, with more than hint of condescension. "Word has already got around that you disturbed the Sultan yesterday during consultation."

The corporal couldn't see where Lahsilli was going with this. "What of it?" she asked.

"I am your *superior* and would never dare barge in on the Sultan! General *Kheller* wouldn't dare barge in on the Sultan!" he said. "You need to learn your place, Stone. Need I remind you that it is by mere coincidence that the construction of the canal is within your parcel and that you weren't hand selected by the Sultan to defend it."

"No need to remind me, Captain," Lais replied through gritted teeth. "Besides, there were extenuating circumstances and I was forced to act."

"Being forced to act does not give you the right to exceed your status."

When they returned to the construction site, most of the soldiers were lingering and awaiting instruction from Lahsilli. Callis Holden had Elian Sole pinned to the ground while Fayne carefully twisted the arrow in the hopes that she could remove it without ripping apart the young ranger's shoulder.

Bracker, meanwhile, had returned to her spot on top of the heap and was surveying the horizon, yet again, for signs of bandits.

Most of the workers were consoling one another and cleaning their own wounds, while many more had taken to extinguishing the vast fires with spoil from the heaps.

"Where do you think you're going?" Lahsilli asked as Lais made for her comrades.

"Like you said, I have two injured soldiers who I would like to check on."

The captain shook his head. "Did you not hear me earlier, or perhaps you were misled into thinking I was joking? You are coming with me to the Sultan before you and your band of hot-headed, incompetent lightweights can cause any more trouble."

"Why? I can't afford to spend time away from my division. Those bandits have gone for now but who knows when they'll be back." She glanced around at the throng of workers, gathered around the top of the construction in a hubbub of trepidatious chatter. Some of them appeared to be collecting their tools and preparing to leave. "Besides, I've built a rapport with the labourers. Who else is going to get them to continue working after this?"

The captain frowned in contemplation. "Good point. Storm'Dune!" he called, looking over to the soldiers.

One of them, a skinnier summer elf whose Noble Guard coat seemed to swamp him, trotted over to Lahsilli.

"Go speak with the workers. I imagine they'll be more

inclined to listen to one of their own."

Storm'Dune dipped his head. "My captain," he replied, in a strong Kelnish accent.

"Reassure them that they will now be under protection of the captain of the West Guard who will personally oversee the construction and eliminate any bandits who tread this way."

"My captain," the solider repeated.

"That is all," Lahsilli said in a tone so flat it could have fitted between the pages of a book.

Storm'Dune politely nodded his head in affirmation and made for the trench.

"It's a shame you lack his manners," Lahsilli remarked, turning to Lais. "You could have so much more potential."

"I save my manners for those who have earned my respect," the corporal retorted.

"Do you think this going to help when I present your case to our Divine Excellency?" Lahsilli asked, his lips curling up into a smile.

Before Lais could reply, they were interrupted by the return of Cedarman who was pulling his limping horse back by its reins. Draped over the saddle was the dead bandit, headdress removed and lifeless arms swinging back and forth like a pair of pendulums.

"Corporal!" It was Callis Holden this time. "Corporal, I think you ought to see this..."

Lais didn't wait to be dismissed by her superior, racing over to her rangers.

When she got there, Holden and Cedarman had removed the bandit from the saddle and had placed him face up on the hot sand. She swiftly leaped from her horse to get closer to the body while a crowd of soldiers congregated around them, curious to see what the commotion was about.

"Out of my way!" Lahsilli demanded as he barged through the divisions. He too jumped down onto his feet. "Well I wasn't expecting that..." he said, speaking everyone's mind.

"A spring elf," Lais stated. "What have the spring elves against the canal? It doesn't involve them at all."

"Nor does it involve you," Captain Lahsilli added. "You" – he waved vaguely at Callis Holden – "find some wraps for this body and take it up to the barracks. I want the general to see it." Then he looked back at Lais. "You're coming with me to the Sultan."

"I thought you didn't like to disturb him?" she replied.

Lahsilli smiled. "I'm sure he'll understand. These are extenuating circumstances, after all."

CHAPTER 21

THE WARDEN OF THE ARCHIVUS

Kaikura had spent all morning trawling through bookshelves and dusting off old tomes in the hopes that she may find something pertaining to the Panamayan spring but, so far, she had only been disappointed. She had settled into a quiet spot on the first floor of the Archivus beneath a tall arched window and was engrossed in a book detailing the history of the Palace of the Sultan from its construction in the fourth dynasty to renovations that took place in the last century.

The author, Fiyra Mesah, had meticulously compiled nearly every transaction that had been made, from quarrying the marble, to carving the pillars, and shaping the gold dome, but not once did she make reference to the Panamayan spring. It was useless.

The other curiosity was that barely anyone else had felt the tremor during the night, though perhaps it was hardly surprising considering how gentle it had been. She had exchanged loose pleasantries with a drunken, homeless elf on her way to the Archivus who, through slurred expletives, reported how the mountain was shaking, but perhaps it always felt like it was shaking on his legs? Whatever the case, the streets had been quiet and, of the handful of folk she had overheard in the library, nobody had mentioned the quake.

Frustrated, Kaikura slammed the book shut, forcing a cloud of dust to burst from between the pages, and received a disgruntled look from a severe librarian who had been returning journals to a shelf opposite.

The librarian scowled at her and Kaikura felt her cheeks blush.

"Forgive me," she said, "but my search for knowledge is being painfully inhibited."

Her apology was met with a roll of the eyes and an audible tut, after which Kaikura felt too embarrassed to hang around. She hurriedly stacked her books, grabbed her satchel, and swiftly vacated her nook.

The lack of understanding was beyond infuriating but there was little option. Kaikura didn't like to disturb her mentor, Sialah Bouwer unnecessarily but, during times of academic plight, she felt she had no option. That's not to say the proprietor would be unwilling to hear her out. It was more a mutual respect for one another's study and the knowing that the brink of discovery may suffer at the hands of interruption.

She swiftly made for the staircase, exchanging a polite greeting with Isiah Fethen, the Proprietor of Botany and Horticulture, as she passed him on the stairs.

His skin looked sallow and his eyes were weighed down by heavy bags. Even his normally luscious red hair seemed lifeless and paler than usual.

"Are you unwell, Proprietor?" Kaikura asked.

Isiah forced a smile, though his lips seemed to resist. "Ah, San Kendi, it is most kind of you to ask," he replied, though lacking his usual charisma. "I suppose I had a rather restless night, that's all. I found myself reading about *hibernigot* beans before bed and then, rather ironically, was unable to nod off! Fascinating plant, but to be consumed with caution..."

Kaikura just looked back at Isiah with a bemused expression.

"A tale for another day. Anyway by the time I did manage to fall asleep, I was disturbed on several occasions throughout the night, though I know not why."

This caught Kaikura's attention; it would have been remiss of her not to ask. "Perhaps the earthquake?"

Now the proprietor's lips did curl up as he laughed heartily. "An earthquake? Very good, San Kendi! Could you imagine? Thousands of years of Panamaya City without so much as a quiver until last night! Brilliant!"

This really had tickled the enormous elf and it made Kaikura happy that she had provided him with some amusement, even at the expense of her own intrigue.

"Have a blissful day," Isiah added in better spirit as he continued down the stairwell, his upper body still shaking as he laughed.

"Worth asking," Kaikura said to herself with a sigh.

At the top of the stairs, the energy from Isiah suddenly dissipated and an eery chill consumed the Proprietors' Corridor.

There was no obvious reason for the unsettling atmosphere, just a dull quiet that sent goosebumps down Kaikura's spine.

She walked cautiously along as if treading heavily may

awaken the dead.

When she got to Proprietor Bouwer's door, Kaikura noticed that it was slightly ajar. Her mentor was someone who valued privacy nearly as much as education and to leave her door open was most unlike her.

Tentatively, Kaikura knocked. "Proprietor Bouwer? Are you here?"

There was no response.

A part of Kaikura wanted to turn on her heel and leave but her hand was already pushing the door open. A sliver of light spilled out of the room, illuminating specks of dust that danced in the gloomy corridor.

She peered into Sialah Bouwer's chamber but there was no sign of the proprietor. The room was a jungle of books and apparatus, though this was far from extraordinary.

Kaikura stepped inside, careful to avoid kicking over something important on the floor. Of the innumerable objects that littered every available surface, it was near impossible to discern which were of value and which had outstayed their usefulness.

It was unlike Kaikura to snoop but her inquisitiveness got the better of her and she found herself instinctively wandering over to her mentor's desk. Sure enough, Sialah, wherever she had disappeared to, had left her latest reading material: a book entitled *The Compendium of Sages*. What was more inviting, however, was a leaf of parchment on top with the words *For Kaikura* scrawled in purple ink.

"For me?" Kaikura said softly, picking up the book and examining it. "I wonder why...?"

As she quickly flicked through the pages, Kaikura noticed that, besides from the cover, the rest of the book was written in a language completely alien to her. Strange symbols and letters, like nothing she had ever come across before.

A chill raced down her spine and she thrust the cryptic book into her satchel, determined to retreat to the sanctuary of her own home.

It was then that she was startled by a voice at the door.

"San Kendi? Forgive me, I was ra-rather hoping to find Proprietor Bo-Bouwer."

"Go-good afternoon, Warden Newblood," Kaikura replied a little shakily, afraid of being reprimanded for entering a proprietor's chamber without invitation.

The Warden smiled at her warmly, his eyes sparkling with kindness. "I suppose she must have gone to the forum," he said, stepping into the chamber and casually examining Sialah Bouwer's eclectic collection of artefacts. "It has been a l-long while since I last convened with many of the sch-scholars," he added, glancing over at Kaikura, who was beginning to feel a little trapped.

"Perhaps you should arrange another gathering?" Kaikura suggested, surreptitiously side-stepping towards the door.

"Ha, quite!" the warden replied. He averted his gaze away from Sialah's collection and turned it back to Kaikura. "You mu-must forgive me, I am keeping you from your studies. Remind me, what is it that you are researching currently?"

"Well, until lately, I had been researching mythical practices throughout the Arvum," she replied, "but I have become a little distracted."

"Oh?" The warden considered Kaikura with intrigue.

"I've developed a recent interest in the history of the Sleeping Giant, though sources are rather scarce. I am determined to research the Panamayan spring as I understand there to be more of a narrative than I previously realised. You wouldn't happen to know anything about it, would you?"

Warden Newblood was quiet for a moment, evidently deep in his own thoughts, and Kaikura wasn't convinced that he had even heard her.

A wave of embarrassment rushed over her as well as guilt for having bored the Warden of the Archivus into a stupor.

"Umm... Warden Newblood?"

He dazedly blinked his eyes open as if he had just woken up, then flitted his eyelids as they adjusted to the light. "My apologies, San Kendi, I know not what ca-came over me! Anyway, I have consumed enough of your t-time. I shall chase down Proprietor Bouwer later. May the Four Good Gods smile upon you."

The warden smiled, then vacated the chamber brusquely, his white and gold-trimmed robe fluttering behind him, leaving Kaikura feeling somewhat uncomfortable.

She took a second to regain herself before hurriedly making for the exit, closing the door firmly behind her.

"What in the Arvum is going on with everyone today?" she asked herself with a heavy sigh as she headed for the stairs.

CHAPTER 22

WILLOW'S BRUSH

"We've been this way," Fjona complained as she clambered over a moss-coated tree stump and ducked under a low-hanging branch.

Her sour mood wasn't helped by the unrelenting rain that by now had penetrated the fibres of her cape and was working its way through to her skin. That, coupled with the fact that she was still feeling riled by the way Todie had spoken to her on the bridge.

"Did you hear me, Harper? We've already been this way."

The sage was a short distance in front of Fjona, halfway up a steep bank that was glistening green with moss and leaves. One hand was using his staff to pull him up the slope while the other clung on to the grainy bark of a pine tree.

"Is that right?" he replied, yanking himself over the brow of the hill and nearly losing an eye to the sharp tip of a branch.

"I'm telling you; I recognise that stump, that slope, that—"

"Yes, I get it! There are a lot of trees and hills, okay? It's a forest!"

Perciville was losing his patience. Searching for the Tree

of Birth was always going to be an arduous process, and he was more than prepared for the challenging journey. What Perciville hadn't been prepared for was Fjona's incessant whinging, which was really starting to scratch at his nerves.

"I'm aware of that but we have definitely climbed this particular slope before," Fjona replied.

Perciville offered her a hand but she grabbed on to a nearby tree instead to help make it to the top.

"And I suppose you recognise this glade, do you? That rockpool, those birds?"

Fjona looked about her. They had entered a break in the trees in the middle of which was a spring that fed several narrow streams, all illuminated by a rare beam of light that had penetrated the thick clouds.

"Well... yes. We have been here! You told me about the silkstars, remember?" Fjona looked over to the beautiful azure-feathered birds.

A small flock had congregated to pluck out frogs and worms that had surfaced under the rain, and were using their long, narrow beaks to tease out critters poking out of the soil. The silkstars were startlingly elegant, with a sweeping, flowing tail of fine feathers and were much larger than the wallowbirds that Fjona was familiar with.

Perciville placed his middle and fore fingers on his temples. "Look, Miss Sarsen, I have traversed the breadth of the Arvum for hundreds of years, visited Willow's Brush countless times and compiled an internal map of the world in my mind. Do you not think I, a sage no less, would notice if we had already been here?"

"Well perhaps you don't know the mainland as well as you

think," Fjona said, sheltering beneath the dense canopy of a tree.

She removed her satchel and extracted a chalky red apple, though she was craving something heartier.

"Please, I'm from the mainland. I certainly know it better than you," replied the sage as he shuffled in next to Fjona.

The rain was falling even harder now and a streak of lightening lit up the sky before them.

"Are you, though? I thought only elves lived on the mainland? I've seen elves and, no offence, but you aren't one."

Perciville looked a little hurt. "I could be an elf."

Fjona was less convinced. "You're not pretty enough. You're not tall enough. The elves I met in Port Widow had grace and charm, and you have..." She smiled cheekily. "Relax, Harper, I'm just teasing you."

The sage rolled his eyes and shook his head.

"Seriously, though, what are you?" Fjona asked. "You seem pretty Myrish to me."

"My ancestors were, but I'm not. I'm Marrowborn," he replied casually as if expecting his response to be sufficient, though evidently Fjona's face told him otherwise. "The descendants of Myrish folk who migrated to the mainland generations ago."

"So there are Myrish people living on the mainland?"

"No, well... sort of. Folk who are from and continue to live on Marrow Myre are known as *Myrish* whereas folk who were originally from Marrow Myre but moved to the mainland are *Marrowborn*. People travelled around more often during the Sagedom but, when it collapsed, war broke out and travel became more dangerous. A lot of folk returned to their native homes, but you'll still find autumn elves in Sallisai'Mae and summer elves in Rosensted, and so on and so forth."

Fjona listened intently. It amazed her how much of the Arvum her parents had failed to teach her about, growing up.

"I didn't realise there are so many different families of elves. I mean, there were the spring elves at Port Widow visiting for Lullatide, and Evelyn's father is an island elf, but I had no idea there are others."

"Believe me, you are only scratching the surface. You'll meet many more on our journey. Here..." he said, wielding his staff.

He pointed it at the ground before them and light flurried out of the head forming a circle of stones and logs on the ground. Suddenly the logs were ablaze with a curiously green fire that spat and thrived in spite of the rain.

Before Fjona could query it, the sage explained, "Green fire. Impervious to water. Now warm up quickly, we can't be hanging around here all day."

She certainly didn't need to be told twice and gladly crouched, holding her palms out towards the flames.

"So your parents, are they Myrish?" Fjona asked.

"I believe it was my six times great-great-grandparents who migrated. Something like that. My parents were both Marrowborn."

"Were? What happened to them?"

"Umm... they died." Perciville replied in a tone implying it should have been obvious to Fjona.

"Oh, I'm sorry."

"Nearly three hundred years ago," he added, "each of them

into their nineties."

Fjona tapped her forehead. "Of course. I'm still getting used to your absurd age! So they weren't sages?"

"No, just me and my brother, Ferod. Now come on, that's enough time sitting around," Perciville said, pulling away from the tree.

Fjona sighed. "But this rain is horrible! I mean, I'm from Wychwold, I can handle rain, but this is something else." She screwed her face up, a thought occurring to her. "Wait a second. Surely you can do something about it?"

Perciville was staring forlornly at the silkstars. "Well..."

"I knew it! You can! For Aserae's sake, why didn't you stop it earlier while we were on the bridge, or perhaps you were trying to teach me a lesson about the harsh conditions of travelling across the Arvum?" Fjona was feeling narked and struggling to keep it out of her voice.

"It's complicated."

"Well you best explain quickly because I shan't be moving until you do."

Now Perciville sighed. "Very well," he said as he warmed his own hands on the green fire. "There are several schools of manipulation: conjuring, infliction, altruism, enchantment, and elemental. For the most part, sages can do as they please without fear of repercussion; I mean you have already witnessed conjuring. However elemental manipulation is different to the others. As a demi-sage, it was ingrained in me that toying with nature bears unknowable consequences, and that a sage should only manipulate the environment out of necessity."

Fjona scoffed. "What's the worst that can happen; the sun

might come out and dry up the spring?"

"Possibly," Perciville replied.

"But that could happen irrespective of whether or not you do it."

"Indeed it might but there is a very great difference between the spring draining by nature or by my hand. Do you not see?"

Unfortunately for Fjona, she did see and she completely understood where Perciville was coming from.

However...

"Well, maybe that is the case but I believe you bringing an end to this weather is out of necessity. I mean, we are lost, we are going around in circles, and I, at least, am soaked through. If we are to find the Tree of Birth before the day is over, I think you need to put an end to this rain."

If anything the deluge was getting worse and muddy water was starting to pool around their feet.

"Maybe so," Perciville conceded, "but let this be a lesson to you, should things go wrong."

He stepped out from beneath the cover of the tree and placed his staff forcefully on the ground before him, holding it tightly in both hands. Focussing his energy, a deep, emerald light shimmered at the tip of the staff, spreading like ripples in the ocean. Then the sage thrust the staff upwards and the light exploded towards the heavens, spreading across the sky like lightening, only brighter and more brilliant.

Within moments, the heavy rain lessened, then became a few drops, then nothing at all.

Fjona was stunned into silence. She had truly believed Perciville was capable, even with his ability dampened, as he had put it, but to actually witness such power was overwhelming.

She moved away from the fire and stood under the natural warmth of the newly revealed sun. "Thank you," she said.

Perciville didn't reply. Instead, he was glancing around the glade as if making sure that everything was as it should be.

Fjona could sense his discomfort. "No consequences, see? It's all fine."

"Hmm..." Perciville agreed uncertainly. "Well, it's dry now, we can get going."

He pointed his staff towards the fire and extinguished it as easily as he had conjured it.

They had barely stepped away from the shelter of the tree when they were disturbed by a high-pitched animalistic cry. The call was met by another, then several more. It was a guttural howl, as beautiful as it was frightening.

Perciville and Fjona stood completely motionless, their eyes flitting about their environs.

"What is that?" Fjona whispered.

The silkstars had barely enough time to react before the first of the predators leaped out from the woodland and caught one of the birds but it's long, sinewy neck. The captured silkstar issued a deafening, gurgling scream before its head was ripped cleanly from its body in a fountain of blood.

"Pettywolves," Perciville hissed. "Run!"

Nearly a dozen pettywolves had taken advantage of the abrupt change in the weather and had emerged from the woodland to hunt down the silkstars.

The wolves were only fractionally bigger than the birds, but they were cunning and highly vicious with razor fangs and sharp claws. Their dark brown fur enabled them to hide in the shadows, and they had learned to communicate with the pack with their bright white eyes.

Not that Fjona had long to admire them. She chased Perciville along the top of the ridge, hopping over stumps and shimmying around trees.

Scurrying feet echoed through the woodland behind her and the pettywolf cries seemed to be getting closer. Evidently they had finished with the silkstars and had turned their noses to a different scent.

Underfoot, the wet leaves had congealed with the mud to form a dangerously slippery paste and it was inevitable when Fjona lost her footing, skidded across the ground and landed on her face in a spread of sticky sludge.

"Perciville!" she yelled, spitting out leaves.

The sage stopped in his tracks and turned to see a pettywolf descending on Fjona. It snarled at her, presenting a jaw of salivating, lethal teeth.

For the first time since meeting Perciville, Fjona felt truly afraid. She managed to shuffle the satchel from her back and held it in front of her like a shield but the pettywolf was not deterred. Instead, it tore its canines into the fabric of the bag and ripped it out of Fjona's clutches – there was a shower of paraphernalia. Dried food, fruits, a glass lantern and clothes dropped into the thick mud surrounding her.

The pettywolf wasn't finished yet, however, and edged close enough to Fjona that she could feel its musty breath on her face.

It was moments from tearing into her neck when a sharp

blue flash shot into its muscular body causing the wolf to spasm. Electricity swirled about its frame before it keeled over on the wet ground beside Fjona and died.

Two further pettywolves had caught the scent and were ready to leap on their prey, but Perciville was too quick for them. He pointed his staff at them, issuing a fatal dart of electricity at them both.

"Stop dilly-dallying," he yelled at Fjona, only partly joking, as he yanked her up by her arm.

"Thanks," she replied breathlessly, wiping some of the leaves from her soiled cape.

Somewhere in the near distance behind them, the shattering howls of the pettywolves sounded again.

Perciville hammered his staff into the ground, his face pensive with concentration. This time, a piercing emerald light shone from its head and a fierce, spiralling wind swirled about them, powerful enough to elevate the pettywolves from the ground. He lifted the staff up, then thrust it into the ground, the wind and the dead wolves scattering in all directions.

"To confuse our scent," the sage explained. "Come on, we need to get moving." He turned on the spot and continued to charge through the woodland.

Had Fjona not been running for her life, she may have had time to reflect on how beautiful Willow's Brush was now the rain had subsided, for better or for worse. The trees were magnificently tall, rich in vibrantly coloured leaves, and ancient beyond comprehension. In places, the trees grew against one another in tiers down the slope and were segregated by narrow streams and trickling waterfalls.

They climbed a steep hill, lit up by pockets of sunlight between the trees, which had grown in a natural avenue towards the top. The ground was rockier here and speckled with luminescent orange mushrooms which grew in shaded clumps.

At the summit, they fell into another clearing, this time occupied by a single tree with incongruously ochre leaves, and moated by a small channel, easy enough to step over.

Fjona could feel a drastic change in energy, the threat of the pettywolves replaced by a soothingly powerful sensation. Even to a novice who had never before visited the Tree of Birth, it was obvious to Fjona that she was standing before something of immense importance.

"Wow," she gasped, looking up at the grand tree which was attracting dozens of small birds that tweeted and twilled in the sunshine. "I imagined it would be impressive but this..."

Perciville was standing before it, plucking a short branch from low down on the trunk.

He hopped back over the channel and headed towards Fjona.

"Here," he said, his eyes twinkling with wonderment.

Fjona put out her hands and accepted the strange, knotted stick, though she knew it to be more. It was short, about the length of her forearm, but was surprisingly weighty considering its size. Its colour was deep brown with a red hue, and it had a small kink about a third of the way up.

"This is incredible," Fjona said as she pinched the stick by its end and pointed it at the ground before her, eager to try it out for size. She closed her eyes. "Then what? I think about what I want to conjure?"

"No," Perciville replied, "you pluck off the berries and eat them."

Fjona opened one eye and considered him. "What do you mean?"

"Look on the other side."

She rotated the stick in her hands to reveal a cluster of small but plump purple berries.

"And these will give me my powers?" Fjona asked sceptically.

"If you mean the powers of an energy boost and, if boiled in sweetened water, then the power of a bowel movement, then yes."

"This isn't a wand, is it?" Fjona said feeling her face redden with embarrassment.

Perciville smiled kindly. "No it is not. It is a stick. The boltberries ought to pick you up a bit, help the adrenaline settle after all the running, though I admire your enthusiasm."

To Perciville's credit, the berries were deliciously sweet and did make Fjona feel better.

"What is this place?" she asked after she had finished eating.

"No idea. I just recognised the tree for having boltberries and thought they might be of use to you."

He looked Fjona up and down. She was completely caked in mud and her cape was ripped and fraying in more than one place.

"Here..." he said, removing his own cape from the satchel.

"Are you sure? You might need it," Fjona replied.

"Believe me, there is no garb in the world that I would choose over my robe. I insist..."

Fjona felt relieved to have exchanged her sullied cape for

a clean one. She left the old one in a bundle under a tree, deciding that it wasn't worth keeping, and swore to herself that she would return when the mission was over to discard of it properly.

"I'm sorry," she said upon her return.

"About what?"

"About the silkstars and the pettywolves."

Perciville gestured for them to keep walking, looking over in the direction of the woods on the far side of the ochre tree. "It's not me you should be apologising to."

"I know but... if I hadn't persuaded you to change the weather, none of this would have happened."

"And I was aware of the risks. Perhaps I should have trusted my instincts more. I guess my judgement was hindered by the fact that we had been walking in circles."

Fjona glared at him. "Are you serious? I told you we'd been to that spot before and you rejected it!"

The sage shrugged. "It's all part of the endeavour."

Now Fjona's face was red with frustration. "What does that even mean? Part of the endeavour. Why don't you use your staff as a compass again instead of leading us aimlessly through the woods?"

"I have been. Still am, in fact. So far as my compass is concerned, we have been walking north-west the entire time."

"Then how is it possible that we have returned to the same spot twice?"

Perciville faced Fjona and winked. "That's the funny thing about the Tree of Birth. It needs a little time to suss out those who wish to find it. I didn't want to mention it too soon, else you may have become distracted, and that would only have caused delays. The fact that we have been walking around in circles is a good thing, believe it or not."

"Because it means the Tree of Birth is interested in me?" Fjona asked, beginning to catch on to what the sage was saying.

"Essentially, yes. It has been weighing up your soul to decide whether you harbour the moral capacity that is required to be a sage and, before you ask, no, I do not know exactly what that entails. What I do know is that it took me two days to even begin retracing my steps and then a further day beyond that to find it. Santhé was certainly the fastest candidate to track down the Tree of Birth for generations. Took her less than an hour, if I recall correctly!"

"What about your brother?"

Fjona hadn't meant to upset Perciville, she was only asking out of curiosity, but it was obvious by the way the sage dropped his head that she had struck a nerve.

"Ferod took nearly a month to track it down," he replied shamefully. "In hindsight I may have been wise to dissuade him then from hunting for the Tree of Birth but my brother never lacked perseverance. It's strange how tenacity can be as dangerous as it can be inspiring. I suppose that is what the Tree of Birth is weighing and maybe that time it got it wrong..."

His voice trailed off into the wind and the two travellers remained quiet as they followed their way along a deer-trodden path.

Before long, the sun began to dip over the high canopy of trees and the temperature was beginning to drop with it. Fjona knew better than to ask the sage to do anything about it just in case she caused him to start a forest fire or accidentally summon a pack of pettywolves again.

In the end she thought it best just to follow the sage's lead and keep her questions to herself for the time being.

Her feet were beginning to feel sore and her shoulders ached from lugging her satchel but she was awakened from her wallowing when Perciville pulled up at the start of a strange woodland avenue.

It was lined by pointed standing stones of a soft golden hue which glowed under the light of hundreds of fireflies that illuminated the shade. The woodland was so dense beyond the avenue on either side that Fjona couldn't even see between the trees, and it was deadly quiet but for the trickling of streams that meandered between the stones.

"Well I never..." Perciville uttered in the silence.

"Where are we?" Fjona asked, but the sage was already excitedly walking along the woodland corridor with more gusto than she had seen in him before.

Fjona began to follow him, her footsteps dampened by a blanket of moss beneath her.

"That's strange..." she heard Perciville say up ahead.

"Wha—?"

She cut herself off as she noticed that what little sky was visible over the canopy was beginning to darken with every step that she took. The gentle timbre of the stream was drowned out by the intermittent cawing of crows in the trees on either side of her and the primal thumping of her heart echoing in her ears.

As she proceeded to walk, the trees lining the way began to

deteriorate. With each step, the next tree lacked the vitality of the previous, until they were void of all colour and leaves, and were being eaten away by rancid black rot. It was enough to make Fjona's skin crawl.

"Perciville? What's happening? Where are we?" Her voice trembled as she spoke, and she could feel the prickling of hairs on the back of her neck as if she were being watched.

Ahead of her, all she could see of Perciville was his silhouette as it flickered in the shallow light of the fireflies.

"I'm not entirely sure," the sage replied, though his voice sounded muffled in the stifled air.

Fjona picked up her pace, closing the gap between her and Perciville, but as she walked, the light from the fireflies began to peter out until only a gentle haze remained between her and the sage. She stopped in her tracks, too afraid to walk any further and be entirely consumed by the night.

"This doesn't feel right." It was the last thing she said before the remaining light of the fireflies blinked off and they were left in darkness.

Fjona tried to scream but her voice resisted. She tried to walk but her legs were wooden. The harsh screeching caws of the crows seemed to amplify and envelop her, making her feel dizzy and sick.

Her breaths became shorter and shallower, depriving her tightening lungs of what little oxygen surrounded her.

A cool, scaly hand suddenly gripped hers and, for a second, she thought she was going to be sick until she realised that Perciville had come back to grab her.

"Thanks, Harper," she managed to say as the hand dragged

her further along the avenue.

Had the sage said a word, Fjona would not have heard him over the deafening cries of the crows. It sounded as if they were laughing at Fjona, taunting her from above the planes of darkness. Even the pitch black felt to be darkening still, but for a faint speck of light in the distance.

She was being tugged so forcefully that she felt as if her arm may pop out at the socket, and her weary legs were burning under the strain but she knew that there was no sense in stopping.

Though Fjona knew not what lay at the end of the avenue, she was acutely aware that where there was light, she would at least be free of the fears that lay awake in the mottled earth around her.

What she hadn't expected to see at the end was a plain wooden door, bathed in a dull light and framed by thick tree roots.

In the half-light, Fjona turned to the robed figure beside her and said, "Thank you for coming back for me."

However, the face that turned to Fjona was not Perciville's. It was gaunt and pale with sunken black eyes and no ounce of humility, as if she were staring into the face of death itself. Its hand felt suddenly colder, and Fjona could trace frail bones beneath its taut skin. She stood frozen as it stared at her, expressionless and macabre. Tears began to roll down her cheeks and her body quaked.

She released its scaly hand and it hung limply by the figure's side as if it were disarticulated from its body.

Then its twisted, black lips curled into a gruesome, toothless smile and Fjona's instincts kicked back in. Still trembling, she cowered away from the living corpse and reached for the knob, praying to the Four Good Gods that the door would be unlocked.

CHAPTER 23

THE COVENANT OF CREATION

Reishir didn't know why he was so nervous as he sat outside the rusty chamber door, his good leg shaking agitatedly as he waited. He was finally getting the chance to be made whole again, but at what cost? It wasn't too late to turn around, was it? Go upstairs, have a drink and mull things over. He had heard that the Denvillers had a temper but apparently the brother wasn't quite so bad. More forgiving, perhaps?

He needed to pee too which didn't help the matter and the stinking drip of groundwater, seeping in from above, only made matters worse.

"Screw it," he thought as he attempted to stand but his gammy leg prohibited him. Instead, he collapsed onto the mildewy ground, his pointed nose scraping along the cold stone. Reishir cursed audibly and thumped a heavy fist on the ground beside him.

He heard the door creak open and light footsteps tapping on the floor.

"My, my, I was not expecting our new recruit to be the religious type," a young voice said above him, "though fate has clearly treated you unkindly. Perhaps you are in need of a new god?"

"Just a new leg," Reishir spat, pushing himself up on his strong arms. He had ripped his breeches in the fall and now the putrid, raw meat that was his leg was oozing out between the stitches.

"Evidently," the newcomer replied.

Reishir could feel them glancing disdainfully at the wound. When he was back on his feet, and using the dank wall as support, he found a spring elf looking up at him. Their features were ambiguous, as was their voice which was reminiscent of a prepubescent boy or a postpubescent girl, and their bald, faintly green head gave nothing away.

"Who are you?" Reishir asked.

"Hmm, no. Let's try and keep you out of trouble. Mister Denvillier will ask all the questions, okay?"

"Are you Mister—" he stopped and smiled with his mouth shut.

"Follow me."

Reishir was shown into a windowless chamber, lit only by candles that adorned the filthy brick walls. The air was almost sweet, and ripe with algae and mould, though at least it wasn't as cold as it had been in the hallway. In the middle of the room was a hefty round table at which sat a spring elf who was dressed in a long black robe. The elf had a smoothly shaven face revealing a strong jaw and high cheekbones. His eyes were a deep blue and danced in the flickering light of the candles, and his hair was like a sandy beach that clung to the nape of his neck.

It was too dark for Reishir to properly tell how many other elves were hanging about the chamber but his best estimate was about two dozen. They appeared to be mostly spring elves, though there were others from across the Arvum, and they were occupied polishing weapons, or conversing with one another on benches, drinking from tankards and laughing.

"Quite the specimen you've brought me, Harlan," said the berobed spring elf. "Please, come join me."

Reishir hobbled over to the table, clutching his leg and wincing in pain. He took a seat opposite the spring elf.

"I trust you know who I am?" The voice was smooth like honey.

"Benjamin Denvillier," Reishir replied, struggling to keep his voice from wavering.

"And what is it that has brought you to me?"

"My friend said you can fix my leg."

Benjamin rose a thin eyebrow and brought his hand to his chin. "Fix your leg? Yes, yes I believe I can do that."

Reishir expelled a relieved sigh.

"And of course, in repayment, you will be invited to join my little organisation."

"That is kind of you, but I doubt I have much to offer."

Benjamin's eyes narrowed and his voice darkened. "I insist that you consider, else I may not be able to help you after all."

Reishir became acutely aware that the surrounding members were all but silent and turning their heads in his direction. A bead of sweat traced the outline of his face.

He felt pain race to his deteriorating leg and the muscles begin to spasm.

"Maybe there are one or two things I can bring to the table," he said.

"I'm pleased to hear it," Benjamin replied, leaping to his feet and crossing over to Reishir. "We don't have many summer elves here but you may already have a vested interest in our latest project. What do you know of the Sultan of Panamaya City?"

Reishir's body tightened, his fat hands clenched, and his breathing became fast and deep.

"I think you will fit in here very well," Benjamin added, "but first things first; I must initiate you."

Benjamin pulled out a sage's staff from inside his robe. It was a murky grey in colour with a spherical crown on top and, when held in front of him, came up only to his chin.

"I suggest you lean back," he told the terrified Reishir.

"No, please..." the summer elf begged. "I have changed my mind."

"I'm afraid it's a little too late for that," Benjamin said as Harlan pulled a damp cloth through Reishir's mouth and tugged at it from behind.

Chaotic white sparks issued from the head of the staff. Benjamin pointed it at Reishir's chest, the sparks shooting into his flesh.

The cries were like that of pigs in a slaughterhouse that pounded at the cavernous walls around them.

Benjamin gently moved the staff as if he were painting murder on a canvas. His horrifying eyes were electric in the glow of the uncontrollable sparks.

When he was done, Reishir hung back in the chair, panting.

His chest felt sore and his thoughts were consumed by a hunger for revenge, though not for what Benjamin had done to him.

"How do you feel?" Benjamin asked.

"I want to rip the Sultan's head from his body and feed it to the dalachites."

Benjamin smiled with his perfect white teeth. "Welcome to the Covenant of Creation." He offered Reishir a hand which was gladly accepted.

"What about my leg?"

Benjamin looked around the chamber. "You!" he said, in the direction of a spring elf who was sharpening a double-edged axe. "I need your assistance."

Reishir's eyes widened. This was not how it was supposed to go. Some friend he had.

The axewoman stood over Reishir and, despite all his ordeals, it was only now that his bladder relieved.

CHAPTER 24

THE TREE OF BIRTH

The moment Fjona was through to the other side, she slammed the door shut behind her and leaned all her body weight against it. It was a struggle to catch her breath between retching but after a few minutes, her heartbeat had settled and she was able to think clearly again.

When eventually she looked up, Fjona realised that the horrors beyond the door were just a precursor to what she now saw. She found that she had wandered into another glade and, like the avenue, it was consumed by an oppressive darkness. Surrounding her, the woods were denser still than behind the door and were veiled in a skin of shadows making it near impossible to tell where the canopy ended and the sky began.

The only light, faint though it may have been, hovered over what Fjona knew must be the Tree of Birth, situated on a slight mound a short distance from the door. From where she stood, her legs anchored to the ground, the tree appeared starkly different from how Fjona had imagined. The trunk was a spiral of fat, twisting roots that formed together midway up, where several chunky branches petered off and leered over its own shadow. It was tall, though not the tallest even in this glade judging by the silhouetted forest surrounding it, and although its trunk was thick, Fjona had certainly seen thicker.

The image of the grand boltberry tree, vibrant and full of life, burned in her mind.

"Is this really it...?" she whispered.

As Fjona took a step forwards, an audible crunching beneath her broke the deathly silence. She gulped. It was pitch black around her feet and she had no way of knowing what paved the way before her.

Tentatively she continued through the haze, feeling the uneven surface with the balls of her feet as the ground continued to snap and break under even her slight weight.

Afraid of what may be lurking in the midst, Fjona knew better than to ignore it. She stopped where she was and crouched steadily onto her haunches, invisible from the chest down in a blanket of blackness. With a shaking hand, she probed the ground around her, wanting to discover what lay at her feet, though equally wishing she would never find out. Her hand drifted through the dark ocean, sinking deeper beneath the surface. Her fingertips felt icy as goosepimples erupted over her entire body.

Then her hand brushed over something. It was brittle and pointed, and cold to the touch. The harrowing face from beyond the door flashed in her mind's eye as she was reminded of holding that lifeless hand. Startled, she nearly fell on to her back but she managed to use her hands to keep steady.

Fjona continued to feel around her. Her hand, hidden in the dark shroud, traced the long, fibrous texture of bone. It was cold and heavy, and felt almost wooden. She ran her palm up, what felt like, an arm then into the space between long, spindly fingers. Creepy, unnaturally long fingers, more akin to talons. Seemingly arthritic, bony...

"No, that's not right..." she muttered, and yanked the dilapidated limb into the air, standing as she did so.

When she examined the article in the low light, she nearly laughed at her own misguided fear. It was only a tree branch. Granted, it appeared skeletal and had certainly felt like it in the mist, but it was far from the images that Fjona had conjured in her head: a plateau strewn with corpses.

Relieved, she discarded the branch where she had extricated it and continued towards the Tree of Birth, now unperturbed by the snapping and crunching beneath her.

The tree was bathed in a pale moonlight, casting long shadows from bulbous knots and narrow splinters. Its bark bore a sordid pallor and was peeling in places, revealing pockets of rot inside. It had not a single leaf on any of its pale branches, of which there were only a dozen or so – one completely black and hanging on by a thread.

Trails of viscous orange sap snaked down its frail, wilting trunk, congealing with dust and grime in fist-sized clumps.

"So what now?" Fjona asked herself, wishing that Perciville would appear to guide her. "Am I supposed to pray to you, or something? Declare my worthiness to the ancient sages and then I get a wand?"

Wind hissed between the empty branches, causing them to clatter together in slow applause.

She remembered how Perciville had knelt on one knee

when he had pledged to her a sagen oath.

Fjona lowered herself onto one knee and bowed her head as if she were in the presence of a queen.

"Oh Tree of Birth..." she said quietly, feeling a little self-conscious despite there being nobody else in earshot, "...my name is Fjona Sarsen. I have travelled from the island of Marrow Myre in the company of a sage, a Perciville Harper. He insists that there is trouble brewing, stirring in the peripherals beyond what we can see. I can feel it too..."

The wiry trunk creaked in a low breeze.

"Though I am unsure of exactly the role I will be playing in preventing these atrocities, it has become apparent to me that I am to learn the ways of the sages. To do so, I must be bestowed a wand with which to harness the art of manipulation for only then may I do my part in all this. Tree of Birth, please hear my words."

When Fjona looked up, nothing had changed. The seminal tree was as rancid and lifeless as it had been when she entered the grove.

"This is great, I am talking to a dead tree," Fjona said to herself. "How could I have been so foolish to have listened to that deranged man? Find the tree of birth, get a wand..." she said, mocking Perciville's voice and standing, her shoulders slumped forwards. "And now I am trying to reason with a pillar of rotting—"

As she took a step towards it, the Tree of Birth began to shift. It was subtle at first but it was definitely moving.

The orange sap started to bubble and the black rot began to writhe.

Fjona was transfixed, unsure whether to turn and run or wait and see what would become of it.

Patches of ashen bark were rippling as though parasites were festering beneath it, and the mound beneath her was trembling faintly.

From the snake-like roots, the Tree of Birth grew upwards several feet and the lower echelons of the trunk were green and bursting with vitality. Then, through the healthier bark, a slender branch erupted, reaching out to the length of Fjona's forearm. It had a silvery hue and served as a spine to several smaller twigs, one of which contained a lowly dark green leaf. The new branch glowed softly at the trunk.

Fjona tentatively reached out for the branch but, as her fingers neared it, a magnetic-like force clasped her hand over it. She gasped in surprise. She wanted to release her hand and pull away, not because she was afraid but because she wanted to know that she could. Despite her effort, Fjona's hand was ensnared.

A strange sensation poured into her skin – a mix between scalding water and electricity.

"Argh, sweet Aserae!" Fjona cried into the dampened void.

With all the strength she could muster, Fjona tugged but to no avail. The branch was too stubborn to snap. Throughout her body she could feel the burning, electrical sensation as if it were navigating her bones and seeping into her cells, filling her body like a stiff drink.

After a while, the energy felt to be retreating, climbing back up her legs and through her abdomen, around her breast, into her shoulder and back down her arm. With little effort, the new branch snapped at the trunk and into Fjona's gripped hand. It had a rough, abrasive skin and was surprisingly heavy considering its size.

Instinctively, she turned it around so that she was holding the thicker end, away from the smaller branches.

The Tree of Birth wasn't finished, however, and a new branch erupted from the same point. It was much larger than the one held by Fjona, and several luscious green leaves bloomed at its peaks. Fjona was forced to step away from the tree before being thwacked out of the way.

A creak sounded from the trunk and the Tree of Birth returned to its motionless state, though now with the contrast between the living growth at its roots and the dying above. For Fjona, the sight was almost as unsettling as when the entire being was decrepit.

Fjona turned her attention to, what she presumed to be, her wand.

"Well you're not quite as polished as I had expected," she said, "but I suppose I shouldn't judge you by your appearance."

Gripped between her fingers, Fjona pointed the stick at the bare patch of ground before her. She closed her eyes, listened to her breathing, then conjured an image of a lantern in her head. In her mind's eye, she pictured a rectangular iron frame, glass panel windows and a tall white candle. She even went to the trouble of imagining her wand materialising the lantern in a wisp of silvery green magic, just as Perciville had done with the port.

Fjona wasn't sure if it was just her imagination or whether the wand did actually tremble gently, as if magic had poured out of it.

Through one eye, Fjona took a peek and was unsurprised, though nonetheless disappointed, to discover that nothing had appeared in front of her.

"Perhaps," she wondered, "I could cast an elemental spell to clear this smog."

She pictured Perciville and how he applied the art of manipulation. He hadn't closed his eyes when he had stopped the rain. Maybe that wasn't necessary.

Fjona pointed the wand at the haze of darkness, then focused her gaze, controlled her breathing, and imagined the fog dissipating.

The longer nothing happened, the tighter Fjona's jaw became as she convinced herself that focus was measured by the firmness of her mandible.

Although the smog persisted, her efforts were not completely in vain. A short distance before the haze, a flat, round leaf appeared to hover no more than an inch above the ground. In fact, it was here where her wand was actually pointed.

However, in her astonishment at the levitating leaf, her focus became distracted and she lost connection. The leaf floated gently back down to the surface.

Fjona smiled gleefully.

"Well I didn't clear it but I have to start somewhere..." she said aloud, preparing her wand to reattempt the spell.

A loud bang at the door startled her, and Fjona flinched. In her excitement she had almost forgotten where she was.

A cold sweat trickled down her forehead as she remembered

the ghostly figure who stood on the other side. There was no choice but to confront them. She could hardly stay in the glade for the rest of her life.

Another bang at the door, sounding powerful enough to knock it off its hinges.

Fjona's hand clenched the wand as she strode determinedly back through the haze, tree branches splitting and crackling beneath her.

At the door, she took another deep breath. With one hand, she pointed the wand upwards in the vague direction of the phantom's pallid face, with the other she reached for the knob.

The door trembled under the weight of another fist.

"Here goes. ." Fjona said, steeling herself.

She swung open the door to reveal a red-faced Perciville Harper on the other side.

"About bloody time." he uttered, "I've been out here for hours!"

"You swine!" Fjona exclaimed, thumping her fist against the sage's chest. "I thought you were that creepy, half-dead monster!"

Perciville looked abashed. "Monster? What in all the Arvum are you talking about?"

"It was—" Fjona cast a glance around the avenue.

An iridescent moonlight illuminated the treelined path which was alive with the speckled flames of the fireflies and the soft glow of luminescent orange toadstools.

"It was so dark. Completely pitch black. You took my hand and led—"

"I did no such thing," Perciville interjected. "I was halfway along the route when I felt a stiffness in the air as if someone had sucked all the oxygen out of it. When I turned back, you had disappeared. I thought maybe you'd been taken by a pettywolf or something. I came looking for you only to look back the other way to see you entering through the door without me."

"What? No, that's preposterous!"

"I agree, but it is the truth. Anyway, the door locked behind you so I knocked until the moon came up."

"But I was only gone a few minutes."

The sage exhaled deeply through his nose. "Look, none of this matters. The point is you met the Tree of Birth and it ceded you a Raw Wand. Let me see."

"A Raw Wand?" Fjona asked.

"Indeed. The first in a series of wands before you get a staff and can call yourself a sage, now may I see it?"

Fjona held the wand out before Perciville. He didn't touch it but instead leaned in with his pointed nose and examined it closely as if it were a rare artefact.

"Astonishing..." he muttered.

"What is?"

"This really is remarkable..."

Fjona closed her hands around the wand. "Perciville, talk to me! What is so special about this Raw Wand?"

"Come, I'll explain as we get moving," he said, and started back down the avenue. Fjona was hot on his heels as he spoke. "It's been centuries since I last laid eyes on a Raw Wand. I suppose it would have been Ferod's when he visited Willow's Brush. As I recall it was spring wood, named for the spring elves. Green-brown in colour, slightly knotted in the middle with a spirally little twig near to where he rested his thumb. It's funny what people remember. My Raw Wand" – he turned his sparkling, bright eyes excitedly on Fjona – "was autumn wood, the colour of port. I think that's why I developed such an affinity for it."

"All very fascinating," Fjona interrupted with a roll of her eyes, "but what has this to do with mine?"

Perciville furrowed his brow. "Well it's curious that in all my years, I have heard only once of a sage whose Raw Wand was silver."

They stepped out of the avenue and entered back into the main wood whose nocturnal inhabitants were beginning to stir.

"Who did that wand belong to?" Fjona asked.

"Yilsommen," Perciville replied, "the very first sage."

While Fjona was left processing this, Perciville had brandished his staff and was conjuring a shelter on a flat patch of ground beside a stream. It was a modest structure, built of mud bricks with a straw roof, but with the night closing in and one or two raindrops in the air, it was certainly better than nothing.

The sage then conjured up another green fire and two log stools, one either side. Inside the mud hut, he conjured two tattered rag blankets and a couple of feather pillows, before making for the stream.

"Very cosy," Fjona marvelled. "I can't believe how quickly you can make camp."

"The nomad life," Perciville replied, conjuring a fishing line out the end of his staff. "I've become quite adept at camping out like this although my skills are currently lacking. Had it not been for the Eight Afflictions, I could have crafted some nicer accommodation and even a bed, but alas..."

He trailed off as he swung his staff, currently serving as rod, over the back of his shoulder, then cast the line into the stream. The line had an odd blue glow that reflected off the viciously sharp hook as it plunged into the waters.

"So my wand is identical to the original sage? Is that significant?" Fjona asked as she watched a school of sizeable fish dart towards the hook.

The moderate water rippled with surprising ferocity as they raced towards the prize, and Perciville was quick to react, reeling the first one in: a large grey trout.

"Absolutely significant, probably," he said as he flopped the trout onto the bank. It wriggled about in the wet grass until Perciville bludgeoned it to death with the blunt end of his staff. "Now get this on the fire, you need a proper meal before tomorrow."

"Why, what's happening tomorrow?" Fjona asked, scooping up the dead fish.

"I'm going to teach you the art of manipulation," the sage replied as he cast the line again.

Fjona rummaged in Perciville's satchel for a cooking knife, sheathed in a leather scabbard. As she proceeded to gut the trout, she asked, "Does this mean I'm somehow connected to *Ilsim*... the first sage?"

A dead, wet fish flew through the air and flopped down in the mud next to her, it's fat tail slapping against Fjona's thigh.

"Perciville!"

The sage shrugged as he came over to join Fjona near the fire, the fishing line now dematerialised. "Couldn't resist," he said with a boyish grin.

Fjona shot him a scornful look then continued preparing the fish.

"*Yilsommen*," Perciville said, "and no, I don't think that you're connected. As far as I know, wands don't work like that. In sagen lore, Yilsommen discovered the Tree of Birth as a child at the turn of, what the sages know as, the Age of Resurrection, many thousands of years ago. When she met the Tree of Birth, it is believed to have been the first time in history that it had ever revealed itself, thus making her the first to ever harness the art of manipulation. Later, when Yilsommen was older, wiser, and immensely powerful, she built the Rock of Caeznor, founded the Sagedom and taught to others all that she had learned."

Fjona skewered the trout on a sharp stick then suspended it over the fire on a makeshift spit.

"What happened to her in the end?" she asked, turning her attention to the other fish.

"As I said before, this took place many thousands of years ago. Everybody meets their end eventually, even sages. Some say she died tragically young considering her strength: a couple of hundred years or so. Others say she lived to nearly two thousand years, or that she submitted her soul to the Tree of Birth and continues to live through the work of the sages. A little airy-fairy for me but perhaps it provides solace to others..."

Fjona had been so hungry that it was only when she had finished gorging on the smoky flesh of the trout that she took her wand and attempted to levitate a small stone beside the fire. After several minutes of deep concentration, the stone still failed to budge.

"I don't get it!" she complained. "It worked earlier."

"You are thinking too much. Focussing too much on being focused. Clear your head of all the nonsense, then try again," Perciville replied having been too preoccupied conjuring a tumbler of whiskey to even look at what Fjona was doing.

"Nonsense?"

"Distractions, then. Try again. Create as clear an image of the surroundings in your head and imagine exactly what you are trying to achieve."

A little hot under the collar, Fjona made a second attempt. This time, she tried to keep from letting her thoughts wander and pictured only what she knew was around her. The mud hut, the fire, the damn little stone which was as stubborn as she was.

Then, after a while, Fjona released her frustration. The image of her surroundings was burning in her mind as if the wand itself were painting it for her. She could imagine the stone raising up from the ground with a dusting of earth spilling off of it. It was as vivid as a lucid dream.

When she opened her eyes, the stone was indeed hovering above the fire, defying gravity and nature itself. Her lips curled into a smile; Fjona was surprised that she was able to maintain the focus this time.

The stone then bobbed up and down, heading steadily towards her.

She furrowed her brow. "Why is it doing that...?"

Her realisation came a fraction too late and the stone plonked against her head, then tumbled to the ground.

With a huff, she turned to Perciville who was sitting on the log stool with his staff pointed at her and a big grin on his face. "Couldn't help myself."

Agitated, Fjona thrust the wand at the sage, manipulating a meagre cloud of dust to plume around him.

"Hey, not bad!" Perciville commended. "Not enough to cause any harm, but see what can happen when your energy is focused solely on one aim?"

Fjona smiled fully. "That felt good!"

"And so it should." Perciville replied, "and on that positive note, I have had a lengthy day and it's all uphill from tomorrow."

He got up from the log stool and stood roughly in the middle of the campsite. Once there, he placed his staff vertically in front of him. A vibrant turquoise light burst out of the head and spread into a small dome around them, then faded to a faint shimmer, like glass. The staff itself hovered a few feet off the ground.

"To keep nasties away," Perciville said simply. "Don't wake me when you come to bed."

With that, he disappeared into the mud hut and tucked up beneath a blanket.

Growing ever sleepier, Fjona stayed up a while longer trying to cast more spells with her wand. No matter how hard she tried, she couldn't seem to repeat either of her successful attempts.

Over and over, she pointed at twigs and stones, in the air

and on the ground, relieving her mind of extraneous thought, but always to no avail.

Fjona found herself staring into the flames of the green fire. Without her wand poised, she concentrated on it, mesmerised by the flickering of embers and the spitting of flames. Almost intrinsically, she lifted her wand and pointed at the fire. In a flash, she imagined it being extinguished, and with a sudden green spark from her wand, the fire went out. Fjona remained still, sitting only in the faint turquoise glow of Perciville's staff. She now felt that she could go to bed with a sense of accomplishment.

Just before she made for the mud hut, Fjona wandered over to the edge of the conjured dome and tentatively reached out for it. Although she could feel the air passing through, her hand pressed up against it, leaving a faint print. She watched the print fade away into nothing and a troubled thought crossed her mind...

Was the dome solely to keep nasties out, or was it also designed to keep her in?

CHAPTER 25

ASCERAT

The snow was coated in a thin crust of ice that crunched beneath Dharla Sarsen's worn boots. It was tiresome to trudge through and she wished they hadn't needed to leave their horses at the Mountain Foot Stables. It was for the best, she knew, and Iser would never have forgiven her if they returned without them.

That's if they returned at all.

She tightened her shawl around her neck as a stiff mountain wind tore through her from the east. Despite being wrapped up with only her eyes exposed, the icy breeze still penetrated her bones.

This is the last thing she needed in the middle of the night – to be out of the tent, tracking footsteps that were already starting to fill in with a fresh bout of snow.

Between the gusts biting at her ear and the audible thumping of her heart, Dharla could just make out a faint sound from beyond the next ridge. It was too difficult to discern over the wind but the noise was somewhere between sobbing and giggling. A higher pitch than may have been expected. More like a child than a fully grown man.

She skirted the edge of a sheer rockface and pressed on into the wind, mindful of the slope beside her that faded into darkness.

"Four Good Gods please spare me," she muttered over, until she was safely around to the other side and was able to move away from the drop.

It was a little more sheltered here as Dharla squeezed between a fissure in the mountain face and into a rocky cove.

The animalistic sound was more distinguishable now. An eerie, uncomfortable giggling in a landscape completely devoid of humour.

Had she not been painfully familiar with the sight, Dharla may have been more afraid.

"Come now, my *derin*. I think it's time you come back to bed." She spoke softly but assertively, all the while maintaining a safe distance from her beloved husband.

"Return with me back to the tent and we can find your clothes," Dharla offered, stretching out a hand.

Ascerat was too preoccupied, hunched naked, but for a loin cloth, over a dead mountain goat. He was sniggering to himself and whispering nonsensically, gummy blood dripping down from his chin and leaving spots in the snow. His skin was a translucent blue – ghostly and cold.

Dharla took a cautious step towards him, the snow crackling beneath her. She could just make out what her husband was saying.

"Not so clever now, oh little *goatie*. No, you beat me, not!"

He violently bit into the goat's neck, tearing through flesh and tendons to an expulsion of blood. The sight caught Dharla in her tracks.

Ascerat's giggle turned into maniacal laughter, echoing off the cavernous walls.

Dharla took another step.

Her husband suddenly looked up at her, no longer laughing. Bright yellow eyes stared back at Dharla as if they were seeing her for the very first time. His face conveyed a look of fear and curiosity which quickly turned into distrust.

In a heartbeat, he thrust away the goat and charged at his wife with predatorial ferocity, blood-infused foam frothing around his pale lips.

From beneath Dharla's coat, she revealed a short staff. It looked like a small shepherd's crook. It was dark grey, with a round bump on top.

She held her breath, tightened her grip and, when Ascerat was close in front of her, she expelled a disparate white light from the staff's head. It shot into her husband's body, forcing him to collapse into the frozen snow and spasm from head to toe.

When Ascerat calmed down, Dharla spoke.

"As I said, my *derin*. Let's get you back to bed."

Acknowledgements

It would be remiss of me to not offer my sincere appreciation to everyone who has helped bring the pages of this book to life.

To Niamh Batsman, a real-world Fjona Sarsen who brought a little magic into my own life.

To Lucas Abbott, the only soul I'd dare trust to read an early draft of my manuscript; your critique was invaluable.

To Victoria Richards and the editing team at Cranthorpe Millner, who gave me and this novel a chance, helped shape it into the finalised work that it is, and who guided me every step of the way.

To Shannon Chapman, whose innovative cover design has perfectly captured the tone of the story.

To Becca Stevenson, for helping spread the word of the *Sarsen Series* and encouraging me to do the same.

To Jenna Richards, for the captivating map designs and making the Arvum just that little bit more tangible.

I greatly look forward to working with you all through Book 2, *In the Heart of a Soulless Vessel*.

The best is yet to come.

Simon

THE ADVENTURE CONTINUES IN THIS
CAPTIVATING SEQUEL

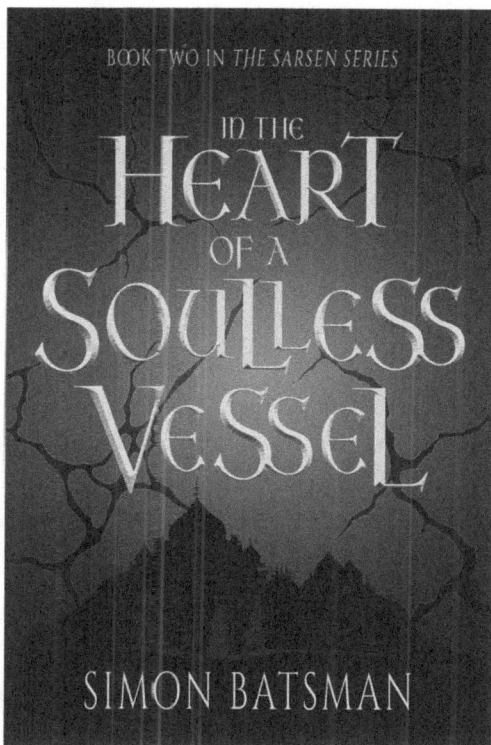

BOOK TWO IN *THE SARSEN SERIES*

IN THE
HEART
OF A
SOULLESS
VESSEL

SIMON BATSMAN

READ ON FOR A SNEAK PEEK...

CHAPTER 1

A MURDER IN ROSENSTED

The Crypt Keeper's Keys had a sour reputation. For generations the dank, claustrophobic tavern had attracted some of the Arvum's most vilified and malicious criminals, from bandit leaders to anti-Sagedom freedom fighters. It was rumoured that many an unsavoury campaign had been drawn up within the same walls where assassins lingered to execute their bounties, and where prostitutes lingered to execute their charm.

Centuries after the collapse of the Sagedom, *The Crypt Keeper's Keys* had become more of a tourist attraction, now there was seemingly less to oppose, and folk across the Arvum would journey countless miles in pursuit of an overpriced drink, just to sit in the booth where an ancient war criminal once plotted against the government.

That's not to say that it didn't still lure in the familiar crowd from decades long past, to stir trouble and conjure devious plans, and tonight was no exception.

Storms were frequent on the east coast of the Arvum during the spring and Rosensted was bracing under the wrath of intense winds and heavy rain. With little else to do in such conditions, it seemed that half the town and her mate were sheltering in the *Crypt*, and getting merry to the backdrop of a lute-playing bard.

In a quiet nook, furthest from the music, Benjamin Denvillier was raising a toast to his companions of the Covenant of Creation.

"What a backwards lot you all are," he slurred, beer foaming over the lip of his tankard, "but I'd be damned if I could find any better across the Arvum." He paused for a moment, then added, "Sages know, I've tried!"

His subordinates laughed loudly, though the sound barely cut over the rest of the tavern.

"With a little help along the way, our numbers are stronger than ever. Take my friend, our newest recruit, Horse Leg over here..." He gestured to a summer elf sitting uncomfortably at the table.

"It's Reishir," the summer elf replied in an annoyed tone.

Benjamin ignored him. "He joined us only a week ago, suffering a rotten leg and harbouring an immense hatred for the Sultan. Well, thanks to me and the Contact, he has an unrelenting hunger for revenge and a nice new leg!"

"Yes, a bloody horse's leg," Reishir muttered, taking a hearty swig of ale.

"Let's hope he doesn't crap like a horse!" Harlan, the young spring elf called out, encouraging further laughter.

Reishir whipped out a sharp, narrow blade and held it to Harlan's neck. Harlan didn't so much as flinch.

"Quiet, squid, or I'll have your head."

"Now, now, Horse Leg, we all give and take in equal

measure. Lower your sword," Benjamin said calmly, with authority.

Reishir remained for a moment before sheathing his dagger.

When the energy had calmed, Benjamin continued. "The Contact has been most pleased with our disruptions to the canal and I can only commend you for your unwavering efforts. What was it you spoke to the Kelnish? *Sil'yhab forlein*? For them, indeed, the worst is yet to come. But for us, I foresee a very lucrative future. Yes, there is much more work to do, but tonight, we must drink to those left behind, drink to what lies ahead of us, and drink to fortify the kinship that has brought us, this covenant, together."

As Benjamin raised his glass, his attention was swiftly stolen as the door to the tavern burst open and a forceful gust billowed inside. It was so strong that, for a moment, even the bard was distracted and performed a couple of dissonant chords before rediscovering his fingers.

Two hooded figures stepped into the quiet tavern, soaked through from the rain. Nearly every face turned to them.

The first figure pulled back her hood and said with a silken voice, "Don't stop on my account."

"Lady Denvillier, please come through! Your brother awaits," said the kind, elderly proprietor of the tavern, who was quick to greet her at the door.

"Thank you, Maurice," Lucinda replied. "Come, Feldin."

Feldin kept his hood on and followed Lucinda around to the rear of the *Crypt*.

"Lucinda, how nice it is that you could join us," Benjamin said, kissing her on each cheek. "Though I must admit, we were expecting you a little sooner."

"It was a job I simply could not rush," Lucinda replied coldly, before turning to address the bandits.

Most of the men and at least two of the women were sitting up straighter and adjusting their shirts, in an attempt to appear half presentable.

"It is apparent that many of the Kelnish workers have fled the construction and their progress has been greatly inhibited. You must be very pleased, not least because my little assignment proved to be something of a success also." She gestured to Feldin. "Show them."

"Of course, my Lady," Feldin croaked, extracting a small parcel from deep within his cloak. With pale, scaly hands, he unwrapped the paper to reveal a sizeable copper key.

"Very fine work, Lucinda," Benjamin mused, reaching out to take it.

Lucinda slapped his hand away. "I will hold on to this for the time being," she said firmly. "We wouldn't want it getting into the wrong hands, after all."

Benjamin turned a little red in the face. "True enough."

There was a moment's awkwardness, until Reishir's new limb caught Lucinda's eye.

"I see we have a new member. Is this handi— sorry, *leg* work of your notorious *contact*?"

"No, actually. I stitched a horse's leg onto him myself."

The bandits laughed again, but were cut short when Lucinda shot them a stern look.

"So your contact was happy to help with *that* then?"

Benjamin shrugged. "Why the interrogation? Look, Horse

Leg came to me with a problem and we solved it. Now, my dear, take a seat, order some wine and let's discuss your visit to the big city!"

The evening wore on and the members of the Covenant of Creation slowly deteriorated into a desperate state of drunkenness.

Much of the *Crypt* had quietened down and the bard had progressed to playing some gentler, slower songs to mirror the mood.

My seaward girl met my hometown wife,
Met my city mistress on a winter's night,
Met my lover's daughter and my Lady Right,
And that foxy whore; not so very tight.

Met my countess, duchess, sage and queen,
And that stableboy I shagged last spring,
Suffice to say she was not pleased,
When I came to bed with little seed.

There was a rumble of laughter from the remaining folk, who were slumped in chairs around the singer.

The Denvilliers and the bandits had stayed in the same booth for the entire evening, a balanced mix of boisterous drunks and resting-one's-head-on-the-table drunks. Benjamin and Lucinda were, of course, the former. They muttered between themselves, as was their want, particularly after a jug or two of wine.

"Father would be proud of us," Benjamin slurred.

"Mother would be ashamed," Lucinda retorted, then broke into giggles.

"Too long have we been *repassed*!" He just about managed to form the words.

"*Repassed?*"

"Re... *prassed*?"

"Repressed!" Lucinda realised.

"Yes, repress—" Her brother groaned, his eye twitching in the low light. "Soon, we'll be celebrated." He leaned in close to Lucinda and whispered, "The Contact says we're going to start quite the revolution!"

Lucinda smiled. "Tell me, how exactly do you plan on doing that?"

For a moment, she thought her brother might reveal everything. But, disappointing as always, he did not.

"You know I can't tell you that!" Benjamin slumped back in his chair, thick red wine sloshing out of his jug and over the table. "After all—"

He suddenly gagged and stopped short.

"Whatever is the matter?" Lucinda asked.

The conscious bandits turned their eyes to their leader and watched as a narrow slit appeared across Benjamin's neck, seemingly from nowhere.

His eyes widened with terrified realisation, and with dwindling strength he scrabbled at his throat. Dark blood seeped between his fingers as he gasped helplessly for air.

Lucinda shot to her feet. "Benjamin!" she cried hysterically.

His life was draining fast, like the blood pooling around him.

"Hel... p... me..."

All the bandits, even those who had been asleep, got to their feet and wielded their weapons: knives, swords and axes, though, having surveyed the tavern, there was no sign of their assailant. In fact, the room was largely deserted and the remaining punters settled around the singer were oblivious to what had happened.

"What are you waiting for?" Lucinda screamed at them. "Find whoever did this!"

Nobody moved.

"Now!"

Commotion ensued as the bandits, Reishir and Feldin among them, dispersed around the empty tavern, weapons raised aggressively. The bard swiftly ended his set and disappeared through the door with his lute, while the stragglers suffered a bombardment of interrogations from the Covenant.

Maurice had ducked behind the bar and was fondling a stone charm for good luck while tables and chairs were thrown about, somewhat unnecessarily.

Meanwhile, in the booth, Lucinda knelt down next to her brother. Tears streamed down her pale cheeks.

"This was never supposed to happen. You're going to be okay," she said shakily.

Benjamin knew only too well when his sister was lying.